THE CLEANSING OF MAHOMMED

THE CLEANSING OF MAHOMMED

CHRIS McCOURT

FOURTH ESTATE

Fourth Estate
An imprint of HarperCollins*Publishers*

First published in Australia in 2012
by HarperCollins*Publishers* Australia Pty Limited
ABN 36 009 913 517
harpercollins.com.au

HarperCollins*Publishers*
Level 13, 201 Elizabeth Street, Sydney NSW 2000, Australia
31 View Road, Glenfield, Auckland 0627, New Zealand
A 53, Sector 57, Noida, UP, India
77–85 Fulham Palace Road, London, W6 8JB, United Kingdom
2 Bloor Street East, 20th floor, Toronto, Ontario M4W 1A8, Canada
10 East 53rd Street, New York NY 10022, USA

National Library of Australia Cataloguing-in-Publication data:

McCourt, Chris.
　The cleansing of Mahommed / Chris McCourt.
　ISBN: 978 0 7322 9415 1 (pbk.)
　Prejudices – Australia – Fiction. Man-woman relationships – Australia – Fiction.
　Broken Hill (N.S.W.) – History – Fiction. Australia – Race relations – Fiction.
A823.4

Cover design by Jane Waterhouse, HarperCollins Design Studio
Cover images: Passenger train by Matthews, H. H., National Library of Australia,
(nla.pic-an23255717) and Indian-Pacific by Buckland, John L 1915-1989, National
Library of Australia, (nla.pic-vn4247797); all other images by shutterstock.com
Back cover image: Picnic train by State Library of South Australia (B 54756/22)

for Verna

I

Gool Mahommed worshipped Allah and Lifebuoy soap, but as he began what was supposed to be his wonderful new life, neither was in evidence.

Allah had come to him at birth; Lifebuoy when he was five, with the English trader. After trying to sell an assortment of knives and trinkets, the trader had flourished his pièce de résistance, a cake of wrapped Lifebuoy, holding it up with a dramatic gesture, telling his Pashtun audience they must have it because cleanliness was next to godliness. Mahommed didn't see any contradiction in the trader's dirty fingernails. All he knew was his own heart, a rush of desire making it pound to the point where he felt light-headed.

He moved from behind the safety of his mother and inched forward. With one hand still clutching her skirt he held up his other, hoping for a chance to hold the soap briefly in his palm.

The trader ignored him.

Mahommed looked up at his mother, leaning out past the swell of her belly in an attempt to catch her eye. She was heavily pregnant, full term for the first time since his birth. He knew that soon she would have no time for him. She had been widowed for six months now. Time was rationed. It would be further rationed when the baby was born.

He intensified the level of his silent pleading, willing his mother to look at him and understand the depth of his need. When that didn't work he tugged at her skirt. She glanced down to brush him away, but before she could do so he smiled at her, putting everything he could into the only weapon he had.

She held his look only briefly, but it was long enough. She returned his smile, curled her fingers around his face, cupped his chin, and told the trader she would buy the soap.

It was her final act of love towards Mahommed. The baby came, another boy. His raspy shallow breaths lasted a day longer than hers and then they, too, stopped. Mahommed was left with only his brothers and the cool clean smell of a bar of Lifebuoy soap. At night he held it to his cheek and wept against it until eventually it smelt of nothing at all. By then it had transferred its magic. A morning soon came when he woke and made his way outside. He rubbed the sleep out of his eyes and was surprised to discover the world had more than one colour. He also smelt breakfast. For the first time since his mother had died he realised he was hungry. He understood these sensations to be gifts from the Soap God, and he was grateful.

In August of 1914, gratitude was not uppermost in twenty-one-year-old Mahommed's mind. He was little more than an untidy bundle, sprawled in the winter sun. His eyes were shut. He was bareheaded. He wore thin cotton trousers, recently stained with grease. His shirt – like his trousers, English styled – was in a similar condition. Over the shirt he wore an old woollen jacket with a tear in one pocket; on his feet a pair of equally old leather boots, painstakingly polished but now etched by the sandstone littering the ground around him. Near him was a cardboard suitcase, held shut by a knotted length of rope. Over him was a crumpled piece of long white muslin cloth; under him a squashed emu bush. He was surrounded by more emu bush, clumps of spear grass, and a few low-growing mulgas.

His nose, pressed against the ground, twitched, feeling the rumble beneath. He lifted his head and opened his eyes, peering into the distance to get his bearings, but saw only baked red-soil desert, stretching to the cloudless sky. Turning his head to the right, he saw more desert, flat and unwelcoming.

He saw the train track when he looked to the left, about two hundred yards away. It was empty from horizon to horizon. The rumbling grew fainter. He frowned, trying to grasp its meaning.

It came to him quickly. It was his fault. What had happened was entirely his fault. He puddled in this unpleasant fact before shutting it out, denying it further access. This was a perfect day. Unlike his first arrival in Broken Hill, this was a day of triumph, a day when all his plans would begin to come to fruition, a day that would mark him for future success, a day when nothing could or would go wrong.

It could still be rescued before it became irretrievably something else. It could still be the best day of his life. But if it was not going to be the last day of his life, he would have to reach the shade of the nearest mulga tree. He got to his hands and knees and crawled towards it. This effort took only minutes but it was enough for the facts to push their way back through the barriers he had erected.

He had fled the train less than an hour ago. The sun had been up; despite being winter the day was already hot as the passenger train belched between Adelaide and Broken Hill, pumping black clouds into the sky.

It had been a long journey; six at night until eight the next morning, with a midnight change at Terowie for the narrower gauge.

He had spent the first part of the journey squashed next to a pumpkin-shaped family of six. Although the mother was aloof, the father was civil, and the children understandably curious.

The oldest boy had stared at him openly. 'What's that on your head?'

His father turned to the boy, to shush him. 'You've seen turbans before.'

The boy ignored the admonition. 'Are you an Arab?'

Mahommed welcomed the question, glad for an opportunity to practise his English. 'I am Afghani.'

'Same thing, isn't it? Where's your camel?'

'I don't have a camel.'

'Why not?'

'I am here to work in the Proprietary Mine.'

'But why don't you have a camel?'

'Because I am working in the mine.'

'Camels stink.'

Before Mahommed could agree with this assessment, the father told the boy to stop being annoying. By now the novelty of talking to a stranger had worn off, and the child occupied himself by squabbling with his siblings.

Terowie at midnight was freezing. Mahommed didn't mind; he felt invigorated. In a few hours it would be daylight and he would be arriving in Broken Hill, eager to make his fortune. He had work, somewhere to call home. His dear friend Abdullah would rejoice at his return, marvelling at the fine young man Mahommed had become. The sun would seek him out to shine on him.

He looked around at the other people waiting to board the express train, most of them single men. A few were alone, as he was; others were in groups of two or three, sharing cigarettes, stamping their feet against the cold. Most waited in silence, shoulders hunched, staring at nothing, their spirits night-dampened. Mahommed pushed his own shoulders back, standing straight. If he was not yet master of all he surveyed, he surely would be soon. He wanted his demeanour to reflect that.

He was among the last to board, and made his way along the crowded corridor. The pumpkin family was moving ahead of him. He hoped he wouldn't have to sit next to them again; their bulk would make sleep impossible.

They stopped in front of him, blocking his view while they found seats opposite each other, staking claims on the racks above. The carriage seemed full; the family was taking its time about allowing those behind it to move forward. He was thinking he might have to go through to the next carriage when finally they parted – to reveal not only an empty seat but the most beautiful girl he had ever seen.

She had green-brown eyes and auburn hair, and breasts he didn't dare look at. The rest of her was a blur of loveliness he was incapable of shaping. She looked up at him and smiled, indicating the seat next to her. 'There's no-one sitting here.'

He stared at her, unable to believe that a goddess would say such a thing to him. 'There is no-one?'

'No.'

'No?'

Before he could think of something else to say that didn't entail him parroting her words, her female companion grabbed her attention and she turned away from him, leaving him stranded.

He tried to remember who he was: a man who one day soon would be master of all he surveyed; a man brought up to treat women with respect. It would be discourteous to reject her kind offer. The train would be moving soon; it would be too late to find another seat. If he hesitated any longer, she might turn back to him and find him still standing; his situation would become even more awkward.

He glanced behind and saw one last passenger, one of the single men, pushing along the corridor towards him. Taking this as his cue, he put his suitcase on the rack above and sat.

He spent the next few hours staring straight ahead, not daring to look sideways, not daring to doze for fear his head might accidentally loll against hers. He heard her whispering with her friend, and, after some time, the measured breathing of sleep. He wondered where she was. He shut his eyes and attempted to join her.

Mahommed had been awake for hours, cursing himself for the scant half-hour he had given over to sleep. A bump in the track had jolted him back to wakefulness and he had been appalled to find himself leaning against the girl. He quickly sat upright. What else had he been doing? Snoring?

He didn't trust himself. He pushed into the corner of the seat, away from her, and stood, getting up inch by inch so as not to alert her to what he was doing. He braved one last look at her, deciding she was lovely even in sleep, and stepped over dozing bodies to the other end of the carriage, where he felt he would be safe from causing offence. He stayed there, leaning against the carriage wall, until the first trace of morning light. When the train blinked past Silverton, he saw others stirring, and moved towards the toilet.

Once there, he reached for a small packet in his coat pocket, and unwrapped a sliver of soap. He had hoped to save it for when he reached Broken Hill, but had not allowed for the possibility of meeting a goddess en route. He wanted her to notice he was clean.

He also wanted her to notice he was handsome. He peered worriedly at his reflection in the mirror, unsure whether or not this might be achievable. The silvered backing of the mirror was scratched and cloudy, softening the sharpness of his features. He turned his face to one side, holding his chin high, searching for a flattering angle.

The train lurched just as he found one. He grabbed hold of a handle near the toilet to stop himself from falling, and noticed a discarded copy of the *Adelaide Advertiser* on the floor next to the toilet bowl. He picked it up gingerly, aware of the probable uses for which it had been left, but after examination decided it was both intact and clean. He tucked it under his arm, gave his hands one more rinse, checked the condition of his teeth, and left the cubicle, clean, refreshed, and confident about his attractiveness. He would open a conversation. She would reply. Who knew where it might lead?

He stepped over the pumpkin children, asleep in the corridor. As he reached his seat, the girl acknowledged him with a smile. In return he gave her a frozen nod.

He cursed himself. He had less than half an hour to make an impression upon her. Once the train pulled into Sulphide Street Station, she would be lost to him. He remembered the newspaper, deciding it could be used both to restore his dignity and buy time in which to plan a conversation.

He opened it and proceeded to peruse it for items of interest, nodding thoughtfully to himself when he came to something worth his attention. He tutted once or twice, in order to make clear to her that he was a man not necessarily in agreement with everything he read, but rather had a mind of his own.

The print swam in front of him, in shapeless clumps of black. Although he could not read English well he could usually make out the occasional word, but now his brain was too occupied by thoughts of kissing her pillowy white bottom to even do that.

'Excuse me …'

Was she addressing him?

And then again. 'Excuse me.'

Disconcerted, he tried to be calm, reminding

himself that this was the opportunity he'd been hoping for. He slowly lowered the paper, peering over it to find her boldly looking straight at him. Behind her, her friend had a hand to her mouth, suppressing laughter.

'It's upside down.'

He stared at her blankly.

'Your paper. It's upside down.'

He looked back at the paper, where he saw a photograph of two soberly suited men. Although they were not acrobats, they were standing on their heads. It took a moment for the implications to register, but when it did they poured in, on waves of shame and humiliation. He wished for instant death. When that didn't eventuate he wished for strength in his legs, and this time the wish was granted. He dropped the paper, grabbed his suitcase from the rack, and fled down the corridor, dodging children as he went.

He risked a glance behind him. To his horror he saw she was hurrying after him, calling, 'Wait, please wait!'

He redoubled his efforts, blindly pushing past the other passengers until he came to the closed guard's compartment. He hurried in without knocking, found it empty, and slammed the door behind him. He continued to the outside door, opening it, hoping to get through to the next carriage.

The bridge between the two carriages provided a precarious perch. As he struggled with the door handle of the following carriage, he tried not to think about the ground rushing by him on either side. He continued to wrestle with the handle, but it wouldn't budge, no matter how he tried. He looked at the ground – could he jump? – but looking at it made him queasy, so he looked away. There was nothing for it; he would have to go back into the guard's compartment.

He re-entered, and found it still empty. He caught his breath, and his scattered thoughts. Mahommed, Afridi warrior, late of the Sultan's army, a man not to be trifled with by a mere girl. He repeated those thoughts, forcing himself to listen. *A mere girl.* What could she possibly do to him?

Before he could answer his question, the door to the compartment opened and she entered, closing the door behind her. She smiled at him and said, 'That was rude, and I'm sorry.'

He stared at her, wishing himself anywhere but where he was. As she held out her hand to him, his eyes lit on the emergency cord.

'I'm Alice. Alice Mercer.'

He was no longer listening to anything but the voice in his head, the one that said, *They laughed at you, the whole train is laughing at you.* He ignored her outstretched hand

and lunged for the emergency cord, yanking it as hard as he could. A bell rang, and the train shuddered to a noisy stop, causing her to lose her balance and fall into his arms.

He felt her flesh pressing against his; her hair tucked under his chin, cushioning it. It was more than he could bear. He quickly disengaged from her, set her on her feet, and made for the outside door. As he opened it, he turned back to her, feeling that he owed her some explanation for his actions.

'My station.'

My station? What made him say *that*?

He hurried out the door to the linking bridge, threw his case onto the ground, and jumped off after it, catching both his coat pocket and turban as he fell. He picked himself up, found his case, and began to run – into the desert, away from the train, away from her.

He heard her call after him, 'You haven't told me your name! What's your name?'

He ran and ran and ran, away from her stupid voice, her stupid face, her stupid mocking questions. He became hotter: the sun burning from outside, his humiliation from inside, until both sources of heat met, searing what was left of him; leaving him unable to do anything but stop and gulp dry air into his lungs, leaving him powerless against her teasing voice, floating through him and asking, *What's your name?*

As his breathing became more controlled, he straightened and looked around, noticing for the first time the emptiness surrounding him. In the distance, the train had started again. He watched it for a while, the one moving thing in the landscape.

He became aware that the end of his turban was hanging down, an annoyance. He yanked it off, and, holding it by one end, watched as it unravelled into a limp cloth pile on the ground. For no good reason other than that by now he was heat affected, the shape of it appealed to him. He began to float it through the still air, concentrating his mind on the ribbon of cloth, watching it as the patterns it formed became something beautiful. As an extension of the cloth, he saw that he had become beautiful, too. He jumped in the air, joining the dance of the turban cloth. He noticed that his legs were not his legs but had turned to jelly, doing a wobble of their own devising, somehow bouncing over the earth, and, how clever, keeping him upright at the same time. He started to laugh, waving the turban cloth at the disappearing train, shouting, his voice full of pride, 'My name is Gool Mahommed! Gool Mahommed, Esquire!'

Then his legs stopped dancing, and he fell to the ground.

2

Alice watched as Irma embroidered an 'R' on a man's white cotton handkerchief. She doubted Robert would notice how neat the stitches were, but she wasn't about to share that thought because Irma was barely speaking to her. She had made her disapproval plain when Alice invited the Afghan man to take the empty seat; now he was gone she was making it plainer. Alice supposed she should use the remaining minutes before they arrived home to apologise for the fuss she had caused, but doubted whether she could feign enough sincerity for the apology to be accepted.

She turned to stare out the window at the red desert plain. There wasn't much to look at; it had been the same since daybreak, and would stay the same until they arrived back. There was the odd distant homestead, the occasional mob of emus and kangaroos.

There were roos in the distance now, but all they did was break up dirty red with jumping specks of equally dirty grey. She squinted and tried to turn the kangaroos into starbursts of colour, but her imagination failed her and they stayed grey.

The few days away with Irma had been an unexpected treat. Mrs Cowie, Irma's mother, had originally advanced the idea, thinking it would be a good opportunity for Irma to buy linen for her trousseau.

Alice had reacted in surprise. 'Robert's proposed?'

'Almost. He's planning to, very soon.'

'How do you know?'

Alice hadn't meant to interrogate her, she was simply curious about her certainty, but Irma shut the subject off. The thing was, she said, her mother couldn't come with her, and she needed a companion, so if Alice would like to join her, she'd be very welcome.

Alice told her it was unlikely they could afford it, but her brother Lewis was surprisingly warm towards the idea, and had insisted she go. He assured her that he and Eileen, their eleven-year-old sister, could manage; that one day soon their lives might change; they should enjoy what they could, while they could.

'Change in what way?' she asked.

Lewis had shrugged. 'We're not children any more. Not everything can stay the same.'

She wondered what he was hiding from her. 'Has something already changed?'

'Alice, if you don't want to go, just say so.'

She hadn't pursued it for fear he would change his mind. Of course she wanted to go; to put behind her, if only briefly, a place with streets called Sulphide and Oxide and Chloride. Where the names matched the fumes spewing out of every boiler stack. Why wouldn't she? Adelaide had streets called King William and Wakefield and Wright. Names of people, names to be proud of. She had found pleasure in walking them, safe in the knowledge they weren't named after a poison.

She and Irma had stayed in a guesthouse behind Rundle Street – chosen by Mrs Cowie as suitable for gentlewomen – and each morning Alice dutifully accompanied Irma on her shopping expedition. By afternoon, Irma, exhausted by the impossibility of choosing between cotton and linen lawn, needed a nap, and Alice encouraged this, taking the opportunity to go walking on her own, without the burden of having to give an opinion about voile.

Halifax Street, Jeffcott Street, Pennington Terrace, Molesworth Street. She held each man's name in her head as she walked his street. She had no idea who these men were, but it didn't matter; they were people who had given their names to the ground beneath her feet. She found it soothing that they had somehow claimed this ground as their own, that such a thing was possible, when she didn't even know how to claim herself.

She had shared this with Irma, which was a mistake.

'That's silly,' said Irma.

'I didn't say it wasn't.'

'I don't even know what you mean by it. How can you claim yourself?'

'That's what I want to find out.'

She had just decided it was not worth pursuing when Irma fixed her with a look that said she was going to pronounce on something.

'My mother's right. She says you're your father's daughter.'

'Well, of course I am. Why wouldn't I be?'

'I don't mean that way.'

'What way?'

'I'm only telling you what she said.'

It went around in circles like that until Alice let it go. Anyway, she knew what was meant. That she was perverse. That she was like him. Maybe she was, although not all of him, not the whisky part. After he died she found what was left in his bottle, only about four inches. He would have wanted to drink it so she did it for him, hoping to find him there. Instead it made her violently ill, and she had never been tempted by whisky again. The empty bottle she had kept for months, hidden in her wardrobe, to be taken out and held when she needed to do so. Eileen eventually found it and queried its presence, and rather than tell the truth, Alice threw it out.

She blew on the window and watched as her breath briefly clouded the view. They were almost back. With each passing mile she could feel disquiet growing, feel herself hollowing into nothing. The imagined possibilities that had come to her on the streets of Adelaide were already poor and faded. In Broken Hill there would only be her home, her work at the hospital, and the poison streets that connected the two. She wondered if Irma, who was looking forward to her return, looking forward to seeing Robert, was ever troubled in this way, but she didn't think Irma would welcome being questioned about it. She wished she had someone more capable than Irma to ask about things that bothered her, but she had no gift for making friends. She and Irma had become tied through their mothers' friendship; it was not something either made a choice about. She couldn't ask Lewis, because he had troubles of his own. She once tried to talk to Reverend Piercey, asking him if a person could be nothing and something at the same time. He had replied by explaining the Holy Trinity, which wasn't much use when what she wanted was for him to explain *her*.

She turned from the window, watching as Irma neatly trimmed the final stitch. Even if Irma couldn't give her answers, she was still her friend. She searched for a light topic that might allow her to unstiffen. 'I read that Houdini can escape from anywhere. That he was tied up in chains and put in a box, which was lowered into a lake, and he freed himself and got out in less than two minutes.'

Irma remained frosty. 'Why would anyone want to do that?'

'Because it's better than drowning.'

'But why do it in the first place?'

While in Adelaide they had seen a magician at a show. Not only was he able to escape from an iron box, but he had also, he claimed, been trained by The Great Houdini. After the show she had waited behind, wanting to touch him, but Irma, afraid of embarrassment, had dragged her away. All she'd wanted was a touch, in the hope of some infinitesimal transference of his powers, but this had been too much potential humiliation for Irma to cope with so she'd had to let the idea go.

The Afghan man had also escaped. The Afghan with his slender, uncallused hands and his manicured nails. No-one had chased after him. Only her, but he hadn't wanted her apology. He had wanted nothing to do with her. She had climbed down from the carriage half thinking she might follow, but he was already too far away.

The train driver had come out to investigate. A fat man joined them and said he had sat near the Afghan during the first part of the journey and he was a strange one. He had turned to Alice for corroboration. 'You were after him. What happened? He nick something from you?'

'No. He didn't do anything.'

She didn't know if she should explain further, but the driver didn't seem much interested. He was irritated by the delay. He made it plain that if a crazy Afghan had decided to jump off the train then that was his business, and no more than could be expected from one of those people. He went back to the driver's compartment, leaving Alice to turn to the fat man. 'Shouldn't we wait?'

'What for?'

'What if something's happened to him?'

He looked at her as though she were stupid. 'In that case there wouldn't be any point in waiting, would there?' He climbed back onto the train.

Alice looked at the surrounding desert. Her desire to make right her wrong was no match for its immensity. She turned and meekly followed the fat man onto the train.

As she went back to her seat Irma looked at her accusingly. 'Honestly, Alice, what were you thinking?'

Thinking? What had thinking got to do with it? She gave Irma a puzzled look. 'About what?'

Irma held her look for a moment. Then, as Alice hoped she would, gave up. 'Never mind.'

It was Irma who saw the first boiler stack. She craned forward with excitement, forgetting her annoyance. 'We're almost home! Look, can you see it?'

Alice didn't have to look; she knew what she would see. One big slag heap, squatting sullenly beneath the stacks. As they drew closer it would divide, revealing itself to be composed of a number of tailings dumps and waste heaps, each overshadowed by its own stack. She'd lost count of the dust storms that picked up this waste and scattered it over the town like a giant pepper shaker; lost count of the times she'd had to bring the washing in and start all over again. But the heaps never got any smaller; she didn't know why the storms bothered.

As the train pulled into the station she shut her eyes to concentrate on feeling happy. Lewis and Eileen would be waiting for her, and she knew Eileen would be excited at the prospect of having her big sister back home; she would have to try to match that excitement.

Irma was already heading towards the carriage door, eager to spot her mother among the crowd pushing forward to greet the arrivals. Alice hung back in the doorway, wanting to see Lewis and Eileen before they saw her.

She found them: Eileen clinging to Lewis's side to avoid the crush, Lewis with a protective arm around her. The sight of him unbalanced her. *He looks so young.* He was three years older than Alice, but she'd never thought of him as being young before. He was scanning the passengers, anxiously waiting for her to emerge.

She stepped down from the train and waved at them. She was back. They would walk the dusty streets to the little tin-walled house in Cobalt Lane, where they could all be anxious together.

3

Mahommed sat on the ground in the scrubby shade. This, he was forced to admit, was a setback; a less auspicious start to his new life than he had imagined. He let this depressing lump of thought sit in his head for a while before dealing with it, shaking it into a new and shiny thought. This was a challenge, not a setback; a small test to remind him what he was capable of. He was Gool Mahommed. It would take more than a bit of sandy desert to intimidate him.

He looked at the railway line. He estimated the train had been no more than fifteen miles from Broken Hill when he fled. Allowing for the uneven ground and the increasing heat of the day, if he followed the track it should take him two hours, three at the most, to reach his destination. These hours would pass quickly if he used them well; by the time he arrived the shops would be open and he could reward himself with a purchase, something that would not have been possible had he arrived at eight on the train, as planned.

He picked up the turban cloth to re-wind it on his head, but thought better of it. All things happen for good reason, he thought; if I am to start, then I should start now. He slung it round his neck, picked up his case, and headed for the track.

He began conjugating aloud before he reached it. 'I like Broken Hill, you like Broken Hill, he / she / it likes Broken Hill.' By the time five minutes had passed he had gone through his repertoire of English verbs, past, present and future. In the ensuing silence his head filled with thoughts he didn't want. They told him he was small and unworthy. *You are nothing. You deserve nothing.* He shook them away and started at the beginning again, this time concentrating on pronunciation.

When he finally saw it, the jolt was almost physical. The slag heap floating, shimmering in its heat haze. He had been picking his way through a particularly rocky stretch of ground when he looked up to check his position, and there it was, looking straight back at him, about a mile from where he stood, as if to say: Here I am, welcome back.

Like Broken Hill? He loved it; how could he not? It was the Silver City. The streets weren't paved with it, but beneath them the ground was full of it, and not just silver but zinc and lead, too. Soon he would be under that ground, growing richer with every ounce he helped scrape out. Let the others hoard their pennies from the camel runs; he would have pounds. He would lay them in front of Abdullah to say two things. Thank you for all you did for me. And I was right.

Broken Hill was where he had lived when he made his first trip to Australia five years earlier. Recruited by a merchant from Karachi, with promises that now made him burn with humiliation – how easily he had been seduced – he had sailed to Port Augusta in the company of a string of camels; eating, pissing, shitting with them, deep in the rancid bowels of the ship. When he went on deck to escape them, to pray, to remove their slops, to remind himself of the existence of the sun, he could see that he was dirty, but it was not until he went back below and was hit by the stench that he understood he was now part of it. He had a small piece of soap with him, but it wasn't enough, the camel stink was layers deep, and anyway, there was no fresh water to waste. He stayed miserably smelly.

In Port Augusta, he resolved, he would politely ask the agent for water to wash. On hearing this, the agent would understand that he was more than fleas and lice and camel dung; that his disgusting presentation was born of necessity, not inclination; that he was a young man of dignity, well worth the pound a week he had been promised. And that would be only the start because, he felt sure, before long he would not merely be working a string of camels, he would own one; then two and three, and who knew what that might bring?

This wasn't blind optimism, but rather, in his opinion, an objective assessment of his capabilities and possibilities. He had a wiry body, muscled by work. Thick black hair and unblemished skin, unlike his poor brother Omar, whose face, thanks to pox, was a landscape of dormant craters. A penis, sturdy and serviceable, although as yet unserviced, if one discounted the efforts of his own hand and one overpriced prostitute. An able mind that had seen him jump nimbly through five whole years at the Little Star Ideal English School, a privilege that was accorded to him, as the favoured youngest, by his indulgent older brothers. A faith that rested comfortably, if a little lightly, on the five pillars. An impressive attention to personal hygiene that marked him a cut above others of his background. And – admittedly, this was not entirely objective – a certain raffish charm, which, coupled with boyish sparkle, would surely ease his way in this far-off land.

The agent, Abdul Rasool, seemed unaware of these attributes. Worse, he was unaware of the details of the agreement that Mahommed had made with the Karachi merchant. There was to be no one-pound-a-week, no ongoing work. There was only a one-off payment of seven shillings, some basic provisions, and a directive to deliver the camels to one Mullah Abdullah in Broken Hill. Take it or leave it.

Mahommed's first inclination was to say he would leave it. His second was to cry. In between was an awful chasm of understanding where he saw he had been foolish to sign a contract in English, which he was barely able to speak, let alone read; foolish to so blithely travel to the end of the earth; foolish to think that any good would come out of sailing to this godforsaken country where no-one, not even Abdul Rasool, knew or cared to know his name. He refused to let himself cry before this man, so moved on to his third inclination. He would take it.

For Mahommed, accustomed to the harsh landscape of the Hindu Kush, the journey was neither overly long nor arduous. He was told to follow the railway line and that is what he did, driving the camels through the cool of the night; finding shade to rest in during the day. The days were the difficult part, the times when he had no alternative but to reflect on his situation. His mortification was still raw, a wound he would pick at for many months; one that would only be healed by constant remembering of the details until, piece by awkward piece, he would rework them into an entirely different mosaic, allowing him to feel that, overall, he had handled things very well indeed. But not yet, not now. Now, mortification fought for space with panic. He had no job, no money, no means of getting home. He had the name of a man who lived near a broken hill. Whether he liked it or not, it would have to do.

That man, Abdullah, took him in, gave him charity, then a job working the camel runs to far outlying properties; helped him save, shilling by shilling, the money needed for his passage home. It was Abdullah who subtly directed his plans, suggesting that Mahommed could satisfy his ambitions better from home than here. It was agreed that the family plot of land was too small to support Mahommed, but surely there were other options? Rather than rail against the merchant from Karachi, why not become one himself? Or an agent, or a supplier for one? Or while he was still young, make *Hajj*, the pilgrimage Abdullah had himself not yet made. Here, he said, there was only dust and despair, burning days and freezing nights and English disdain.

'I could work in the mines,' suggested Mahommed, tentatively searching for a reason to stay. He knew that in the past, one or two of the Afghans had found work as miners.

Abdullah sneered at the suggestion. 'There is no work. They are on strike. Them and their unions.'

Mahommed, in town for supplies one day, had been stirred by the sight of thousands of men and women marching down Argent Street in support of their rights. There had been some sort of mine lockout; he didn't know why. All he knew was the urge to be one of them, shouting slogans with them, happy in the belief that together they were powerful, strong and right. He didn't want to spend his life creeping away. The English didn't, so why should he?

Abdullah whisked these thoughts out of Mahommed's head, replacing them with his own. Mahommed was sixteen, Abdullah nearly sixty; how could his own thoughts compete? By the time he had enough money saved for his passage there was no longer any doubt in his mind that home was where he should be. He left, with Abdullah's blessing and good wishes.

On the journey back to Afghanistan, away from Abdullah's influence, Mahommed started having a few ideas that hadn't been planted by someone else. Although Abdullah was respected in the camp, and was, in Mahommed's opinion, deserving of that respect, in the town itself he was considered part of a homogeneous mass of Afghanness. Not above, not below, just interchangeable with all the others. Mahommed considered the possible reasons for this, lining them up neatly in his head.

One: the turban. In his year at Broken Hill he had come to a rough understanding of social structure among Europeans, and one thing was clear – men of standing could be bareheaded or hatted, but they were never turbaned. If they were hatted, they doffed their hats at certain social moments, such as meeting women, and, he'd been told, when entering church. Mahommed briefly wondered if the impossibility of doffing a turban had anything to do with the lack of them among men of standing, but decided in the end that it was simply an ingrained, and therefore inexplicable, prejudice in favour of rabbit felt over soft, clean muslin.

Two: the camels. Although the English made use of the camels, they were contemptuous of those who worked them. This was odd, given that they didn't seem to feel that way about men who kept pigs; nevertheless, that was the way they felt.

Three: the language. Although English was more polluted than Pashto or Dari, and, to Mahommed's ear, unattractively guttural, it was the language of the ruling class. Abdullah had never acknowledged this fact, and had limited his use of it to the most basic exchanges. It was an understandable arrogance, but Mahommed felt it was probably held against him.

Four: the slaughter. As Mullah, Abdullah was responsible for the correct slaughter of livestock. The English ate impure meat, leaving the blood to congeal with the carcass. Worse, they insisted that everyone did the same, marshalling butchers into unions, forcing them all to follow the same unclean practices. Naturally enough, Abdullah refused to join, a refusal that did not endear him to local officials.

It was a depressing list, thought Mahommed, and completely irrational. But if one put personal feelings aside and viewed it from a distance, there was one thing that could be learned from it: the English were simply not very bright. Having latched on to that insight, Mahommed held it tight, needing to ward off the troubling question that followed: if they aren't very bright, why are they in charge of so much? And, more importantly, how did they manage to invent Cuticura soap?

By the time he disembarked in Karachi, he had spent weeks swirling these questions through his mind, and had come up with numerous answers. I am much younger than Abdullah, he thought, and therefore more able to understand the world. If I had not listened to him, and had instead made my own way, the English would have soon recognised my inherent good qualities.

Although the English are not very bright, they have the ability to stride confidently across the whole world, and that is a skill worth learning. If I had spent more time with them, I'm sure I could have learned that skill. He also thought, because there was a limit to how long one could think of only one subject before getting bored, you can see by my eyes that I am an interesting young man who thinks interesting things. And, coming up on deck one night when the ocean was silent and slippery black, seamlessly joining with the sky, he looked out with wonder and thought, the universe is very big. I must grow to meet it.

None of this was any help to him back home. Two of his brothers' wives had had more children, meaning there was less room than ever, but apart from this nothing seemed to have changed. Except him. He saw his old life with new eyes and found it barren, bleak, and boring. He lasted three weeks before deciding Abdullah had been wrong. He determined to return to Broken Hill, where he would work in the mines, study the ways of the English, and become rich. This cheered him up and gave him a purpose.

He calculated how he could earn money for the voyage, but these calculations did not take into account the existence of the Ottoman Empire and Turkey's apparent ownership of Afghanistan. They also did not take into account the expansionist plans of the Sultan, the visit of the army man, or the disloyalty of his oldest sister-in-law. Despite his protestation that he was only seventeen, not nineteen, the age for conscription, he was bundled into the Turkish army, where he proceeded to endure more misery than he had ever known existed. He didn't know why Italy wanted Libya; he didn't know why Turkey wanted to keep it. He only knew he wanted to come out of the army alive. Mahommed got his wish. The Italians got Libya.

Five years ago, he had offered his belly to the town like the kicked dog he was. But now he was a man, ready to meet it on equal terms. He felt his heart beating against his ribs. It was anticipation, not fear. He increased speed, leaving the train line as he reached the outskirts of the town. At first it seemed almost the same as it was when he left, only more importantly itself, but when he looked for the Williams Street reserve, he lost his bearings and slowed, unable to recognise anything at all. He looked around, bewildered, until it came to him that in his absence the town had grown, spreading past the reserve in a grid of new streets. He found Williams Street and turned left, hurrying along to Bromide Street, where he turned right, towards Argent Street. He stared openly as a truck drove past him, heavy with wool bales, heading, he assumed, for the railway station. When he had been here before, there had been only bullock and camel trains taking goods to and from the outlying stations – when had trucks joined them? And streetlights? When had it been decided that Bromide Street was important enough for streetlights?

He ignored the little tacked together shacks with their flour bag curtains and bare earth yards; of course not everything would have changed, he understood that. But streetlights meant money. A lot of it. Despite his exhaustion, despite his thirst, he picked up his pace, puffed up with the absolute rightness of being back here at such a time of prosperity.

He turned into Argent Street, quickly finding shade under the covered awnings of the main street shops. He was by now in desperate need of water and was momentarily tempted by the bar of the Royal Exchange Hotel, where miners from the midnight shift were already sluicing the aches from their bones. But he wasn't sure how a request for water would be received, or whether or not there would be a charge, so he continued on to Boan Brothers where, once he had shown her that he had enough cash for the purchase, a shop girl sold him what he most desired.

He was nearly done, concentrating on little more than putting one foot in front of the other. He turned into Chloride Street, then Crystal Street, where he forced himself to concentrate, scanning the front of the buildings for the one he wanted, until finally he saw a sign, which said:

Adrian Kadran Esq.
Naturopath and Herbalist
Practitioner of Scientific Method

Underneath that one, another, announcing:

Alhambra Boarding House
Proprietor Adrian Kadran Esq.

Clutching his suitcase and his freshly wrapped parcel, Mahommed hurried inside.

Mr Adrian Kadran led him along the dingy labyrinth of corridors to the cheaper single men's accommodation. Glancing briefly back, he said, 'You have confirmation of your employment?'

His voice was well modulated, without a trace of Indian lilt. Mahommed tried to emulate it. 'At the Proprietary Mine. Starting tomorrow.'

'You realise that reading lessons are sixpence extra?'

'We agreed four.'

Mr Kadran seemed to sense his uncertainty. 'Intensive lessons are six. A necessity in your case, I would have thought. However, it's entirely up to you …' He let the words hang as he stopped at a door, unlocking it to reveal a plainly furnished room with a single bed, a wardrobe, a chair, and a washstand. 'Breakfast is from six-thirty until eight. If you have any problems …'

Mahommed stopped him before he could leave. 'There is one thing …'

Mr Kadran picked a piece of fluff from his woollen suit jacket, and watched it float to the floor of the room. 'Yes?'

Ignoring the pained irritation of his tone, Mahommed put his case down, and opened his parcel, revealing a wrapped cake of Alpine soap. 'Read it for me?'

Mr Kadran raised an eyebrow, making it clear he felt the request was strange. 'Alpine soap. The absolute top-notcher for rejuvenating and preserving the skin. Has proved a boon to thousands for shaving purposes.'

As he handed the soap back, Mahommed nodded, satisfied. 'Sixpence.'

'Agreed.' Mr Kadran turned to go, stopping briefly at the door. 'Personally, I use Rexona.'

He left, shutting the door behind him, leaving Mahommed looking at the soap wrapper with concentration, trying to make the swimming letters fit Mr Kadran's words. 'Top-notcher for rejuvenating and preserving, top-notcher for rejuvenating …'

He unwrapped the soap, placed it next to the washbasin, and proceeded to fill the basin with water from the jug sitting next to it. He unbuttoned his shirt, preparing to wash. He willed himself to wait, knowing this moment could exist only once.

He lasted fifteen trembling seconds before grabbing the soap, dipping it in the water, and beginning to lather. After the long desert walk, his thoughts were as slippery as the soap, but one stayed firm, growing till it filled his whole being.

I have begun.

4

Abdullah was the one who mattered. The one to whom Mahommed had written, explaining his decision to return. He knew he would be expecting him, so, after washing and performing *Salat ul Zuhr*, he opened his case and took out his offering of dates and *bhang*. He looked at them, already sensing their inadequacy. Well, they were what they were. Abdullah would be so pleased to see him that the size of the gift would be irrelevant. He picked them up and tucked them safely inside his shirt.

Still, he hesitated before setting off towards the camel camp. Aware of his hesitation, he tried to identify its source. But it was lost to him, and he knew he couldn't spend the rest of the day standing in an empty room waiting for it to appear. He opened his door and went out into the hallway, looking to see if it was clear before locking the door after him, pushing his hand against it to make sure it was secure. He went downstairs and out the door, turning right in the direction of Williams Street and the camel camp.

His unease grew as he turned into the crooked end of Williams Street. The bustling centre of town was behind him, the distances between the houses he was passing increasing. He had thought by now the growing town might have spread as far as the camp, but it was soon obvious he was wrong. It had been ten minutes since he had passed a house, the last one little more than a rudimentary shack. Ahead of him stretched at least a clear half-mile of scrubby mulga. The road itself was empty. What little pedestrian traffic there was when he started out had now vanished. Apart from an occasional dray there were no vehicles. No-one has a reason to go there, he thought. Only me.

He slowed as he neared it, his boots like lumps of lead. It was his former home. He wanted to feel excited about seeing it again after so long away, but the only thing he felt was a deadening sense of suffocation.

Unlike the town, the camp hadn't grown. His memory had told him it was larger than this, but now he saw it for what it was; nothing but a couple of scrubby acres, one a holding paddock for the camels, the other something similar for the Afghans.

There was a desultory, shabby air about it that he had never before noticed, a give-up-and-die crumbling edge to the old shacks and their dusty forecourts. Near the shacks was the one-room corrugated-iron mosque where Abdullah led prayer. Mahommed remembered the mats, pushed edge to edge when all the men were inside, so he knew it had been small, but *this* small?

He wanted to flee before he had even entered.

He heard the tinkling of *zungwalla* over in the camel paddock and looked across to see a man hobbling a camel. He looked familiar to Mahommed, and he narrowed his eyes for a better look. It took a moment before he recognised Wadud, one of the men who had been here before. Wadud had a wonky left eye, courtesy of a camel kick, which gave his face a lopsided sinister cast, but Mahommed had liked him, and remembered the tolerant good humour that belied his appearance.

The tightness in his chest eased. The condition of the camp wasn't important; it was the men who lived in it who mattered. They were his friends; he was happy to be among them. He hurried on, eager to see Abdullah after being so long apart from him.

He found the old man on his hands and knees, clearing debris from the ablution pool next to the mosque. He wanted to rush into his arms, to hug and kiss him, to feel his bony warmth. But Abdullah barely reacted to his presence. 'You're back.'

'Yes.'

Abdullah climbed slowly to his feet. He took in Mahommed's Western dress, his shirt tucked in to his trousers.

'You look English.'

Mahommed's instinctive swell of pride was quickly replaced by the realisation that it was not a compliment.

'You're staying in the town?'

'Yes.' He had known this point would be tricky. 'I'm working in the mine. I have a room nearby.' He handed over the gifts, needing to cover an awkward moment. 'I have thought of you often, Abdullah. And always with thanks.'

Abdullah nodded stiffly, accepting the gifts and thanks as his due. When Wadud came up to welcome Mahommed, Abdullah moved away on some chore, and had spoken little to him since.

'We were completely surrounded ...'

Mahommed paused his story, trying to gauge Abdullah's reaction to it. It was night, there was a fire and, thanks to a freshly killed goat, a plentiful communal meal. There were old and new friends to embrace and impress. Along with Wadud, Sherdil had instantly recognised him, greeting him as a long-lost friend. He remembered old Jemadar, of course, but most of the others he didn't know, although they too greeted him with warmth. He enjoyed the temporary stature that, as the latest news bringer, he was being accorded.

Only Abdullah was less than effusive about his return. He joined the others for the meal, but was so far showing no interest in Mahommed's tales of adventure. Mahommed added detail, hoping to break through his shell. 'There seemed no way out, but I was fighting for both Allah and the Sultan and this gave me added courage. So that night, when the enemy were sleeping, I crept into their camp ...'

'Was there no-one on watch?' This from Jemadar, whose unhelpful interruption threatened to derail his story.

Mahommed stayed in charge. 'Three men. But one by one I silently slit their throats. And then, when I had loosened the horses ...'

'They must have made a noise.' Jemadar again, with rather more vigour than his frail physical appearance would suggest.

He responded firmly. 'They didn't. So when I had loosened the horses, I crept ...'

'Silently?'

Mahommed cursed himself for starting this story. But he couldn't retreat without losing face. 'Yes, of course silently. I crept to their cannon, I turned it round to face their camp, and then I lit it and blew them all into the sky.'

He glanced at Abdullah, sitting across the fire from him. He didn't expect him to believe this tale of courage yet hoped he might have been entertained by the telling. But the fire shielded Abdullah's eyes, and Mahommed saw nothing.

When the fire died down, Abdullah stood and left without comment. Mahommed, torn between bewilderment and irritation, watched as he headed towards the camel paddock. He knew that neither of these feelings would lead to anything useful, and was annoyed with himself for turning back into the immature boy who had left. Despite the lack of invitation, he stood and hurried after him.

Abdullah was checking the hobbles on his three camels.

'Would you like me to help you?'

'There is nothing to be done.'

Mahommed wanted to confront him; wanted to say, *Do you know how far I have travelled today to see you?* Wanted to say, *Does that mean nothing to you?* Instead he put his head down and busied himself filling a small pipe with *bhang*, waiting for Abdullah to tell him, as he surely would, what terrible crime he had committed.

After seeing to the camels' needs, which tonight entailed a lot of fiddling about, designed, Mahommed suspected, purely to make him wait, Abdullah finally deigned to speak. 'You should not have come back.'

Mahommed exhaled, passing the pipe to him. 'I had hoped you would be pleased to see me.'

'I hoped you would understand why I sent you home.'

'Abdullah … the conditions in the army were not quite how I described them.'

'I have allowed for that. But your term is over.'

'And my family is poor. And the Russians and the English are always causing trouble and making life difficult.' This was true in a general sense, although Mahommed had never met a Russian.

'Life is difficult everywhere.'

Mahommed had forgotten how gloomy Abdullah could be. He countered, 'If you feel that way, why don't *you* go home?'

'Because it is no longer there!'

Mahommed didn't know why Abdullah seemed so angry. He hadn't told him anything he didn't already know. That Abdullah had come to Broken

Hill after the Chaman earthquake was no secret. Nor that the earthquake had taken members of his family. Mahommed didn't know the details because Abdullah had never offered them for discussion. But it was twenty years ago, almost Mahommed's lifetime. Surely whatever pain had been caused was long gone.

'Your memories are still there.'

'None that I wish to stir.'

'If you are so adamant you won't go back, why do you keep trying to persuade me to?'

'Because you are young, you still have a chance to make something of yourself.'

Mahommed held his ground. 'Which is exactly what I plan to do here.'

Abdullah took a long draw on the pipe, holding the smoke in before he spoke again. 'My point, which you are not allowing me to make, is that they don't want us here. We don't belong.'

'But if we did belong, they would want us.' Mahommed's tone intensified as he tried to clarify his position. 'If we worked like them, and looked like them, and sounded and acted like them, then they would want us, and we could have all the things that they have.'

'We would still be who we are.'

'Exactly. Which would make us doubly blessed.' He took back the pipe, declining to argue further, preferring to give in to the image of Alice, which was sliding in to the corners of his mind, taking a free ride on a puff of *bhang*.

Abdullah looked at him, disdain dripping. 'You've become a fool.'

The words slapped Alice out of his head. Abdullah didn't wait for him to protest. He headed back to his shack, leaving Mahommed alone with the camels.

It was still early; in the distance he could see some of the men moving about. He'd lost all desire to talk with them. As he left, he kept to the edges of the camp to avoid being seen and began the empty walk back to his room in town.

5

Slow. Breathe slowly. If she concentrated on nothing more than breathing, she would be alright, she could last till daylight. The window faced east; her bed, wedged against it, would catch the first morning rays. She would be alright.

She always woke first, even after nights when she could sleep. Eileen's bed, across the room from hers, caught the sun five minutes later, but even then she had to be roused, crumpled and sleepily complaining. Lewis, in their parents' old room, would rise a little later, remaining monosyllabic until she had made the tea. He would thaw after that, probably more as a favour than by inclination.

It had been a strange homecoming. After the initial greetings, Lewis had seemed overly interested to know whether the trip to Adelaide had settled her. His word:

settled. It made her think of dust. He hadn't seemed at all interested in the details of what she and Irma had seen and done.

She had never travelled so far from Broken Hill before, and never to a big city. Eileen, envious of the treat she'd been given, had questioned her relentlessly, demanding detail upon intricate detail.

Lewis told her he had heard that France had declared war against Germany. That England would probably soon join in. But news travelled slowly to Broken Hill through the filters of distance. Had Alice heard anything more?

Alice told him what she knew. Only the headlines, which Lewis had already seen. She had never been to any of the countries involved and knew little about them. She found it hard to sort out exactly what was going on. It was probably just a storm in a teacup, which would soon be over. Lewis disagreed. He seemed to want her to be wrong. She didn't argue; she didn't much care. It was nothing to do with her. It was nothing to do with him either, so why was he being so insistent?

Slowly. Breathe out. Then in. She didn't understand where it came from. Not a nightmare. She'd had plenty of those, where the sheer terror of what was happening – being chased, or eaten alive, drowning, dissolving, all manner of indescribable horrors – was enough to hurtle her, at the last possible moment, into the relative safety of wakefulness. This was different. This was dreamless sleep, which for no apparent reason would suddenly catapult her into being awake, only to find that the sheer terror was on this side of the divide, pressing against her from all sides, overwhelming her with such force that even breathing was beyond her.

She made herself go through the list. My bed, my room, my home, my brother, my sister. She went through it again, lingering on each word, drawing strength from the commonplace safety of each item, each person. My bed, my room, my home, my brother, my sister.

Eileen hadn't liked the dress material Alice had bought for her in Adelaide. Aqua-blue brocade, shot through with pink. Eileen, with eleven-year-old tact, said it looked Chinese. Well, it did, it was — wasn't that why it was beautiful? But Alice knew there was no point in making it up for her, she would never wear it.

The magician's assistant had worn a dress in nearly the same colour; not Chinese, but sparkling and exotic nonetheless. She had worn it when she climbed into the box and allowed the magician to close the lid; allowed him to thrust the sword right through her body ten times. Alice had been on the edge of her seat, already seeing bright red spurts of blood pulsing out and staining the blue dress. But there were none, and the magician released his assistant unscathed. Alice thought maybe that was the power of aqua blue, and said as much to Irma. Irma scoffed, and said it was a trick, making Alice wish she had never opened her mouth.

Yes, it was a trick, but wasn't everything? When she was younger she had played a game, avoiding the cracks in the footpath to safeguard herself against marriage to a black man. It was common knowledge this was one of the worst fates that could befall you, although she wasn't sure what form the black man would take. Not an Aborigine, not a Chinaman, not an Arab. She had guessed something halfway between a Negro and a giant golliwog, and thinking about it gave her shivers to the point where she would jump on the cracks just to see what would happen. She knew that probably nothing would; the relationship between cause and effect had never seemed to her to be all that definite, so why not jump on a crack? Why not allow it the power to marry her off to a golliwog? Why not allow a blue dress the power to ward off the thrust of a sword?

Breathe in. Out. Slowly. The trembling had stopped; she was starting to feel calmer. As yet there was no sign of the headache that often accompanied these sudden awakenings; perhaps she would be lucky today and manage to avoid it altogether. She sat up and pulled a corner of the curtain aside, looking out at the dark street. She wondered if that man was still out there, running away from her across the desert. He wouldn't have done so if she hadn't given in to the moment of casual cruelty that had caused him to flee. Her words had been spoken lightly; they weren't intended to wound. But, she now realised, what else could they have done?

She hadn't wanted him to leave. He had been an unexpected visitor to her thoughts, and she had wanted him to stay. It was more than his hands. It was his face, so completely open, even though she knew it couldn't be; that the whole point of a face was to hide what was behind it. But even if she was wrong about his face, she was sure she wasn't wrong about what she felt when the movement of the train caused their shoulders to briefly touch. He may have felt nothing. The carriage was dark; he may have been asleep. Now, thanks to what she did, she would never know.

She wished she could turn the clock back, but that was a trick she knew was beyond her, so she simply added cruelty to her ever-growing list of character faults. She let the curtain drop and lay down again. It was cold. She pulled the quilt closer and faced the window, waiting for the sun.

6

Adrian Kadran's private suite was much grander than Mahommed's humble room. It consisted of his bedroom, a private living area, a bathroom, and a consulting room-cum-study. The consulting room was where he received patients, and was the only room outsiders were allowed to see. Consequently, it was the one on which he had lavished the most care. In an alcove, discreetly curtained off, he had an examination bench. More visible was a mahogany desk and three chairs, the largest for himself, the other two for patients. He also had two brown leather chesterfield settees, facing each other, a bookcase filled with English literature – largely unread – and walls hung with paintings, framed patient testimonials, and three professional certificates.

He was especially fond of the paintings. Most of them featured various aspects of English country life, as lived by the gentry: fox hunting, fishing, garden parties and the like. He liked to place himself in the scenes, say, for example, riding to hounds, calling *tally ho* and *pip pip* and occasionally blowing a bugle, and always, *always*, with a young lady in the background, silently gazing at him with heartfelt admiration. But if he was fond of the paintings, he was proud of the testimonials. He had laboured over them for hours, trying to find the right blend of gushing gratitude and scientific verisimilitude. Too much gratitude and there was the danger of arousing suspicion; too much science and there was the danger of the reader falling asleep before reading it in full. He considered he had done an excellent job in finding the balance.

The certificates had been bestowed upon him by the Oxford College of Scientific Enquiry, The Cambridge Institute of Herbal Science, and the York Naturopathic School, for passing courses in Empirical Medical Diagnosis (Honours), Modern Herbalism (Honours), and Scientific Naturopathy. He had considered giving himself an honours pass in Scientific Naturopathy to match the other two, but had reluctantly decided against it, feeling that three honours passes might indicate cold intellectualism, whereas two would indicate a more modest and approachable humanity. Gaining these certificates had required a great deal of work and concentration on his part, what with the scrolls and fine penmanship – slightly different in each case – that they required. If it were possible, he was even prouder of these than the testimonials.

But it was the testimonials he was concerned with now. He looked sternly at Mahommed, who was standing in front of one of them, trying to decipher its meaning.

'As you can see, written English is customarily more formal than spoken English, although when in doubt it is preferable to lean towards the formal in both instances. Continue.'

Mahommed peered at the words, struggling. 'For six months I ress … I ress no ben … ben … beneff …'

Adrian was already bored with the lesson. It was all well and good that the chap was trying to better himself, but this was the English language being mangled, and it deserved better. He took over, rattling through the words, hardly needing to look at the text. 'For six months I received no beneficial results from doctors, but immediately I started your treatment I felt better, and miraculously, I continue to do so.' He had toyed with leaving the 'miraculously' out, but on reflection had decided it was necessary, to best convey his grateful patient's state of mind.

He flicked a glance at Mahommed. 'Continue.'

'For five months now, I have passed co … co … co …'

'Coarse.'

'Coarse and fine gravel to the extent of four ohun … ons … ohnc …'

Making no secret of looking at his watch, Adrian put an end to this painful attempt. 'Four ounces, and about twenty gall stones, the largest measuring three quarters of an inch in diameter. Etcetera, do you see?'

There was a knock at the door. Adrian didn't wait for Mahommed's answer, feeling he'd given more than enough to this lesson already. He went to the door and opened it to a man in his early thirties. It was Robert Brosnan, one of his patients, a good fifteen minutes earlier than he should have been. Adrian greeted him warmly, making no mention of that, nor the air of feverishness that accompanied his arrival.

'Robert, do come in, I've been expecting you.' He guided him in and fussed him into a chair before remembering Mahommed's presence. 'You're doing splendidly. Here, practice on these.' He grabbed a few testimonials from the top of his desk. 'Apart from anything else, I think you'll find them uplifting.'

In one gliding motion he bundled Mahommed out the door, shut it after him, manufactured a new face, and turned back to Robert with professional concern. 'Your arm, please.'

Robert held out his arm for Adrian to take his pulse.

'It's racing,' said Robert. 'I already know that. Between my superiors …'

'Who are not so superior?'

'Exactly. And they expect me to provide reams of certification on all the new building work that's going on when not one of them has an engineering qualification, so they have absolutely no idea what they're asking me for. And between them, and now the butchers' union, which is pushing me to prosecute more of those wretched Afghans when quite frankly they should all be encouraged to die of botulism.'

Adrian concentrated on Robert's pulse, letting the words spill out.

'And of course, on top of all that, there's Irma.'

'Ah yes. A lovely young woman. A fine family.'

Robert let that pass. 'It's too much for one man, simply too much, and I've a mind to tell them all so.'

He stopped, watching as Adrian finished with his pulse. 'It is racing, isn't it?'

Adrian moved behind his desk and sat. 'More than I would like, yes.' He frowned, considering the matter. 'Is the tonic not calming you?'

'It is. It was. Actually, that's why I'm here. I appear to have run out.'

Adrian noted the shiftiness of his response. 'Already?'

'Only because I accidently spilled the bottle. Damn clumsy of me. Lost half of it down the sink.'

'Ah.' Adrian could see half moons of armpit sweat pushing through the thick wool of Robert's jacket. 'You'd like me to make up another prescription? The same as before?'

'Yes, thanks, Adrian, if you would.'

Adrian stood and began to fetch the ingredients he needed. He sensed Robert building to another request.

'Er … how about making up a bigger bottle? Only to save me coming in again quite so soon.'

'Yes of course. Very sensible idea.'

Adrian turned his back to Robert as he began making up the prescription. It was the only way he could hide his face.

Irma walked along Argent Street, towards the Council Chambers. Robert had arranged to meet her at Brown's Tea Rooms for lunch at twelve, but when she poked her head in, he wasn't yet there. No matter. She would go to his office and surprise him. It was a direct route between Brown's and the Council Chambers, so there was little chance of her missing him if he was already walking her way.

She had been pleased to discover he wasn't waiting for her because it gave her the opportunity to visit him in his office. Chief Sanitary Inspector; that was the sign on his door. She knew about things like chiefs because her father was Chief Teller at the local branch of the Government Savings Bank of New South Wales and he also had a sign. He didn't have his own office, though, more a sort of box with clear glass around three sides. Robert had a proper office. To gain entry, she had to approach Mary Hamilton at the reception desk and tell her to let Robert know that Irma Cowie was there. She had only done it once before and it had given her pleasure, because it was obvious that Mary was herself attracted to Robert.

Not that Irma had reason to doubt him. In fact she was certain that a proposal of marriage could not be too long in coming her way. She had already spent a lot of time rehearsing the dramatic possibilities of the word 'yes'. What else could she say to a man who was in every way perfect?

Of all her friends only Alice had been less than enthusiastic about him. But Alice was strange in her opinions. She took likes and dislikes to people, usually for no reasons that Irma could fathom. She didn't have a young man of her own so she was possibly jealous. How could anyone not be jealous of Robert?

If he had one fault it was that he worked too hard, to the point where he had once or twice fallen asleep at the office. Only last Saturday night, at the Theatre Royal watching *The Thrilling Adventures of Protea, the Lady Detective*, he had actually dozed off in his seat. An almost impossible feat since Protea's adventures had kept the audience in a state of continuous excitement for a whole hour.

She worried about him. Once they were married she could put her foot down, but he was touchy about such matters. She had asked if there was any way in which he could reduce the hours he worked, but he hadn't considered the question worth discussing let alone answering. And when she suggested it might be a good idea to go to the doctor for a tonic to reduce his tiredness he said that was completely unnecessary; he was already seeing Adrian Kadran, and didn't see any point in consulting more than one medical man at a time.

She stopped near the Chambers to adjust her hair and admire her reflection. She didn't like Adrian Kadran. She didn't care what Robert said about him, he was a big fat Indian, and nothing was ever going to change that, no matter how hard he scrubbed.

She entered the Chambers and was disappointed to find that Mary was nowhere to be seen. She coughed once or twice, to announce her presence, but it had no effect on the invisible Mary. She would leave a note telling her how sorry she was to have missed her while visiting her good friend Mr Brosnan. That would do it.

She walked along the corridor towards Robert's office, stopping outside the door to admire the sign. Chief Sanitary Inspector. She wasn't sure exactly what a Chief Sanitary Inspector did, but she knew it was important. She tapped on the door. What a surprise it would be for Robert to find her here. By now he should have been making his way towards Brown's Tea Rooms, but she understood. He was terribly busy.

She tapped again. 'Robert?'

She looked down the corridor towards the reception. She wouldn't like Mary to find her loitering outside the door when all visitors were supposed to wait until directed in. Even if she *was* practically Robert's fiancée.

She gave another tap, calling his name again.

She heard the front door of the Chambers open. Maybe another visitor, or an employee, perhaps even Mary. She couldn't stand out here forever. Turning the handle, she pushed open the door, and entered.

She was hit by the sour smell of vomit, a great wall of it, making her gag. Robert, slumped motionless in his chair, opened his eyes and looked at her, vaguely registering her presence.

He said, 'Hello, Irma. What're you doing here?'

What am I doing here? What are you doing here when you're supposed to be at Brown's with me, at a good table, with other people noticing us, thinking what an attractive couple we make? Instead you're here, doing … doing … Robert, what are you doing?

All she said was, 'I've come to surprise you.'

Robert replied in a peculiarly flat monotone: 'Oh. That's nice.'

She watched, horrified, as his eyes glazed over and shut. They opened again as he leaned forward, aiming for the wastepaper basket he had recently vomited in. He missed, spewing the disgusting muck over his shirt and jacket. He sat for a moment, as if trying to grasp what he had done, then fell forward on to his desk, head down.

Irma thought she might faint, but she couldn't. There was no-one to pick her up. She had to do *something*, though, because Robert was clearly very ill. That's what it was, he was sick, probably some germ, and she had to help him. She would, of course she would, but why couldn't they be sitting at Brown's with none of this having happened?

Behind her the door opened wider, and Mary Hamilton entered. Irma tried to appear dignified, to rise above – above whatever this was. 'Mr Brosnan has taken ill.'

Mary looked at him, then turned back to Irma. 'You'll have to clean him up.'

'Me?'

'I'm not going to do it.' Mary shrugged. 'Not again.' She turned abruptly and left, shutting the door behind her.

Irma knew she would have to start somewhere. She wasn't strong enough yet to deal with the vomit, so she moved to the desk and picked up the half-empty bottle of Adrian Kadran's tonic, found the cap, and screwed it back on.

7

On his first day Mahommed was terrified. He would have shut his eyes but was afraid the other men in the cage would notice, branding him useless before he had begun. The shaft was narrow, each turn from the winder-driver up above making the cage jerk. He expected it to crash one too many times against the rock wall of the shaft, for the rope to break, for death to greet him in the fetid air waiting far below. He looked sideways at Andy Jones, the crew foreman he had been introduced to only minutes before, but Andy seemed unconcerned. He took comfort from that. He gripped his shiny new shovel – four shillings' worth, to be taken out of his first week's pay – and decided he would live.

The cage reached the cavern at the bottom with a thud that made his knees buckle. Dark, lit only by scattered carbide lamps, the cavern was bigger than any house he had ever been in. Once his eyes adjusted, he could see passages leading off in many directions. The other men got out ahead of him, but before he'd gone far, Andy remembered him.

'Hey, Ghan. Cuddy's over here.'

Mahommed had no idea what he was talking about, but hurried after him, not wanting to be left behind. Andy turned into a makeshift rest area, with a couple of rough tables and chairs, next to which were equipment lockers. As he opened one of the lockers, he indicated Mahommed's shovel. 'Put it in here. You won't be needing it.'

Mahommed hesitated, puzzled. 'I am not working today?'

Andy didn't conceal his irritation. 'You'd better be. So put it in, I'll explain when we get there.'

Mahommed did what he was told, waiting politely while Andy and the other men gathered their tools and their lamps. He followed when they moved off, taking a narrow sloping tunnel barely head high. That first walk to the stope seemed to take forever; he stumbled after the others on the uneven floor, doing his best to avoid the overhanging rocks, which came at him from all sides. He found the air hard to breathe, and, even with the lamps, hard to see through, but he knew better than to ask anyone to slow down for him.

There were ladders, and more tunnels, and more ladders again, and with each downward step the air became closer and the sound from distant firings louder. He thought they might go on forever; that a hole might open up to reveal China or America or whatever country existed on the other side. But at last they stopped, and as the men laid down their tools, he saw they had reached the stope.

He turned to the man nearest to him, asking what he hoped was not a stupid question. 'How deep are we?'

The man shrugged. 'About a thousand feet. Give or take.' He grinned at Mahommed through the gloom. 'Got to you, has it?'

'No.' He tried to sound as if he were merely curious. 'No, not at all.'

He soon discovered why the shovel was not needed. Andy indicated an ore-laden box truck, and told him it had to be pushed along the track to a shaft where the ore would be taken away for processing. When it was emptied, he was to bring it back, and once filled, he was to repeat the process, again and again until the shift was over. Andy didn't bother with further explanations, leaving him to join one of the other men in readying the drill.

Mahommed looked at the truck, guessing it to weigh more than a ton. He estimated his own weight to be around a hundred and fifty pounds, but whatever it was, it would have to be enough. Aware that some of the others were watching him, he gripped the edge of the truck, dug his toes hard into the ground, and pushed.

Nothing moved; only his toes, sliding backward in the rubble. He tried again, this time digging his toes in deeper. They were all watching him now; this spurred him on, his fear of failing in the eyes of these men greater than his fear of a ton of rubble. He pushed harder, every muscle taut with the effort, and was at last rewarded with the creak of wheels as the truck began to roll forward.

His progress was slow. The track constantly needed to be cleared of debris, and each time he stopped to attend to it, the effort of making the wheels turn again seemed greater. His hands were greasy with sweat and his ears hurt from the constant firing blasts. His lungs felt raw, his back ached, his eyes streamed from dust. He had no idea of the time; no idea of how long this would have to be endured until he could ride back to the surface.

He had taken four loads to the shaft and back, and was returning with a fifth. The truck had stopped, blocked by a rock that had fallen since his most recent load. He removed the rock, heaving it onto the rubble, and leaned against the truck, catching his breath, trying to summon the energy to keep going.

And then it happened.

It took him a moment to grasp what it was, and a little longer to understand it was coming from within. The most wonderful feeling of euphoria, filling his whole being, lifting him up from the gloom of the tunnel. He was in Broken Hill, working as a miner, earning wages. He had planned it, hoped for it, worked for it – and it had happened! He was here where he was meant to be, and if the truck was heavy, then he was strong and would grow stronger. It was only his first day; of course he found it difficult. Of course the sounds of hammering and firing, echoing through the boulders, assaulted his eardrums; of course the air was thick, and the heat nearly unbearable. None of that mattered; he would work hard; he would watch and learn. He was here! And doing work that had nothing, nothing at all, to do with camels!

The euphoria was fleeting, but its place was taken by calm contentment. The work was still arduous; the truck still had to be pushed, inch by inch, along the track, but his initial agitation left him. He pushed the truck every day for a week, and when he rode down in the cage at the start of each shift, he held his back straight and his eyes wide open.

At the end of that week, one of the men took most of the skin off his knuckles after a firing, and Andy told Mahommed to swap with him, so that the injured hand could be kept out of harm's way. After that he began shovelling, using his new shovel to heave the freshly blasted ore into the truck. Andy worked with an Irishman called Kevin to bore the holes with the pneumatic drill, readying the ore for the next firing. Two others did the barring, the most difficult job – prising down the loose rocks left after a firing with long metal bars.

By now Mahommed was comfortable with the routine, and had grown to like the work. He liked the feeling of existing in a nether land that had no reality beyond itself, no apparent relationship with whatever was going on above him.

What he liked even more than the work itself was the leaving of it, the shift's end, which came for him in two parts. The first was in the shaft, in that split second before he left the underworld, when he was suddenly pushed into the light to rediscover the existence of the overworld. He would feel light-headed, and would stay pleasantly light-headed through the second part, the shower he took in the makeshift wash and change house outside the mine. While the other men shared a smoke and had perfunctory showers, he would luxuriate in his, gliding the wet soap over his body, enjoying its silky feel on his skin. When the work became too hard, and exhaustion threatened to overtake him, he would think about it waiting for him, and it would see him through.

'Come on, Ghan, smoko.' Andy nodded at the shovel.

Mahommed took his mind from the shower. 'Thank you, but I am not tired. I will keep working.'

Andy hesitated before replying. 'Suit yourself.' He headed off with the other men towards the cuddy, where they could smoke without inviting dismissal.

Mahommed fought the temptation to join them. He *was* tired, but he wanted to prove his worth as a hard worker and he wasn't sure he had done that yet. Apart from Andy and Kevin, there were three others in the crew: Bruce, Dave, and another Kevin. He had carefully learned and practised their names, in order to greet them all warmly at the start of each shift. In return they called him Ghan, something he thought of as an affectionate nickname rather than a slight. He knew it would take time, but he planned to become their friend. If the price of that friendship was a few more blisters, then so be it. He kept working.

The day shift finished at four o'clock. With no English lesson scheduled, the rest of the day was his to do with as he wished. Today, as he often did, he went for a walk.

He cleared the northwest outskirts of town and climbed up to White Rocks until he found a boulder smooth and weathered enough to sit on. The outcrop of quartz had pushed itself up into a hill, and, although barely worthy of that name, it was set high enough for him to look out over the town while the afternoon sun massaged the aches from his back.

He could see the mine from where he sat, and tried to trace the route he had just taken. He had walked the back streets, loitering when he came to an opened door or an uncurtained window. The big houses, the ones he aspired to, were too set back from the road for him to see into, so he had contented himself with peering in to the small pressed-metal cottages that made up a large part of the town's housing stock.

One house, with curtains pulled open, offered no sound or movement to indicate anyone might be inside. Its emptiness drew him in, as did the metal gate, with its broken catch. He looked up and down the road to make sure no-one was watching, then slipped through the gate and went right up to the window. It took a moment for his eyes to become accustomed to the gloom, but when they did he saw a small neat room filled with dark furniture. There were decorative pictures on the wall, a couple of stuffed chairs with cloth protectors on their backs, and behind them a dresser. On top of the dresser, in pride of place, were some ornaments, underneath which were round lacy doyleys, to both show them off better and to protect the dresser from scratch marks. He imagined himself sitting in such a room at the end of a day's work. He would relax in one of those chairs, reading the daily paper. There would be a pleasant domestic hum coming from the kitchen, and at just the right time – when he was ready to turn to the next page – Alice would come in and …

'You! What're you doing there?'

He spun around.

An elderly matron from next door was standing in her front garden, accusing him over the fence.

He thought quickly. 'I am looking for my friend, Mr Andy Jones, but I see I have the wrong house. Do you know which is the right house?' He smiled politely at her.

She looked suspiciously back at him, her brows knitted. 'No. But that's not it.'

'Thank you very much for clearing that up for me.' He smiled again, and hurried on his way, before she could tell him – as who knows, she might have – that Andy Jones was her son and it was highly unlikely he'd be friends with the likes of Mahommed.

★

He gave up trying to locate the house from the clutter of roofs below. Behind him the sun was setting; once it was gone he would have to hurry to beat the cold back to the boarding house.

He looked to his left to try to find the camel camp, but the distance hid it. The preparations for the evening meal would be beginning, and those men returning from a trip would be attending to their camels, their weariness from the past few days or weeks fading at the thought of a hot meal, a fire, and the good company awaiting them. He had none of these; thinking about them made him keenly aware of the emptiness gnawing at him. He didn't allow himself to call it loneliness; he told himself it was just a stage to be gone through, something unavoidable, which would soon pass. Like his time at the Little Star Ideal English School, which was neither Ideal nor English, where he had spent his school nights curled under a desk in the empty classroom, because his family had deemed it too far for him to make the journey home each night. Like the feeling he had when he went back to Afghanistan and discovered Suleiman, the youngest of his brothers, the one he had been closest to, had married. Had sloughed him off like winter snake skin: grown out of, unnecessary. These things had passed, and this would, too. Feelings could be shrunk, stepped over, and left behind. One only had to keep looking ahead to strip them of their power. He had done it before; he would do it now.

He stood and began to walk home, taking the long way back so as to avoid any temptation to detour in the vicinity of the camp. He had so far spent very little time there. Abdullah hadn't reproached him for this – not directly, not in so many words – but Mahommed knew he felt wounded by his absence. Mahommed heard the unspoken question: *aren't we good enough for you?* – and wasn't sure what answer he could give if Abdullah ever voiced it. *Yes, you are good enough for me, but I live in hope that one day you won't be? Or, if I spend too much time in the camp I will be seduced by the familiar rhythms of its heart and lose my resolve? Or, you are limited in understanding and I want more than you can possibly grasp?* None of these answers would do, and if his absence caused them both pain, the truth would have caused more.

There were other truths he did not want Abdullah to know. He still performed *Salat*, but observance was already starting to leach out of him. The *Salat ul Fajr*, yes, every morning, on a mat in his room, facing northwest to Mecca, of course. *Maghrib* and *Isha*, he observed these too. But *Zuhr* and *Asr* – most days he was down at the stope. He had no mat there, and anyway it was filthy, there was nowhere to wash, nowhere to kneel and no way to fix his direction. He had worried about this for the first couple of days, sifting through his mind for an acceptable solution, one that would offend neither Allah nor Andy. He thought perhaps that during smoko there might be an opportunity to casually turn away, maybe even to kneel, but he couldn't see how even a ritual purification could be carried out without drawing attention to himself. For the first week he enacted the prayers in his mind. Then he gave up, knowing that Allah would see through this as the shoddy compromise it was.

It was in the evenings, at dinner in the boarding house, that his resolve to avoid the camp was at its weakest, and tonight was no different. He sat in front of his meal, pushing it around the plate with his spoon, while around him, at the long wooden tables, the other single men were eating with apparent relish. How could the English eat such disgusting food? Not only was the mutton dry and sinewy but, discounting the occasional maggot, the stew it was boiled in was completely unflavoured. The woman Adrian Kadran had hired as a cook was sweaty, lardy, and not friendly. Mahommed didn't think she would take kindly to helpful suggestions regarding the judicious use of spices, so he kept his feelings about cinnamon and cumin to himself. Later, when he had made his way sufficiently in the English world to purchase some sort of business – he was leaning towards the idea of a small department store

– he would go back and eat some meals at the camp. But as yet he had no solid buffer against its seductions, so he stopped playing with his food and forced himself to eat. He made a mental note to tactfully ask Mr Kadran for his opinion about the efficacy of Cockle's Antibilious Pills, which were advertised in the *Barrier Daily Truth* as being good for indigestion.

After dinner he went, as usual, straight to his room. He didn't drink alcohol, so there was no point in attempting to join the other miners at the pub, and besides, he wanted to save his money for more important things. Going for a walk was out of the question; he had done enough walking, and he didn't want to risk his feet taking him to the camp. It was confusing, this emotional push–pull of the camp, and until he had risen completely above the temptation, he thought it best to keep right away.

Anyway, he liked his room, liked the fact that it belonged to him and no-one else. It was dingy and the walls had old leak stains coming from the ceiling. The mattress was suspect and lumpy and the bed creaked. The chair was wobbly, missing a rung. He didn't care. He had never had a room to himself before, not one with four proper walls, not one where people knocked before entering. This was academic because the only people who knocked did so because they'd mistaken, often after a drinking session, his room for a friend's, but nonetheless, it was *his room.*

He had made a start at decorating it. Instead of completely blank walls, he now had two soap wrappers pinned up, one Rexona, the other Alpine. After he had taken the soap out, he smoothed the wrappers carefully, ironing out the creases in the paper with the warm palm of his hand before pinning them flat against the wall. He was not so foolish as to think they were art, but he liked looking at them. They reassured him; encouraged him in his belief that he was becoming a new and superior type of man. Sometimes, when his open window caught a faint breeze, the naked light bulb above his bed would sway, catching the polished sheen of the wrappers, highlighting the lettering. *Rexona. The Universal Favourite. Alpine Soap. The Absolute Top-notcher.* Depending on the light he could sometimes make the lettering say *Gool Mahommed. The Absolute Top-notcher.* This made him laugh.

Once inside his door, he followed his regular routine. He performed *Maghrib* on the floor at the end of his bed, then rolled up his mat and put it away carefully in his case. He had a key to his room, but wasn't sure there weren't others floating around. Not that anyone poking around would necessarily steal his mat, but they would probably step on it with dirty shoes, and he wasn't prepared to risk that.

Then, duty done, he began to study, using Mr Kadran's testimonials as reading texts. He would have preferred something else, but these were the texts Mr Kadran had given him, to be studied by the next lesson.

He read them aloud, stopping occasionally to make note of the words he didn't understand. He wrote them carefully in pencil on a piece of paper he had scrounged; he would ask Mr Kadran about them during the lesson.

'Dear Mr Kadran, it is with a thankful heart I write to you. Upon taking your powder and medicine, whatever it was, I have now extruded all that was troubling me. These were a number of coagulated slimy lumps of skin and flesh, and five or six hard stony lumps of indeterminate composition.'

This took Mahommed quite a long time. He had absolutely no idea what the woman was talking about. Extruded? Coagulated? He read the first part again silently, trying to make sense of it, before reading on.

'I am now returned to my previous pink of health, and hope and pray, Mr Kadran, that God will grant you a long life so that you may continue aiding humanity in the same wonderful way that you have aided me. I remain most gratefully, Beatrice Williams.'

Mahommed still had one more testimonial to read tonight. He glanced at it, trying to work up some enthusiasm for the task. Like the first, it was largely incomprehensible, but he noted that the second writer had also extruded a number of substances. And, unless he was mistaken, had extruded them from a larger number of bodily orifices than was physically possible.

He didn't want to think about it. It was only an hour after he'd forced himself to eat dinner, and the details of another testimonial would not be conducive to good digestion.

He put it aside, still feeling he should be doing something constructive to improve his mind. After a moment he had an inspiration. He would practice his writing by making a list of things he needed to do in the near future.

He turned his scrap of paper over, licked the lead of his pencil, and began to write:

1. *Learn to read English better.*
2. *Develop modulated vowels although perhaps a little less modulated than Mr Kadran's whose own vowels seem a little fruity. In my opinion. I may be wrong.*
3. *Save money from the mine. Start a successful business that has nothing to do with camels.*
4. *Become sophisticated. Find out what coagulated means.*

5. *Purchase a Lounge Suit as advertised by F.J. Palmer
   & Son in the Barrier Daily Truth. Discover the
   purpose of a Lounge Suit. Purchase a doyley.*
6. ~~*Lay Alice down onto the ground and lift up her
   skirts. Let her see admire my penis before I thrust
   it into her and make her moan and writhe.*~~
6. *Become pure of heart.*
7. *Make Hajj.*

He had been in Broken Hill for two weeks. He hadn't
seen Alice in this time, and he didn't look for her.
He couldn't be sure that she even lived there. He had
practically forgotten her. She had been nothing more
than an unpleasant ripple upon the now calm water of
his days. She had been a she devil sent to tempt him,
and he had emerged unscathed and victorious and much
improved in character. She was probably nothing more
than a stupid Methodist who in a few years would turn
into Mr Kadran's lardy cook, eating boiled cabbage and
mutton without spices and not knowing how to wash
her hands before she did so. Also she had the strangest
eyes, light brown and green with flecks of gold that
flashed and called you in, asking you to drown and be
glad of it, and oh you would be, because to drown in
Alice would be a little death worth …

He pulled himself up sternly. *Make Hajj.*

8

It was vanity's fault. There he was, earning and carefully saving his money, learning English and dreaming about a shipping business. He had briefly put aside the department store idea, reasoning that even if a shipping business seemed fanciful, well, so what? It didn't matter, given he wasn't planning on sharing the idea with anyone else. Wherever his dreams eventually took him, he knew he was steadily improving both himself and his prospects with sensibly small, incremental steps.

Then vanity reached out and shook his brains from his head.

It was Saturday morning. He had come off from the midnight shift an hour earlier, and, unable to face another breakfast at the boarding house, was going to the bakery to buy a loaf of bread.

He should have walked right past. He would have, but an unexpected hole in the footpath forced him to veer left, and he found himself looking in at the window of Millers General Store and Emporium, where a male mannequin was wearing what was advertised as a fine-cotton dress shirt. He had no intention of buying it, but surely there was no harm in inspecting it for future comparison.

So he went inside, noticing that the tip of the mannequin's nose had chipped off, leaving a flaky white plaster hole. It might not have been an omen, but if it was, he would later regret overlooking it.

The display of shirts was near the front of the store, and he went over to look at them. They were six shillings each. He had twelve shillings and eight pence saved from his wages, and given the probable cost of buying a shipping business – he knew it wouldn't come cheap – he was not about to hand over nearly half of what he had for the sake of a new shirt. He fingered one of them, coveting it, imagining how he might look in it.

'May I help you?'

He turned from his reverie to see a young man, about his own age, looking disdainfully at him. His manner made it clear Mahommed wasn't good enough to be in this store let alone buy anything from it. And that was where vanity mingled with pride to make him answer, 'Yes. I would like a cake of Cuticura soap and a small bottle of lavender water, please.'

The man, presumably the manager, remained superficially polite. 'Certainly.'

'In the meantime I will think about these shirts.'

He saw the man turn to his young assistant, indicating he should keep watch on Mahommed, as though he were a thief and a murderer and a rapist, if not worse. He saw the boy react, sniggering with pleasurable embarrassment.

He should have walked out there and then. He didn't want the lavender water, he didn't need the soap, and he knew that getting out of buying the shirt was going to prove difficult. Instead, he turned back to the shirts, picking one up to study it for quality. *Hmm. The stitching is not too bad; the weave is a little coarse, not quite what I am used to. Perhaps I will look elsewhere.* He calmed himself. With luck he could carry it off.

'I think that would suit you.'

Mahommed spun around, and came face to face with *her*. Her and her friend from the train. They were standing in the doorway, the door closing behind them. She was smiling at him, teasing him. He put the shirt down, hating it.

'You got off at the right station, then?'

Mahommed stared at her.

'The train,' Alice prompted.

He tried to sound dignified. 'It was a little further than I expected.'

'I thought it might have been.'

It was time to cut his losses. He would go now, walk out the door without looking back, head to his room and lie down until his heart returned to a regular rhythm, allowing him to pretend this had never happened. But in the time this message took to reach his feet, it was too late. The man was already returning from the back of the shop, carrying his purchases.

'Soap and toilet water. That's one and fourpence.'

One and fourpence? Nearly a shilling for the lavender water? He fumbled for the money, avoiding looking at Alice.

She showed no such delicacy, continuing the conversation as though it was perfectly normal. 'Have you met my brother, Lewis?'

Her *brother*?

'How do you do, sir.' He knew it was cowardly, but what was the alternative, spit in his face? Five seconds of pleasure, a lifetime of consequences.

Her brother made no reply. Alice continued, ignoring his discomfiture. 'And my friend, Miss Irma Cowie.'

'How do you do, Miss Cowie.'

She mumbled a reply without looking at him and began sidling over to Alice's brother, subtly indicating her disapproval of Mahommed's presence.

Then, after introducing Alf, the assistant, Alice gaily included the man now coming in through the door. 'And Robert Brosnan, our Chief Sanitary Inspector.'

Mahommed nodded at him, recognising him from Mr Kadran's study. In return, he was ignored.

Alice moved a little closer to Mahommed. There was by now an edge of hysteria to her gaiety. 'I'm sorry, I've forgotten your name,' she said.

For a brief moment, he held her gaze, knowing he would never forgive himself for looking away. 'I am Gool Mahommed.'

And there it was, surrounding them, a fevered brightness that didn't feel like it was of his own making. There she was, with her frank open stare, looking at him like no woman had ever done before. Not a goddess, just a young woman with green-brown eyes and a puzzled air that seemed to say, are you feeling this too? And if you are, what will we do with it?

Then it was gone. Maybe it hadn't been there at all. Maybe, he thought, it was nothing more than a momentary flight from his present humiliation, invented by him as a few seconds' refuge. Or nothing at all, just that girl again playing tricks with his mind, and what had he come to, letting her do it?

He felt hot. Despite the relative coolness of the store, his body was burning, choking him with heat. He had to get out of there. He forced his eyes away from Alice, found the money he was searching for, took his parcel, nodded in lieu of a spoken goodbye, and hurried out, hardly aware of the ringing of the doorbell behind him.

Alice watched him go. The exhilaration she had felt in his presence was gone. Taking its place was silent disapproval, coming from behind. She turned, already resentful of what had been taken from her. 'He was a customer. Shouldn't you all have been more polite?'

'Alice … he's an *Arab*.' This was from Irma, who was doing her best to look frightened by the encounter. Alice assumed it was for the benefit of Robert. There had been some unspecified tension between them recently, which had apparently required soothing.

Robert, playing his part, moved to Irma and placed a comforting arm around her shoulder.

Lewis moved to straighten the unwanted shirt. 'Did you have to do that?'

'What? All I did was introduce someone. Or is that not allowed?'

'If you're angry at me, if you have some reason to want to embarrass me, then say so now, because you have to *stop*. I need to be able to count on you.' He made a gesture of frustration, and turned his attention back to the display. Unlike Irma, Lewis seemed genuinely upset by what she had done. She didn't know why that was when all she had meant to do was keep a moment going for as long as possible.

She said, 'I'm not angry.'

She wanted to add that he could always count on her, but she wasn't sure that he could. While she was thinking about this, Lewis finished what he was doing and moved to rejoin the others. She did the same and smoothed things over with Irma, who, she was happy to note, appeared to have got over her displeasure.

Alice was even happier about something else. She had his name.

9

Mahommed hurried along Argent Street, aiming for the anonymity of a near side lane. He doubted anyone would bother following him, but he kept his head down, not daring to risk a backward glance. He didn't like what he was feeling; he wanted to not feel, and in the quiet of a lane he would have a better chance of doing that.

He reached the lane, turned into it, and was immediately confronted with, not safety but a commotion. There was shouting, laughter, boys, and an old man on the ground. It took a moment for his eyes to adjust to the darkness, a moment to grasp what was happening.

'Stop them!' It was Abdullah on the ground, a sack of flour spilled around him. Three boys were taunting him, dragging his turban from his head, snorting pig noises at him as their feet stamped up a cloud of white flour dust.

'Oink, oink, oink!'

Abdullah raised his arms in a futile gesture of protection, but one of the boys already had the turban off. Mahommed ran towards them, sickened by what they were doing. 'Leave him alone!'

The boys ignored him, and began to toss the turban one to the other, making a game of it. One of them darted past Mahommed, heading back towards Argent Street, holding one end of the turban high, the rest of it trailing behind. Mahommed reached out to grab the trailing end and yanked him back. He had begun reeling him in, the heat of his recent shame now joined by rage at what this boy was doing, when the two other boys left Abdullah, running to join the tug of war.

He could see their faces, alight with whatever mindless pleasure they were taking from this contest, and pulled harder, determined not to let them win. But their combined weight was too much for him. Inch by inch, they dragged him back towards Argent Street.

He could hear Abdullah's voice behind him, urging him to let it drop, could see passers-by stop, attracted by what was going on, but it was all through a fog; the only thing clear to him was that he could not, would not, let go.

He gave a hard tug and found he was pulling against nothing. The boys, apparently tired of the game, had let go of the turban, and were already running off, disappearing into the gathering crowd.

Mahommed lost his balance, staggering as he tried to regain it before he crashed to the ground. He fell with a smashing sound, which he knew came not from him but from a breaking bottle of unwanted lavender water. He looked up, and for the first time became aware of Alice, standing with her friend and the Sanitary Inspector man, the three of them among a knot of onlookers peering down at him. He averted his eyes and picked himself up, pretending he hadn't seen her, but Abdullah reached him before he could move away.

'We'll tell the police.'

Mahommed was appalled by the idea. 'No.'

'Yes.'

'No.'

He wasn't prepared to argue in front of Alice. He grabbed Abdullah's arm and hustled him back towards his bag of flour, trying to ignore the haze of lavender fumes surrounding him. He gave Abdullah back his turban, then began to scoop what flour was salvageable back into the bag, keeping his back to Argent Street. He hoped that by now Alice and her friends had moved on, but if they hadn't, he wasn't going to look up and acknowledge their presence.

'Didn't you see what those boys did to me?'

'Abdullah, of course I did. They bring shame to their families. But what can we do?'

Abdullah finished re-winding his turban. 'I want to make a formal complaint. It is my right.'

'Nothing will come from it; we both know that.'

'It's a matter of principle. Why should I put up with what they do?'

'Are you still angry because of the fine?'

'The fine is irrelevant.'

Wadud had told Mahommed that Abdullah had been fined recently for unauthorised slaughter. It was apparently something to do with his continuing refusal to join the butchers' union, although the details were murky.

He pressed Abdullah further. 'Because complaining about those boys won't change anything.'

'It's not about their fine. But I'm tired of constantly lying down for these people. Where is the dignity in doing that?'

Mahommed took in his hurt, tired face and gently reached out a hand to him. 'Come. Forget this. Let me take you home.'

'Anyway, there were witnesses.'

Mahommed pulled back his hand, horrified by the idea of Alice as a witness. 'Do you really think they would speak up for you?'

Abdullah looked at him coolly. 'Then give me the flour. I'll go by myself.'

Trapped, Mahommed gave in, unable to desert the old man in this way. Cursing himself for every decision that had led to him turning into the lane, he hefted what he had saved of the flour onto his shoulder and accompanied Abdullah towards the police station.

Halfway there, Abdullah stopped to sniff the air, and gave him a puzzled look. 'Lavender?'

They waited half an hour, loitering near the counter in the hope of being noticed. There were three policemen on the other side, and as far as Mahommed could tell, they were doing nothing pressing that would prevent them from attending to him and Abdullah. He hated occasions like this, when he was forced to admit the social divide. The fact that an old Aboriginal man, his hat in his hands, had been already patiently waiting on one of the chairs when they came in, did not make the wait any more palatable.

'You should tell them they must see us.'

'You think they can't?' Mahommed could hear the shortness in his tone, regretting it immediately.

Of course Abdullah was angry, of course he chafed at the condescension, but why did he choose today to do it so publicly? Hadn't his own day already been bad enough?

He swallowed his annoyance and moved closer to the counter, directing his words to the policeman who was nearest. 'Excuse me, sir?'

The policeman, head down, appeared not to hear him. Then his shoulders heaved as he sighed, conveying his lack of interest. He pushed his chair back and stood up, moving over to the counter. 'Alright. So what's the problem?'

'There is no problem, sir, only a small happening.'

Without even turning, Mahommed could feel the look of disgust from Abdullah as he shoved him aside.

'The problem is, I have been assaulted, and I wish something to be done.'

He went on to tell the policeman about the boys. They had thrown rocks at him without provocation, had forced him to the ground, had spilled his flour, had torn his turban off, hurt and insulted him beyond measure. They were criminals and he wanted them charged.

Mahommed watched the policeman's face throughout this recital. Whatever interest he had in listening to this story was gone. He had stopped taking notes, had put his pen down.

'The trouble is, if no-one saw it …'

Mahommed nodded his agreement. 'Unfortunately for us, nobody.'

Abdullah's voice became louder, more strident. 'There were at least ten witnesses.'

'But if they're not here, they're not much use. I can't tell you your business, but it might make things easier if you –' He indicated Abdullah's turban. 'Look, you could wear a hat. That'd be alright, wouldn't it?'

Mahommed nodded again, doing his best to be agreeable.

Abdullah, stony faced, looked at Mahommed, then turned and went out, trailing his silence behind him.

Carrying his flour for him, shepherding Abdullah back to his shack in the camp, Mahommed tried to make himself small, aware that he was in disgrace; that he hadn't supported Abdullah as much as he should have. Had, in fact, cravenly worked against him.

He tried to justify his stand. 'It isn't weakness to understand that lying down sometimes makes us stronger.' As though he had taken a well-thought-out intellectual position on the matter.

Abdullah didn't answer. He lifted the flap that served as a front door to his shack and went inside.

Despite the lack of invitation Mahommed knew it was expected that he follow. But he wouldn't, not just yet. He would make Abdullah wait; make him think the sack of flour was unattended outside the shack, that he had gone. Make him lower, if only slightly, the perceived height of his moral ground.

He looked around, taking in the well-worn path leading from the shack to the ablution pool and the mosque in front of it. His indignation wavered. He knew Abdullah's anger came not only from his failure to support him at the police station. But how could he tell him that even now the sounds and smells of the camp were courting him; that every day it took all his strength to withstand its seductive overtures?

One day he would come with money in his pocket. He would build Abdullah a house. Buy him camels, a ticket home; whatever he wanted most. And then he would explain, and Abdullah would understand.

He looked over towards a shack where ten-year-old Zainie, one of Jemadar's two daughters, was preparing food for the midday meal. Ibram, eight, was nearby with little Partimah, drawing circles in the dust with sticks. Partimah had been a baby when he was here before. There were rumours then that Edith had cuckolded Jemadar, but Mahommed thought these grew mostly out of wonderment that such a dry old piece of sinew could still sire a child.

Abdullah, who was younger than Jemadar, had no children in Broken Hill. Whether this was because of some private distaste for black women, Mahommed didn't know, but he thought having children here would have made Abdullah a happier man. He had heard that a daughter had survived the earthquake, but even if that were so, she would have been married and gone to her husband's family long ago. But children here would still be young, a comfort, something to take his mind from his daily troubles.

Well, it was too late for all that now. And he couldn't make Abdullah wait any longer. He picked up the bag of flour, and pushed aside the flap.

Rugs covered the dirt floor of Abdullah's home; rugs and woven cloths the walls, granting it an air of opulence that disappeared upon closer inspection. Mahommed barely noticed them, so familiar were they to him. This was the home that Abdullah had so generously shared with him when he had first come to Broken Hill, delivering his camels.

Abdullah had clearly not wanted him, had not wanted the responsibility of another life. Mahommed had spent his first night at the camp alone, huddling ever closer to the dying embers of the evening fire. The image of him shivering outside in the desert had finally been too much for Abdullah, and the following night he reluctantly invited him inside, supposedly for a night, but as it turned out, for more than a year.

Ignored, he sat cross-legged near the entrance, watching as Abdullah carefully removed his turban, putting it to one side. He squatted on the floor opposite Mahommed, still not looking at him, his sparse grey hair fluffing up like an old dandelion.

He said, 'Eighteen years, and they are as strange to me now as they were when I first came here. At first I would weave thoughts of home inside my head and live inside them, but I don't let myself do that any more.'

His sadness enveloped them both, binding them with silence. After a moment Abdullah continued, idly tracing a pattern on the rug he was sitting on. 'My thoughts I can control. But my dreams roam unbidden … and sometimes, when I least expect it, they gather up memories of the life I once had and place them in my heart and force me to look at them, and each time it happens I have to make myself remember how to breathe again, because part of me no longer wants to.'

Mahommed found himself unexpectedly fending off tears. Not just for Abdullah but for himself, for the humiliation they had both endured, for the shattered lavender bottle, for the look on Alice's face, for the broken plaster nose on the poor mannequin. He blinked, sweeping these thoughts to the edges of his mind's eye.

Abdullah was looking at him, as though measuring him up. He said, 'Help me.'

Moving to one side, Abdullah lifted up a corner of the main floor rug and started rolling it back upon itself. Intrigued, Mahommed helped him roll the rug back, revealing two planks set in the dirt floor.

Abdullah removed them one by one, carefully leaning them against the wall. As he did so, Mahommed leaned over the cavity the planks had been covering, and saw a long object wrapped in cloth. He was now even more intrigued. That he had secrets from Abdullah was one thing; it had never occurred to him that Abdullah had secrets from him.

'What is it?'

By way of answer Abdullah reached down for the object and lifted it out. He gave it to Mahommed, and indicated that he should open it.

Mahommed didn't need to open it to know what it was; the weight and feel of it in his arms was enough. He put it on the ground and unwrapped it, revealing a carefully maintained Snider rifle. 'This is yours?'

Abdullah nodded. He had, he said, been given it in lieu of a shipment payment many years ago. 'If I were

the man I used to be, I would not let them get away
with what they did to me today.'

'Then it's a good thing you're *not* the man you used
to be. They were just boys.'

'Who have fathers who teach them to hate.'

'Like you want to teach me?'

Before the words were out he knew he shouldn't
have uttered them. He'd never spoken to Abdullah
with such disrespect. He waited for admonishment, but
Abdullah ignored the words, letting them slink into the
walls around them. He picked up the rifle, cradling it in
his arms, looking along its sights.

Mahommed squirmed as the rifle turned his way.
'Why are you showing it to me now?'

Abdullah took his eye from the rifle and held it out
to him. 'Look through it. Tell me what you see.'

'I've used a rifle before. Many times.'

'Tell me.'

Mahommed humoured him and did as he was told.
He pointed it away from Abdullah, and focused it on a
detail of one of the rugs. 'There is a tree in a garden. In
the tree is a bird.'

'Is the bird smaller through the rifle?'

'No. Larger.'

'And clearer?'

'Yes. It's clearer. Beyond the bird, everything else fades away.'

'Yes.' Abdullah held out his hands for the rifle. 'That is why I am showing it to you now.'

Mahommed was aware he was being taught something, but if that something was an instruction to open his eyes, then he had done that by himself, years ago. He wasn't prepared to risk a sneer by saying this, so he changed the subject. 'Do you know how to use it?'

'Not very well. But it doesn't matter. I have no bullets left, nor money to buy them with.'

'That's probably another good thing,' said Mahommed, attempting a small joke.

He smiled at Abdullah, hoping for one in return. He had already humiliated himself in front of Alice; being out of favour with Abdullah had not improved the day.

Abdullah lowered the rifle. He put it on the ground and began to re-wrap the cloth around it, making it clear the subject was closed.

IO

Alice's shift at the hospital started in an hour and she should have been getting ready. Instead she was in her bedroom, one wrist tethered by kitchen string to the bed head, the other in the process of being similarly tethered by her assistant, Eileen.

Alice gritted her teeth in concentration. 'Tighter.'

Eileen, though doing her best, lacked the required degree of professionalism. She pulled the knot tighter, until the string dug welts into Alice's flesh. 'You'll never undo it. You'll be stuck here forever.'

'No, I won't. Now turn around, don't look.'

Eileen did as she was told, moving to the window and looking out. Alice knew she didn't understand why they were doing this. Knots were of no interest to her. Alice had tried to explain it wasn't about knots, but she hadn't succeeded.

Eileen fiddled with her plait, filling in time. She said, 'When you went to Adelaide, I was afraid you weren't coming back.'

Alice hadn't wanted to come back. Waiting at the ticket office with Irma she had scanned the other destinations. Melbourne? She could take the train there and get off and walk about until she became so tired she would float away, little pieces of her dispersing into nothing. It didn't have to be Melbourne. Anywhere would have done. In the end, the line moved forward, and she obediently paid for her ticket back to Broken Hill.

She ignored Eileen and concentrated on her task, making her wrists smaller, edging the knotted rope over.

She said, 'For instance, if a robber came and took your money and tied you up, or if someone threw you into a lake and tied an anchor to you, or, if there was a speeding train and you were tied to the tracks, or if someone was dragging you on a rope behind a runaway horse, or …'

… or if a foreign man called Gool Mahommed took revenge on her and wrapped his long dark fingers around her neck and tightened them until she begged forgiveness and then could no longer do that because the words were choked out of her to the point where they were just breath and then not even breath …

Eileen interrupted her, exasperated. 'But none of that's ever going to happen.'

Unable to help herself, she turned around to see Alice free herself from the last of her tethers.

Alice stood up on the bed, triumphant, and jumped up and down, laughing. 'With one bound she was free!'

There was a tap on the door and Lewis poked his head around. Alice stopped jumping.

'Eileen wants to join the Girl Guides. We're practising knots.'

She ignored Eileen's look of indignation. If Eileen didn't understand, then Lewis certainly wouldn't, so she wasn't about to explain, although it was obvious he knew she was lying. She got off the bed. 'And now I have to get ready for work.'

'Keith's just dropped by. I thought you might make us a pot of tea.'

'What's he here for?'

'I imagine because he felt the need of some company.'

She could feel Lewis's irritation. She wasn't responding the way she was supposed to.

'Then perhaps Eileen could make the tea for you.'

'I was hoping *you* would.'

'I'm sorry, Lewis, I can't afford to be late.'

Eileen pushed forward, wanting to be away from them.

'I'll make it, I don't mind.'

Lewis waited till Eileen was gone, keeping his voice low so as not to be overheard. 'It's not me he's come to see. You know that, don't you?'

'No, I didn't.'

Another lie. Another look on Lewis's face acknowledging the lie.

'Give him a chance, Alice. You might find you like him.'

'I do like him.'

'Then, at the least, you could be civil.' He left, shutting the door after him.

Alice resolved she would do as asked. She changed into her uniform, pinned her hair, and went out to the kitchen where she chatted pleasantly to Keith, agreed with his opinion on the weather, made her apologies, and took her leave. Keith had brightened at her presence; she hoped her efforts towards him would be enough to make Lewis like her again. He used to like her all the time, but that was when they told each other everything. Now they were grown up, they each had a store of things they kept to themselves.

She shut the front gate and hurried up Cobalt Lane, making towards the hospital. She always hurried from home. When she was very young she had thought of cobalt only as a pretty blue, but when she discovered it was also a magnet, her feelings about the lane changed, and getting out of it became a contest.

She reached the end of it and slowed her pace. Despite what she had told Lewis, she wasn't late. If she went slowly and kept her eyes open, she might see Mahommed again. She supposed he lived at the camp – most of them did – but he had gone to Millers so he obviously had at least occasional need to come into town.

What she would do if she saw him she didn't know. If she spoke to him, all she could say would be, *I don't know what I want from you but I would like to find out.* And if she said that, how would he respond? She reached the hospital without seeing him. She took one last look around, as though a look by itself might cause him to appear. Fits and starts of decisions, she thought. Ragged end bits of half-formed longings. That's how she lived her life. Her father had at least tried to do more, but all she ever did was wish. Irma was wrong: she wasn't her father's daughter. She was her mother's.

The thought gave her no comfort so she put it away. She went inside, reported to Matron Guthrie, and began her shift.

II

Was it a week, two weeks ago? Mahommed had banished the day from his memory, wrapped it in an impenetrable box out of which time and place could not escape. It simply hadn't happened, although in the space where the memory would have been there was something dark and lumpen, and try as he might, he couldn't find an alternative memory to fill it. But one would come.

He had not seen Abdullah since the episode with the Snider. Abdullah's clear intention was to draw a line in the sand between us and them. Us being Abdullah and Mahommed and the others in the camel camp, and them being nearly everyone else. He owed Abdullah, he knew that, but just because Abdullah was determined to be miserable was no reason for Mahommed to join him. They had only spent one year in each other's company, and that was five years ago. It was possible he had invested too much in the memory of that year; possible that the differences between them were too wide to bridge. Where he looked outward, Abdullah looked inward. Where he was optimistic, Abdullah was not. Where he was ambitious, Abdullah's horizons had shrunk.

For example, there had been a photograph in yesterday's *Miner* of the very latest, so the caption said, in submarines. One of two recently purchased by the Australian government, it was floating in Port Jackson, and had three sailors standing to attention on its deck. Mahommed was sure that if Abdullah had seen the photograph, he would have glanced at it, turned the page, and thought no more of it.

On the other hand, he, Mahommed, had looked at it and sensed commercial possibilities. There was, after all, no absolute law that said a shipping line had to have all its ships above water and if he had a submarine (or two), it could well be a useful point of difference between his line and, say, P&O. He assumed a submarine cargo hold would not be large, but thought the fact that cargo could be carried safely under water, away from marauding pirates, might well be a selling point when trying to procure contracts.

He wasn't completely unrealistic. He knew the chances of his ever owning such a business were slim.

But what he couldn't accept was the idea that it was better to look at the ground rather than the sky. He cared for Abdullah but would not – could not – allow himself to be infected by his negativity.

So for now he would keep to his plan. He would work hard and save money. He would continue with Mr Kadran's English lessons even though by now he knew more about the workings of the human body than he had ever wanted to know. He would become friends with his fellow miners. He would eat boiled mutton and learn to like it.

Of all this he was determined. So much so that, as of yesterday, he had become the proud owner of a finely worked linen and lace doyley.

It was afternoon. He had been shovelling at the face of the stope for five hours without a break, but he wasn't measuring time. He was worrying about the measurements of his doyley, at present sitting under the water jug in his room. The base of the doyley was seven inches in diameter and the base of the water jug six inches, which left only an inch of lace frill visible. And the water jug bulged out from its base, so from certain angles the doyley wasn't visible at all, not even the frill.

He could put something else on the doyley, something smaller that would display it to better advantage, but he didn't have anything suitable. Bebarfalds was advertising china vases at sevenpence ha'penny (sixpence for postage) and he thought he could probably purchase something similar locally, but then he would have to buy something to put in the vase, which would cause the initial cost of the doyley to spiral out of control. He should have spent the extra money and bought a bigger doyley. He could still do that, but then he would be left with the problem of the too small doyley, all because he hadn't thought it through properly in the first place.

'Smoko!'

Andy's call dimly registered through the clutter of doyleys and vases. The others – Bruce, Dave, and the two Kevins – downed tools, grateful for the chance of a break. They'd just finished another firing; any barring down could wait.

Andy looked at Mahommed. 'Come on, Ghan, smoko!'

Mahommed continued to shovel. He could sense Andy's irritation; perhaps, while daydreaming, he had slowed his pace.

'Are you listening? We're taking a break.'

'Thank you, but I am not tired.'

Andy advanced towards him. 'When I said *we*, I meant all of us.'

Mahommed stopped shovelling. By the look on Andy's face he knew he must have made some error of judgement, but he had no idea what it was.

'Yes. Yes, I understand.'

'No, you don't. You wouldn't have the foggiest idea.'

Mahommed stayed still, not daring to contradict. He glanced across and saw the other men watching in silence as Andy, jaw thrust forward, wound himself up.

'Like about how bad the conditions down here would be if we hadn't fought for the little we won. We bust our guts every shift, and no-one up top has a clue what we put up with. We're not slackers, we can't slack with the way they're talking about layoffs, and the last thing I need is some halfwit Turkey lolly making me look bad by saying no to a smoko!'

Mahommed wanted to appease him but was still not entirely sure what he had done to offend. In the background, he saw Dave move forward to Andy.

'Leave him be. He doesn't understand.'

'Which is what I'm saying.'

'Well, now it's said.'

This seemed to have a calming effect on Andy.

Mahommed waited, bracing himself for a further explosion, but none came.

'You're a hard worker, aren't you, Ghan?'

Mahommed responded nervously, unsure what this new reasonable manner signified. 'I am trying, yes.'

'Reckon you might be ready to give the barring a go?'

'Yes, of course. I will do anything.'

Andy picked up a bar and indicated a mass of overhanging rock. 'Just poke it in there, nice and easy. When you're ready, bar down.'

'Why don't we wait till after smoko?' said Dave. 'Probably not a good idea for him to be doing it on his own.'

'You saying he's not up to it?' Andy turned back to Mahommed. 'You're up to it, aren't you, mate? In fact, way I read it, you're asking for it, right?'

'Yes, indeed. I am asking for it.'

Andy handed him the bar. 'When you've got it down, shovel it into the truck, same as the rest.'

Mahommed climbed up onto a fallen rock, and reached up to wedge the bar in. Under other circumstances he would have been pleased to be given this new responsibility, but he was troubled by the feeling that all was not as it seemed. He concentrated on the job at hand, unsure about how far in he should push the bar. He wanted to ask Andy for advice, but held off, not wanting to admit his ignorance.

'Alright, let's have that smoko.' Andy indicated to the other men that they should move off.

Dave stayed where he was. 'We can't leave him barring by himself.'

'He knows what he's doing.'

'He doesn't. Blind Freddy can see that.'

'Blind Freddy's not here.' Andy looked up at Mahommed. 'You're right for a bit, aren't you?'

As Mahommed turned to answer, he pulled the bar with him. The overhanging rock, loosened by the last firing, tilted down a few degrees, then stopped. From behind it a stone, no more than a pebble, bumped down the side of the face.

'You idiot,' Andy shouted. 'Watch what you're doing!'

He rushed in and grabbed the bar from Mahommed, causing him to lose his balance and fall. Andy tried to bar the overhanging rock into a safer position, but as he did so the pebble was joined by another, then another, until suddenly it was no longer single stones falling down but rocks, and not just from where the bar was wedged but from the roof as well.

Dave darted forward and grabbed Andy. He shook him hard, dragging him, shouting at him. 'Andy, get out! Now!'

There was a crack as the overhanging rock broke in two and smashed to the ground next to where

Mahommed still lay. With rocks now tumbling around them, Andy ran back with Dave along the tunnel, scrambling after the others, shielding their heads with their arms as they went. Mahommed looked up as Dave briefly turned back towards him.

'Come on, Ghan, run!'

Mahommed picked himself up off the ground, making to follow, but the curtains of dust falling and rising through the semi-darkness were already making it impossible for him to see where he was. As he stood, blinded, a rock crashed off the wall into his shoulder, an invisible hand shoving him hard, forcing him to his knees. He put an arm up to shield his head, and with the other reached out to where he hoped the wall would be. Ignoring the pain in his shoulder, he found a hold and dragged himself up again, knowing that to lie down would be fatal, that his good friend Andy would not save him; knowing that this mine that had been his cocoon could soon become his grave.

He pushed himself against the wall, afraid to move forward. The noise of falling rocks was terrible. The wall itself was shaking as though behind it the whole world had been unleashed. He couldn't stay, he knew that much. Raising both arms, he inched forward, eyes instinctively closed in defence. If he could make it to the truck, he could use it to shield himself. It was strong, made of thick hammered iron. If he could crawl under its overhang, he might be safe until all this had passed.

He would have to reach out for it, feel for it, knowing that any second a rock could crash into his outstretched hand, smashing his fingers into bloody pulp. But there was no choice. With one hand clawing the wall, he used the other to reach out ahead of him, feeling blindly for the rim of the truck.

Two rocks smashed into his hand in quick succession, but he refused to let himself flinch. He knew the truck could be no more than a couple of feet away; that he could make it, that he *would* make it, that he was Gool Mahommed, Afridi warrior, late of the Sultan's army, and …

An outward rush of breath vomited all thoughts away as a rock crashed into his back, felling him instantly. His face scraped against the ground, grinding his cheekbone. As he opened his mouth to breathe it filled with dust and grit, choking his silent *Noooo* before it had time to find voice.

He forced his eyes open and saw that he had been facing the wrong way, not going towards the truck, but away from it. He was puzzling over how he could possibly have made such a mistake when another rock hit him and everything stopped, the puzzle unsolved.

12

There was only the darkness of total black with infinite time stretching it in all directions, beyond imagining. And then a moment came when an edge appeared, one not so black, and this not so blackness began to lap at the shores, shrinking everything slowly back into something that was, something that had been and once more would be.

Slowly, so slowly.

Others were aware of him before he was. His mind was elsewhere, waiting for his body to be once more worth taking hold of.

A day came when he found himself. The first thing he discovered was pain. At first all over, so much that it was all consuming. Then little by little the pain separated into distinct places – his shoulder, his back, his cheekbone – until he could feel them all as separate parts of him, the throbbing here, the stabbing there, the ache somewhere else.

Voices intruded. Not words but murmurings, sounds that were not his. He was aware of being touched. Sometimes the touching added to his pain but he wasn't afraid, somehow grasping that causing pain wasn't the intention.

He stayed in the darkness, sensing he needed to stay there longer.

He could smell something. Soap. Not Rexona. Not Lifebuoy. But soap, nevertheless. He thought he had forgotten smells, but here they were back, all around him.

There was another smell, another vaguely familiar fragrance, mingling with the soap. A body smell, not earthy or dank but light and fresh-air filled.

Skin. He could feel skin. Soft smooth skin gliding over him, gently caressing, soaping him with cool water, teasing him with the lightest of touches.

He opened his eyes, only a faint flutter at first, then more, so that darkness gave way to a shape hovering over him. He watched the shape for a moment as it moved around him and found form and then, as his eyes opened wider and the shape came nearer, he finally hurtled into full wakefulness and found himself staring into the face of Alice.

He shut his eyes again, thinking he had made a mistake; then opened them again just as quickly. She was still there, leaning closer, starting to speak.

Appalled at being put into this position, he squirmed in the bed, feebly batting her hands away while readying himself for flight. He would escape from her, he would climb out of this bed and …

He looked wildly around him, taking in his surroundings for the first time. What bed? Where on earth was he, what was he doing here? Why was she touching him, playing with his body? Was it *Maghrib,* perhaps there was a day when he hadn't performed it, not just *Zuhr* and *Asr,* and Friday prayers, was there a chance he had missed it more than once while trying to avoid Abdullah? He couldn't remember, everything in his life seemed to have happened so long ago.

As he attempted to sit up, Alice gently pushed him back. He was weightless, like a feather, and although his mind fought her fiercely, his body conceded defeat.

'It's alright, you're safe. You're in hospital.'

Hospital? He looked around and saw she was telling the truth. He was in a ward of some kind. Curtains partitioned his bed from the rest of the room, but through a gap he could see there were other, similar beds.

He was bandaged. Around his torso, around his shoulder. Bandages, holding all his pain together.

'You were in an accident. In the mine.'

He stared at her blankly, uncomprehending. Then finally the pieces of him came fully together and he remembered too much: his dying but not dying, the scraping of his cheekbone against the rocks. He reached up, expecting a weeping sore, and found a hard crusty scab.

'It's been nearly two weeks.'

Her white apron, shiny with starch. Who was she, what was she doing to him now? Dipping her cloth into a bowl, reaching towards him to touch him, it was wrong …

'No!'

'It's only soap and water.'

'No, no, you must not!'

'Fine. Stay dirty. If you don't believe in washing then who am I to change your mind?' She picked up the bowl of water.

'No, please, it is not like that.' To have her think that he was dirty – *her*, a lardy unwashed Methodist with, he noticed, a light and not unattractive dusting of freckles on the bridge of her nose – was more than he was prepared to countenance.

She stopped. 'What is it like then?'

'You are a woman,' he explained. 'It is forbidden.'

★

Oh, that. Forbidden.

Why was everything forbidden? Even the things that weren't expressly forbidden ended up being so one way or another. Like taking the train to Melbourne rather than back to Broken Hill. No-one would have physically stopped her, dragged her back in chains, but the voice that had said, what about Eileen, and what about Lewis? had made it a kind of forbidden. Like laughing last Sunday when the Reverend Piercey said God knew what was in all their hearts, because God couldn't possibly know what was in her heart – if he did he would have struck her dead years ago. But she hadn't laughed, she had stopped it from coming up, so Irma needn't've looked at her in that horrified way.

Even her work here in the hospital, Lewis wanted that to be forbidden. It was beneath her, he said, which was completely untrue because she had examined herself good and hard and had long ago come to the conclusion that there was little inside her of much worth. So how could the work be beneath her? And Eileen didn't suffer for it, it was only three or four days a week, which Matron Guthrie allowed because she knew their circumstances and because she was short of willing staff. Why didn't Lewis understand that she needed this job, that staying in this town depended on anchors?

She had told him that one of the Afghans had been hurt in the mine and was in the ward, though she hadn't told him which one. As always, he refused to react to news of another accident. Twenty-nine men had been killed in the mines last year. The black flag had hung limply at half-mast over the Trades Hall too often. Two of the men had been Lewis's childhood friends. He had not considered a wounded Afghan worth talking about, beyond giving her a warning that she should have as little to do with him as possible.

Well, too late. And too late for Mahommed to tell her it was forbidden to wash him. Did he really think they could leave him to lie there for nearly two weeks, dust and blood encrusted, hardly a person at all, without washing him?

She was not there when they had brought him in, more dead than not. She knew there had been an accident, in itself not uncommon – wasn't that why they were having yet another enquiry now? This one had been something small, only one man hurt, an Afghan at that, so it had barely been remarked upon.

At first she didn't realise it was him. His shoulder had been dislocated but somehow no bones had been broken. His insides, of course, were a dreadful mess. There was internal bleeding and leakage of an indeterminate amount of blood and fluid. His face, one side of it scraped nearly raw, had puffed up, as had his body, making him look like a dead animal, skin stretched tight, bloated in the sun.

But he wasn't dead. And it was definitely him.

She hid the shock of recognition from Matron Guthrie and the other nurses and aides. She wasn't ashamed of knowing who he was, but was keenly aware that if she showed any sort of proprietary interest she might be directed away from him.

She was matter of fact and practical in helping with his care, although that first day she had to stop herself from finding excuses to attend to him. She wanted to climb into the bed with him and fold her body around his, but why was that? She barely knew him. She would never have actually done it, but why was it even in her head?

In the afternoon a senior nurse had removed his catheter and taken it to the utilities room to prepare another. Although she had no reason to be there, Alice found herself by his bed. His top sheet had been pulled to one side, exposing him, his penis lying vulnerable against his thigh.

It was not the first one she had ever seen. Lewis's, when they were both small children, and perhaps her father's when she was young enough for it not to matter, although she had no recollection of that. And here in the hospital, old ones and young ones, too many to count. The old ones were stretched and sad and purple-red veined, the younger ones all shapes and sizes, but they all had one thing in common: they seemed to be peculiar afterthoughts to the bodies they were attached to. Unlike Mahommed's, which, to her mind, simply formed a perfectly natural extension to the rest of him.

She reached out a hand to touch it, resting her fingers lightly on it. Briefly, but long enough to be surprised at her boldness. Well, Reverend Piercey, what do you think God made of that?

He lay in his bed, unclaimed. Charlie Main, the paymaster at the mine, supplied a boarding house address for him but when Matron Guthrie telephoned Adrian Kadran, the proprietor, he seemed uninterested beyond the fact he rented a room to the man and rent would soon be owing. He told her that someone in the camel camp might know more about him. Matron Guthrie had more important priorities than an unwanted Afghan, but eventually filtered this information down to the nurses where it finally found Alice.

She was curious about the camp. As children, she and Lewis had once ventured into it, lured by the promise of sweets and fruit being handed out after a funeral. The food smells, the music and dancing; she had never before felt so transported to another world. Outside of her dreams she had never even known other worlds existed, but here was one where a man with a mirrored cap and kohl round his eyes danced in curled up shoes to the beat of a drum and the strange twanging of a painted *santur* dulcimer. Right in Broken Hill. She had wanted to stay there forever but, after accepting their oranges, Lewis said the camp was dirty and made them leave.

She left work that afternoon determined that if no contact with the camp had been made by the end of the week, she would do it herself.

She saw them in Garnet Street. An Aboriginal woman in the company of two young Afghan girls, crossing the road towards her. She hesitated, her mouth dry. She'd never initiated a conversation with such a woman before, but if she didn't speak soon, she would be gone.

'Excuse me, I'm sorry to bother you.'

The woman grabbed hold of the younger girl's hand. Alice thought she might flee at any moment.

'Do you know a man called Gool Mahommed?'

Looking away from her, the woman shook her head, but the older girl tugged on her blouse. She said, 'We *do* know him, Edith. He's Abdullah's friend.'

★

Early the next morning an elderly Afghan man had appeared outside the hospital and, after identifying himself as the Mullah Abdullah, had waited patiently to be let in. He had come every day since to wash Mahommed and help him eat the meals that Zainie, the older of the two girls Alice had seen, brought daily from the camp. The nurses were allowed to change Mahommed's bandages, but Abdullah, who considered himself to be in charge, firmly rebuffed any attention not specifically medical in nature, and politely refused to deal with the hospital staff any more than was absolutely necessary. Alice, knowing any offer of help would not be welcome, kept her distance.

Mahommed winced as Abdullah held his arm and scrubbed it roughly.

'You've grown soft.'

'I nearly died ...'

'And you exaggerate.'

He had cried when Abdullah had first appeared by his bed, his tears welling at the sight of his friend. The old man had not acknowledged them, nor mentioned the strained circumstances of their last meeting. He showed no interest in the details of the accident that had brought Mahommed here; gave no indication that he was there for any other reason beyond duty.

He took the other arm and scrubbed it even harder. Mahommed thought he was punishing him, but didn't say so. He responded with childlike passivity, too weakened physically and emotionally to do otherwise.

He had no womb to crawl back into. For now, Abdullah would have to do.

13

Carrying a lamp, Alice moved quietly through the darkened ward, checking on patients. She didn't normally work at night. Her evenings were mostly spent preparing and cooking dinner for Lewis and Eileen, but she had offered to fill a sudden nursing shortfall. Lewis wasn't happy about it, although she had pointed out that she would leave them a perfectly adequate cold tea. She added that if he was really unhappy about it she would stay at home, as long as he was comfortable with the idea of patients dying, with a great deal of accompanying pain, as a result of her absence. That had settled the argument.

They had had a number of arguments recently. She had felt him watching her ever since her return from Adelaide. He had used that word again, *settled*, more than once. As though she could now safely be put down and forgotten about. She didn't tell him she felt more unsettled than ever; as if she had been given the key to a gateway, but was allowed to do no more than peer through it before it was shut in her face. She couldn't tell him that. She had never told him she felt trapped, so how could she tell him she felt more trapped?

She soon discovered why he was saying these things. She had been washing up after dinner and he was helping her, something he didn't usually do. Eileen was in the bedroom, studying for her weekly spelling bee.

He said, 'Those Germans.'

'Yes.' She put a clean plate on the draining board.

He said, 'It's bad alright.'

She thought about calling Eileen in to help. Whatever he was trying to say, her presence would make him think twice.

'Arnie Jenkins has enlisted. At Railway Town, yesterday.'

She shrugged, as though it was of no great consequence. 'He's a single man with no dependants. Better in the army than in the hotels.'

'They're paying five shillings a day. Six for those who serve overseas.'

She put the last plate down and pulled the plug out of the sink, concentrating on the water swirling away. 'That's what they say. It'll be over before anyone gets there.'

'Men with dependants, they take two shillings a day out for them. So they're looked after.'

She turned to face him. 'And that's what you'll tell Eileen, is it?'

They heard her coming out from the bedroom, and by tacit agreement changed the conversation. But it stayed between them, and no amount of pretending it wasn't there would make it go away.

She hesitated outside Mahommed's cubicle, listening to the sound of his regular breathing. He was the only reason she was there tonight, she knew that. She was mostly comfortable about lying to others, but never to herself; she was rigorous about it.

She had tried to accept that he wanted nothing to do with her. But their eyes had met once, hadn't they? He had held her look and told her his name and if she had imagined that, then her grasp of what was real was shakier than she thought.

If he would only acknowledge her, she could get over it. If he would only talk to her, she would see him for what he surely was, a foreigner with nothing to offer her, except the chance to say his name, Mahommed, Ma-homm-ed. If she could speak it to him, perhaps she could stop herself from obsessively rolling it round and round in her head.

She moved to the side of his bed and watched him as he slept. His face was narrow, drawn. Now that his body was no longer swollen she could see he had lost a great deal of weight from his ordeal. But he was recovering, growing stronger. A few days at most, Matron had said, and he would be gone. Alice would be left with nothing more than the memory of a name.

His top sheet had come adrift. She put the lamp down and began to tuck it in, a tiny chore she eked out as long as she could. Just when she thought she couldn't make the moment last any longer, that she would have to either leave or touch him, he opened his eyes and looked at her.

Alice kept her voice low so as not to wake anyone else. 'I'm not allowed to wash you, and I'm not allowed to feed you. Now you're probably going to tell me I'm not allowed to tuck you in.'

'It is allowed.'

'It is?'

He nodded.

He had run out of strength to fend her off, and reasons why he should. He had, he knew, overreacted to their encounters. He had placed so much importance on his return to Broken Hill, but he could not continue to blame this girl for everything unpleasant that had happened.

Alice finished tidying up his sheet, lingering. She said, 'Would you like a glass of water?'

'No. Thank you.'

'Are you sure?'

'Yes. I am sure.'

She turned to go. He didn't want her to.

'Would it be possible to leave me a lamp?'

'What do you want it for?'

He gestured towards his bedside table, to the neat pile of Adrian's testimonials. 'I am not so tired. I was hoping to do a little reading.' Whatever else she might think of him, he wasn't going to allow her to continue to think he couldn't read. He tried to reach out for them, but she anticipated his need and picked them up.

She looked at him frankly. 'Mahommed?'

The sound of his name surprised both of them. No longer rolling around inside her head but given soft voice, heard only by the two of them.

'About the train. I really am sorry.'

Mahommed resisted, struggling to revive his disdain for her. But he had mislaid it. All he could feel was a surge of warmth and goodwill, of relief as he let all those other things go. He found that he was returning her smile.

'It is only with English that I have some small

difficulty.' He indicated the testimonials. 'I have been taking lessons from Mr Adrian Kadran.'

'The herbalist?'

Mahommed nodded.

Alice knew very little about Adrian Kadran beyond the fact that Robert Brosnan consulted him on a regular basis about some unspecified ailment. Irma had confided as much to her. Irma found these consultations troubling, although she wasn't able to say why.

Alice looked at the top testimonial. 'To whom it may concern, I had suffered from a duodenal ulcer for eight years, but when I took Mr Kadran's powder ...' She looked back at Mahommed. 'Is this your reading lesson?'

He nodded. 'Some of the words are a little difficult for me.'

'I'm not surprised.' She hesitated. 'If you like, we could go over them together.'

'You are busy.'

'Nothing that can't wait.'

She gave him a space to decline her offer. When he didn't take it, she moved to the curtains and pulled them shut. As he propped himself to a sitting position, Alice perched on the edge of the bed. She shared the testimonial with him, so that they could both see it.

He read, 'When I took Mr Kadran's powder, my con ... considerable dig ... dig ...'

Alice helped him out: '... my considerable digestive derangement ceased instantly.'

'What does that mean?'

'I've no idea. I think he cured her.'

'It seems Mr Kadran cures all his patients.'

'Maybe you should be letting him treat you. We don't have anything like his success.'

Mahommed, shyly emboldened by the curtained night, said, 'I would rather be treated here. By you.'

'Well, I don't suppose Mr Kadran would tuck you in.'

She looked away, embarrassed. They read through one more testimonial before putting it aside, in silent mutual agreement that they had risked as much as could be risked in one night. Alice bade him goodnight in a friendly but professional manner, moved off to check the patient in the next bed, and left the ward.

Mahommed stayed awake for a long time, thinking about her eyes, before drifting off to sleep where he enjoyed a satisfying dream about the three submarines in his hugely successful shipping empire.

The policeman, Constable Keith Fitzpatrick, shifted his weight from his left foot to his right. 'The thing is, Andy feels it was an accident, and if you're happy with that, then I think he'd be happy with it as well.'

Andy, standing next to the policeman, nodded soberly. Mahommed found their deference disconcerting. First the policeman, who'd given no indication he remembered Mahommed from the police station, had introduced himself and enquired after Mahommed's health. And then Andy, treating him as though he were somebody worthy of respect. The situation was both pleasant and odd.

They were on the sheltered verandah attached to the main hospital building, where Mahommed had come to sit on a small iron chair, placed to catch the healing light, yet avoid the burning heat of the sun. He had come here yesterday, helped by a nurse. This morning, buoyed by Alice's late-night visit, he had walked here by himself. He felt well enough to contemplate the resumption of his life; to feel that that resumption might even be a desirable thing.

He looked at Andy, feeling no ill will. An accident. Yes, it could well have been that. And men say things in the heat of the moment; he thought it reasonable that Andy might now regret the words he had said. He said, 'Yes. I am happy.'

Andy nodded again, mumbling to his feet, 'I'd appreciate it.'

The policeman had a report of the accident in his hand, and a pencil. He said to Mahommed, 'Like a lot of the men, he's got a family.'

'Yes indeed. I understand.'

'You sure you're alright with this?'

Andy looked at the policeman, sidelong. 'He said he was.'

'I need to be certain.'

Mahommed could feel some tension between them, and did his best to smooth it away. 'I assure you, I am happy.' He accepted the pencil and paper from the policeman, and had a quick look at the words, clumping in front of his eyes. If Andy and the policemen hadn't been there he would have been able to unclump them, but he didn't want to keep them waiting, so, at the bottom of the page, where indicated, he signed his name.

Once they had left, Mahommed pushed himself up from the chair. The sunlight had shifted, making it too hot to stay on the verandah. He thought if he went back to his bed he would be cooler, and beyond that there was the possibility he might be able to see Alice when she arrived for her shift.

He used his hand as a guide, touching the wall as he shuffled along the verandah towards the doorway to the corridor. Walking was still an effort for him, but although his legs were heavy he felt happy, infused by a healing lightness. Andy had as good as apologised to him, and Alice had shown him warmth; that these two unexpected things had happened in less than a day was a minor miracle in itself, and he could already feel his body trying to catch up with his newly lifted spirits.

He reached the doorway, and stopped to let his eyes adjust from bright sunshine to gloom. He shut his eyes to hasten the process, and when he opened them again he saw, at the other end of the corridor, the policeman talking with Alice.

They were framed by a circle of light from the hospital entranceway, turning them into little more than scissored silhouettes, and he couldn't make out what they were saying; their words reached him as only a low murmur. But he saw what the policeman did. He saw him reach out and brush her cheek with his hand. He saw her accept the gesture.

He didn't want to see any more. He turned into the ward, hurried to his bed and began to dress, stumbling over the effort of trying to fit his left foot into his right shoe, fumbling with shirt buttons he'd forgotten how to use, hurling his few possessions into his case. Feeling faint from the exertion, and the knowledge that he had been a fool.

Keeping his head down, he lifted the case off the bed, trying not to think about how heavy an almost empty case could feel. By the time he reached the end of the bed, he had to stop for breath. He forced himself to keep going, ten steps to the end of the ward, and then out. Where to? Not to Abdullah, too many explanations, back to his room, yes, his room, five more steps, and …

'Mahommed?'

She was in front of him, blocking him.

He fixed his gaze on a fly crawling across a wall. 'I am well now. It is time to leave.'

'The end of the week, that's what the matron said.'

'You are all very busy. It is better I go now.'

'It is not.'

The fly changed direction, dragging Mahommed's gaze with it. He found himself looking directly at Alice, with no way of letting his gaze fall.

He said, 'I am healthy now and I must start work again. Thank you for your consideration.' He walked around her and headed outside, not letting himself breathe until he was out of her sight.

She wanted to chase after him. But she couldn't, because Matron Guthrie had appeared and was asking questions. She produced answers as best she could. Then, accepting Mahommed was gone, moved to his bed to strip it. She gathered his sheets, smelling him, keeping him close as long as possible. She was about to head to the laundry with them when she saw the neat stack of papers by his bed, forgotten in the rush.

She picked up the top one and learned that Adrian Kadran, not content with curing digestive derangement, had done wonders with the overwrought debility of one Edna Hooper's sluggish liver, and that she would be 'eternally (and forever) grateful'.

Alice pictured Edna, contentedly emanating gratitude until the last breath of her happy old age, all because of a cured sluggish liver. She tried to dislike Edna for this, but ended up disliking herself for her mean spirit.

She put the testimonials into the waste basket by the bed and prepared to leave with the sheets. She hesitated, reasoning that just because Mahommed had gone didn't mean they were hers to throw away. She picked them back out of the basket and headed out to the laundry. She would decide what to do with them later.

14

Adrian Kadran, looking at Irma from across his desk, decided, not for the first time, she was rather pretty. Much more so than her friend, Alice Mercer, who was too angular for his taste. Unlike her, Irma had a round pink marshmallow face, the kind that could be moulded into any number of pleasing expressions.

He was surprised when she came to see him, but any frisson of excitement disappeared in the wave of controlled hysteria she brought with her.

'Miss Cowie, how pleasant and unexpected.'

'I assure you, it wasn't pleasant for me.'

She remained standing by the closed door. Adrian could see she was uncomfortable about being here. His rooms were not in a part of town she would normally choose to visit, and he felt she wanted him to know this.

'Please, won't you sit? There is no problem that can't be solved, but first you must share it with me.'

He gave her an encouraging smile and eased her into a chair, making soothing noises designed to drain away her discomfort. He moved around the desk to his own chair and sat. He leaned forward, his hands clasped together, presenting, he hoped, a professional and kindly demeanour. 'I find the beginning is often a good place to start.'

Irma fiddled with the clasp of her handbag, struggling for the words. 'It was weeks. Weeks and weeks ago, when we were going to have lunch at Brown's, which I was looking forward to, and I've tried since then to put it out of my mind, hoped it could all be explained, wished for some resolution, but there hasn't been one, and I wouldn't normally come here or interfere in any way at all, but when I raise the subject, which I'm apparently not allowed to do, even in the mildest way, so, so, so … I didn't know what else to do.'

Before Adrian could unscramble this, Irma reached into her bag and produced a near empty bottle of Brosnan's tonic. She clutched it tightly in her plump hand and, giving only sparse details of the incident, told him she had come across an unwell Brosnan. She was wondering if it might have been a reaction to the medicine he was taking.

Adrian relieved her of the bottle, and made a show of studying it. 'I think that's highly unlikely.'

'I even had to help him home, and once there, he fell asleep on the sofa, without a word of thanks or apology.'

'That must have been very upsetting for you.'

'Not that one was necessary, because he couldn't help being sick and I was only too happy to help him, but … Mr Kadran, I was very distressed.'

'Of course you were. I completely understand.'

He resisted the urge to slap her face; to feel his fingers melting into the marshmallow, leaving red welts behind. Instead he gave her a glass of water, and, returning to his chair, allowed her to see he was struggling with a weighty decision.

He was, he said with finely tuned gravitas, going to take her into his confidence. 'Mr Brosnan has been suffering from a rare acute catarrh of the stomach.'

Irma frowned. 'He has?'

'It is a very serious condition, one that can only be cured by modern science, time, and loving patience and care. The science, I can dispense; the time, only God can provide. And if Mr Brosnan were fortunate enough to find someone kind and generous enough to provide the others …'

He let it hang for a moment.

'Someone like me?'

Adrian didn't answer. He indicated the tonic bottle. 'This, Miss Cowie, is all that stands between Mr Brosnan and complete debilitation. We are only fortunate that upon being assailed by a sudden manifestation of the catarrh, he had the presence of mind to administer a larger dose than had been prescribed. When you found him, he was taken ill. But without this medicine, you may have found him … well, I'd prefer not to say.'

Irma's eyes grew wider. 'Dead?' she whispered.

Adrian looked delicately away. 'My dear Miss Cowie. He has been trying to shield you.'

'But why would he do that?'

'Because of the high regard he holds you in. The highest regard. He has told me this himself.'

'He has?'

'He has.'

From there on, it was plain sailing. Irma, damped down and flattered, agreed that the best thing all round would be to allow him to continue treating Robert as he saw fit; that with Irma's patient and loving help, they would soon have him back to his previous healthy state. They also agreed that this conversation would remain between the two of them.

Relieved by this agreeable outcome, he saw Irma to the door, barely refraining from placing a too familiar guiding hand on her back as he shepherded her out. I mustn't, he thought. Never again. He shuddered, recalling a hasty departure from Melbourne three years earlier. *Never.* Too much discipline for that.

The wretched Brosnan, on the other hand, clearly had no concept of discipline. Although the word 'laudanum' had never been spoken by either of them, it was understood that the tonic was meant to be no more than an occasional pick-me-up. Something pleasant. Something which, when finally drained, would stir in one the desire for perhaps just a soupçon more. Another consultation paid for, another bottle purchased. But this weakness of Brosnan's was deplorable. Oh dear. All very complicated when it needn't be.

Robert lifted his pen from the paper and examined the words he had just composed. *A well-made man is usually made well from his many parts.* He read it twice before giving in to a sigh of dissatisfaction. It was good, but unlikely to be added to any canon of higher thought. If he'd taken his tonic it would be better, but, in light of the unfortunate event, he'd made a decision not to take any while at work.

He took out his watch and looked at it, willing the hour hand to move. Four hours before he could leave the office and go home. He heard footsteps in the corridor, the *tap tap tap* of a woman's heels, and quickly dragged some files from his in-tray, using them to cover what he'd been writing.

The footsteps receded, going past his office. Good. The last thing he wanted was that nasty Mary Hamilton spying on him. The dreadful girl was only on the reception desk, but she mistakenly thought that gave her licence to spread unpleasant falsehoods about him. Nothing overt, nothing he could put his finger on — but he knew she was doing it. A sly look here, a raised eyebrow there, and before he knew it he was standing in front of his superiors defending his work output. Admittedly he'd fallen a little behind, but he'd been ill. And no thanks for soldiering on regardless, no thanks at all. He'd like to have her dismissed, but the situation was delicate. Who knows what she might say? The girl was probably angry because he preferred Irma. She'd set her cap on him and he'd taken it right off again. For heaven's sake, she should realise she wasn't in his league. Then again, neither was Irma.

Hector Cowie had stopped him in the street last week, full of false bonhomie. He had mentioned, apropos of absolutely nothing, that he would be very happy when Irma, his daughter, was finally off his hands. When that day came, Doreen could get back to her proper job of looking after him instead of fussing about with the contents of Irma's glory box.

He said it with a chuckle, adding that whoever landed Irma would be a lucky man. Robert pretended not to hear, but that didn't stop Hector. He continued, trying to make himself clear, 'A very lucky man.'

Robert considered Hector a twerp. The thought of him as a prospective father-in-law was enough in itself to turn him against the idea of marrying Irma. Although he had to tread carefully. Since the incident, she'd been sympathetic about his illness, but her concern was superficial. She had somehow used it to wedge herself more firmly into his life, something he didn't want.

The only thing he really wanted – and the certainty of this had come to him only recently – was to be alone.

Over the past weeks a pattern had been forming in his life, and he believed it was the correct one. After work he would return home and take a small dose of his tonic. He would consider going out to have a drink with friends, perhaps dinner at a hotel; but more often than not his stomach would still be troubling him, and he would put off the decision by taking another dose of tonic. After that he would be free of pain, allowing the realisation that he and his surroundings existed in perfect harmony, without need of outside company.

The thoughts he harnessed at these times were of the highest level. His mind soared. It was unlikely there was a person in all of Broken Hill who would have been able to join him in such rarefied atmosphere. He had begun to make written notes about the inspirations that came to him on these nights, his hand cramping as he pushed it to keep up with the torrent of ideas flowing through him. He would assemble the notes in proper order later; for now it was enough to put them on paper before they escaped. Publishing them was an option he had considered. He knew that being a Sanitary Inspector was merely a stepping stone to his true calling as a philosopher. It would, by necessity, be a lonely road. Irma would not travel it well.

The footsteps passed by again. Philosophy. He'd read a book about it when he was hoping to be accepted by Sydney University. Well, enough of the book to get a general idea. The Utilitarians sounded alright. Something about happiness being maximised and pain minimised. It was largely a waste of time because the university didn't see his potential and his father pushed him into the stagnating pond of the Public Service. Nevertheless, the ideas in the book stayed with him. He was grateful for that.

He turned back to his work. It was obvious he needed to make a successful prosecution soon, one that would be noticed. An Arab would be best. That old Mullah had been fined before; it shouldn't be too hard to win a prosecution against him.

His telephone rang and Mary coolly informed him that a Mr Kadran was on the line and wished to speak with him. Matching her tone, he informed her he would take the call.

Adrian quickly came to the point, and told him about Irma's visit.

Robert's initial reaction was alarm, but Adrian assured him all was well.

'I've been discreet,' he said.

'How discreet?'

'Very.'

'You told her I was ill?'

'In general terms only. But I spoke to her about the importance of calm, and I impressed on her your need for solitude. Also that overt sympathy would be much less efficacious than peace and quiet.'

A cloud lifted from above Robert's head. He thanked Adrian for the intervention, and ended the phone call feeling much brighter.

He took out his piece of paper from underneath the files and looked at it again. *A well-made man is usually made well from his many parts.*

He thought about it. *Often made? Generally? Always?*

Concentrate, he told himself. This was important work.

15

After leaving the hospital, Mahommed had dragged himself along Blende Street, heading towards Mr Kadran's boarding house. Initially, anger and shame had carried him, but before long these were not enough and he had to pause, finding a fence to lean against, wondering at his weakness. He had been fit, able, he thought, to do the work of ten men. Now he could barely move.

If he kept walking straight ahead, he would reach the turn off to the camel camp. Abdullah would provide both ministration and remonstration. He thought about these, balancing one against the other. He forced himself to continue walking, turning into Bromide Street, away from the camp.

At the boarding house he let himself into his room to find a note under the door from Mr Kadran, reminding him that he owed two weeks' rent. He put it aside to be dealt with later, and lay down on his bed, exhausted, too tired and weak to think about anything. He slept through the rest of that day and into the early morning of the next. He dreamed of little, and whatever it was, it didn't include submarines.

He wasn't worried about lack of money. He had enough saved to pay the rent that was owed, plus enough for two weeks more. He was philosophical about not having worked for the last few weeks, sure that once he started work again, he would soon make up the lost earnings. This was why he had been willing to let Andy's involvement in the accident go: he had to work with these men again, and a thousand feet under the ground was not a place to be harbouring resentment.

There would be a little compensation money. Not enough to cover the shortfall, but his understanding was that there would be at least one extra week's pay waiting for him. One week's pay wasn't much, but it was something.

Or so he had thought.

When he went to the site office to discuss his situation with Mr Angus Milne, the Site Manager, Mr Milne had seemed surprised to see him, and said as much.

'You took a bit of a beating down there.'

'I am well now. I am as strong as before.'

That wasn't quite accurate. He still had headaches, which sometimes lasted through the night, and he could see for himself that his muscles had wasted. But that was from lack of work, not too much. He could cope, he was sure of it.

Mr Milne was of a different opinion. 'Why don't you leave it for a few weeks?' he said. 'Get yourself a hundred per cent.'

'I am already a hundred per cent.'

In the background Mahommed could see the paymaster busying himself writing up his pay envelope, making it clear he was not part of the discussion.

Mr Milne stood, readying himself to leave. He had his Site Manager's face on, the one he put on when he wanted to let people know he was more important than them. Mahommed had seen this face before, on occasions when problems underground had caused the miners' output to slow.

'The thing is, we're not taking on any more single men at the moment.'

Mahommed frowned. 'But I am already working here.'

'Not for the last few weeks you haven't been.'

'I was in hospital.'

Mr Milne grabbed his coat from the rack and shrugged it on. 'I know that and I've taken it into account, but it doesn't change the fact that I only need men who can do a full day's work.'

'But I am a hard worker. Ask the other men.'

'I did. Sorry, but the decision's made.' He pushed past and was out the door before Mahommed could protest further.

He stayed where he was, trying to come to grips with the situation. He was marooned, he knew that, but he couldn't understand how it had happened.

He heard a cough, and turned to see the paymaster holding out an envelope. 'It's what you're owed. I've made it up to the pound.'

Mahommed hesitated. If he took it, it would mean accepting his termination, and he didn't see why he should do that.

The paymaster held the envelope out further. 'Take it,' he said. 'It's yours, you earned it.'

Mahommed hesitated a moment longer, then reached out and took it.

He began to look for work elsewhere. Each mine he went to being a little smaller than the last, a little further from town; the story always the same. The European war. They weren't laying off yet, but they weren't hiring; or if they were, they weren't hiring single men. Nobody mentioned foreigners, Turkey lollies, Afghans.

They didn't have to; it was in the air. Mahommed tried hard not to breathe it in.

The last mine was over an hour's dusty walk from town. He went early, getting there before the two other applicants. All three of them waited in silence for the arrival of the manager. The other applicants were older than he was; one he judged to be about forty-five, the other in his mid sixties, although he had about him such an air of defeat it was hard to tell for sure.

When the manager arrived he hesitated, then nodded at the younger of the two men. He'd give him a try out. The older man, accustomed to failure, went away without arguing the point. Mahommed watched him trudge off, refusing to join him. He was younger and fitter than the man who'd been hired. Surely he deserved at least a chance to prove himself?

He went over to the manager. 'I will do anything. I am prepared to work very cheap.'

'Not in this mine. The union'd string me up.'

'I will work very hard.'

The manager sighed, swatting a couple of flies from his eyelids before he explained further. 'Look, I'll be honest with you. We don't hire foreigners here because they don't speak the language and it can make for accidents down below.'

'I speak English,' said Mahommed.

'Yes, but I can't make exceptions, because then where would we be?'

Mahommed paused, trying to make sense of it. Given he didn't know who 'we' were, he had no idea where 'we' would be. He knew where *he* would be – down the mine, working and earning money, which was the whole point of this increasingly futile exercise.

The manager, taking his pause for agreement, suggested, 'Try the Proprietary Mine. They're still hiring.'

It took Mahommed longer to walk back from the mine than it did to get there. It was late morning, already burning hot. Whole families of bush flies stuck to his shirt, or crawled inside, dogpaddling through rivers of sweat. He was physically fitter than he had been when he left hospital a week ago, but still weak enough to feel debilitated by the heat. When he came to the fork in the road that would take him to the camp, he wasn't strong enough to stop his feet from heading in that direction.

He entered the camp, burdened by flies and a brooding sense of his own failure. He looked for Abdullah but found only old Jemadar, who, on seeing Mahommed approaching, signalled to his wife Edith that she should leave what she was doing and go inside their shack. She did so, slipping in like a shadow.

Mahommed wondered what would cause a woman to leave her people and throw in her lot with an old man like Jemadar. He knew they didn't always stay but Edith had been with him long enough to produce Partimah. Zainie and Ibram were from Nita, the previous wife, but when she left, Jemadar had insisted on keeping them.

Jemadar told Mahommed that Abdullah was on a station run with his camels; he had been gone now for five days. He was expected back tomorrow, perhaps the day after. Surely he had told him this?

Mahommed bridled at his patronising manner. He informed him that of course Abdullah had told him, but he had numerous complicated businesses to attend to at present, which were so filling his mind that details of Abdullah's movements had temporarily escaped him. Aware that all Jemadar wanted was a chance to winkle these non-existent businesses out into the open, he thanked him for his time, refused his offer of a glass of tea, and took his leave.

He continued on into town, where he detoured to buy a cake of Puritol soap he could ill afford. He needed it to plug the hole in his heart that Abdullah's desertion had created. It should be he who fended off Abdullah, not the other way around. He knew he should have told him he had left the hospital, should have shown the old man more respect, more gratitude than he had. But why couldn't Abdullah have passed a message on to tell him he would be away? Surely he knew Mahommed was weakened, might need him? Didn't Abdullah love him like a son, although it was never spoken? It was understood, all this was understood, wasn't it? Thinking about this made him feel miserable, so he added a small tin of Sanatogen – two shillings and sixpence – to his purchase, reasoning that it would help restore him to health. He would go home, he would wash, and he would make a start on the Sanatogen. Life might look better after doing that.

It didn't. As he sat naked on his bed, reading an advertisement in the newspaper borrowed from reception, he discovered – as claimed by the advertisement – a great controversy going on about the best soap to use for the complexion. None of the soaps in question was Puritol, the new bar of which was sitting, freshly unwrapped and waiting, on his washstand. There were other controversies, mainly to do with war, but he wasn't interested in the activities of Germans. The Germans had caused some of his present difficulties, and he didn't want to read about them. He put the paper aside.

He looked at the opened tin of Sanatogen and made himself eat another spoonful. It was horrible stuff. All it did was make his tongue feel furry. He wished he hadn't bought it. It was an extravagance he couldn't afford. He sucked on it, straining it through his teeth, trying unsuccessfully to make it palatable. If someone could invent this muck and persuade intelligent people to buy it, then why was his own success proving so elusive? And why was Abdullah not speaking to him; why did the English take his job away? Why did Andy betray him, and why did Alice … ?

No! No to that place in his heart where a tiny metallic shard, glinting cold, had taken up residence. Was lying there dormant, waiting for …

No!

He put the lid on the Sanatogen and pushed it away. He picked up the Puritol and sniffed it. It smelt medicinal. But then, medicine was probably what he needed. He added the smoothed-out wrapper to the growing gallery on the wall. He moved back to the washstand, dipped the soap in the water and lathered up, spreading soapy plugs over all those gaping holes.

Halfway through this process, he found himself warming to Puritol. What it lacked in fragrance it compensated for in superior latherability. In this he judged it on a par with Cuticura, perhaps even nudging Cuticura out of its present top position. He would perform a proper test later and determine the absolute merits of each.

But for now he gave himself to the bubbles; his hair, his face, his whole body encased in the silken protection of the weightless white foam. He floated with the bubbles, drifting ever closer to the promised godliness, knowing he could never quite touch it, but …

The soap slipped from his hands, splashing into the basin. He wiped his eyes before opening them and fished it out, placing it beside the basin. He looked at it balefully, seeing it for what it was. It had no power; it was only soap. It could not give him work, could not return Abdullah's regard, could not make Alice see inside him. It could make him clean, that was all, but who now would ever know or care?

He was startled by a rap at the door. He wasn't expecting anyone. It was probably a mistake, a sober rather than a drunken one at this time of day. He grabbed his towel and tied it around his waist.

He opened the door a few cautious inches before opening it fully to admit Mr Kadran.

'There's a young woman to see you. A Miss Alice Mercer.'

Mahommed suppressed a wave of panic. 'To see me?'

'Apparently.'

'Please tell her I am not here.'

'I've already told her you are.'

'But it is not possible.'

'The same thought crossed my mind when she asked for you.'

He looked at Mahommed, clearly unimpressed. 'Perhaps a little attention to your grooming?' he suggested, before briskly heading off down the corridor, letting Mahommed know he was a busy man.

After a few frozen seconds, Mahommed shut the door. What was she doing here, what could she possibly want? He thought about barricading himself in and refusing to come out ever again, but the rational part of his brain told him this was not a viable option.

He would have to go down and get it over with, whatever 'it' was. He whipped the towel off and, working quickly, began wiping the bubbles off the rest of his body.

16

Alice sat on the single wooden chair in the reception area, waiting for Mahommed to appear. She was out of place here, a novelty, she knew that. At first she smiled pleasantly at the single men passing in and out, but quickly tired of being misconstrued. She retreated into her space to wait more privately.

She was prepared to sit for as long as necessary, although she wasn't sure he would agree to see her. She had offended him in some way. She thought it might have had something to do with Keith, although she didn't know what.

The day Mahommed had left the hospital, Alice had arrived for her shift, and, after casual questioning, had been told he was on the verandah. Waiting until she could find an excuse, she had gone to find him. When she saw him outside with Keith and Andy, she stopped, unnoticed. She saw him sign the form Keith gave him, and understood.

She waited inside for Keith as he came along the corridor. Andy, ahead of him, gave her a cursory nod and hurried out, but Keith stopped to talk with her.

She said, 'You're making him lie about it, aren't you?'

'No-one needs trouble. He understands that.'

'I'm sure he does. After you found twenty different ways to tell him.'

Keith ignored her accusation, reaching out to brush her cheek with the back of his hand. 'I'm very fond of you, Alice. You know that, don't you?'

She had endured his touch for as long as was polite before moving away, telling him they both had work to do. And that was all. If Mahommed had seen anything, there was nothing to see.

She had almost let the matter rest. She could hardly force herself on him; she barely knew him. Lying awake at night, after an evening when she had snapped for no reason at both Lewis and Eileen, she had tried to understand why he mattered to her.

He was in her life so lightly, had touched only minutes, hours; not once a whole day even, not if she discounted her compulsive inner ramblings, which had him with her constantly. He had come from somewhere she knew nothing about, to a land that he knew little about. He had done this without blinking, without once grasping the impossibility of doing such a thing, whereas all she had done was wait and watch as another day was added to her tally of yesterdays. Was that it? The second-hand shine of possibilities?

She was not affected in this way by Keith. He was a decent man. He could offer her a home, a space in his heart. But she didn't want a space in anyone's heart, she simply wanted space. She wondered if that was also a cause of this obsession; that Mahommed asked nothing of her.

He saw her, sitting alone in a quiet circle of dignity, hands in her lap, wearing a pale-green blouse with frills down the front, separating her breasts into two green hills. She looked up at his approach, offering him a tentative smile of recognition.

He responded with distant formality. 'I'm sorry. I did not mean to keep you waiting.'

She shook her head. 'It was rude to come unannounced.' She reached into her bag and pulled out a bundle of testimonials. 'You left these behind. I thought you might need them.'

She held them out. He took them, keeping his fingers well clear of hers.

'Are you still reading?'

'Of course.' He didn't tell her that today all he had read was a soap advertisement and the side of the Sanatogen tin. He wished she would stop looking at him. If she would only stop then he could end this encounter and put her out of his mind forever.

'We've got a library at home. It's only small, but you're welcome to borrow from it.'

He stared at her, not knowing how to deal with this offer, which had dropped into the conversation so unexpectedly.

'That's if you'd like to.'

'No, thank you.'

'Why not?'

'I don't think Constable Fitzpatrick would approve.'

'What's it got to do with him?'

'You have, I think, an understanding.'

'We do not.'

'Still, I would not wish to offend anyone.'

'You're offending *me*.' Her voice had risen, attracting the attention of a couple of men passing by. She lowered it. 'Mahommed … do you have any idea,' she asked, her voice shaking, 'how difficult it was for me to come here today and speak to you?'

All he heard was *Mahommed*. No-one else had spoken his name since he had left the hospital. He had been nameless. He didn't want to be nameless, not any more. By the time he understood she needed a reply she had turned and hurried out the door, a flash of green already gone before he started after her. She had said his name and now she was gone. If he let her go, no-one might ever say it again.

She was hurrying and he had to walk fast to keep her in sight. He had angered her. He knew if he let this slender fraying string between them break, it would stay broken. He followed, on the other side of the road, keeping distance between them, having no plan beyond the act of following.

She turned a corner and he lost sight of her. He picked up speed, worried by the thought of her disappearing into a maze of side streets before he could see where she'd gone.

He reached the corner and looked around, seeing nothing but an empty street tailing off to nowhere. He peered into the distance at a figure coming into view, crossing the road a hundred yards away. A man, not a woman.

Mahommed stopped beside a hedge, realising the futility of chasing after nothing. He heard a noise. A heaving noise, someone gasping, gulping. He moved cautiously to the source of the noise, to where the hedge was broken by a gate, and came upon Alice. He could see she was having trouble breathing. Reaching out a tentative hand towards her, he asked, 'Are you alright?'

She stiffened.

He tried again. 'Are you alright?'

'Go away.'

He held his ground.

Alice turned from him, moved away from the gate, and continued up the street.

He followed. He was Mahommed, Afridi warrior, hunter of pale-green women. He hadn't come this far to leave it like this. 'Please wait!'

She kept going. 'Why would I be so stupid as to imagine you'd be interested in looking at my books?'

He increased his pace until he was practically alongside her. 'Because I no longer have anything to read. See?'

He tossed one of the testimonials aside. 'No more stomach growth!' He tossed another into the air. 'No more gout!' And another. 'No more derangement in intestinal passage! I am free of all these things!' He scattered the rest into the air. 'So I am now ready to read more.'

Alice brushed away a stray testimonial that had blown onto her blouse. She said, 'You don't need books.'

'I do.'

'You don't. My father used to read to us. He didn't want Lewis going into the mine. He thought if we could have education, however we got it, that it would save us.'

'He was right.'

'He wasn't. It didn't save my mother.'

Mahommed was having difficulty following. 'Your mother died in a mine?'

'Typhoid.' She cut off his awkward attempt at condolence. 'It didn't save my father, either, because he died four years ago.'

'A mine?'

'In a way. He'd left the mine and got a job as a clerk.'

'A very fine job.'

'He hated it. He only did it because of a deathbed promise to my mother. But on Sundays he used to forget about the promise and go searching for a silver lode he told us was out there.'

None of this was making it clearer for Mahommed. 'He found silver?'

'No. Only an abandoned hole left by someone else doing the same pointless thing. I hope he died happy, but he probably didn't.'

Mahommed tried to find some words of sympathy that would be acceptable to her, but she was already moving on.

'And education didn't save me, because with Lewis working, there was no-one else to look after Eileen.'

'But you love her?'

'It still doesn't make him right. I suppose it's possible that if they hadn't read books they might have died even earlier, but I don't see how.'

She stopped and turned into the small frontyard of a cottage with pressed-metal walls. It was like the doyley cottage.

Mahommed hovered at the front gate. It was one thing to follow her along the road uninvited, but to go any further might occasion a cry for help, and although he was willing to risk affronting her, it was a long time since he had wished her harm.

Reaching the front door, Alice stood on her toes to feel for a key that lived on the ledge above it. She unlocked the door, and put the key back on its ledge.

She looked back at Mahommed. 'Are you going to stay there?'

'No.'

'Where are you going to go?'

'I am deciding.'

'Well, while you're doing that, do you want to come in?'

He entered the parlour, glimpsing a couple of bedrooms, a kitchen out the back. The parlour had two comfortable chairs, two wooden chairs, a gun cabinet and a small sideboard. Mahommed could see that the sideboard, with a mirror and carved panels, was older than the chairs. He ran a finger along the top of it, feeling the cool smoothness of the worn timber. 'It is beautiful.'

Alice barely looked at it. 'My mother brought it with her. She told my father she wouldn't come here otherwise. She said she knew the sideboard couldn't tell her where she was going, but it could at least tell her where she'd come from.'

She pointed past doyleys and glass dishes to a framed photograph showing a man and woman in their thirties. 'That's them.'

Mahommed looked closely at the photograph. The man was looking straight at the camera, but the woman was gazing slightly to one side, as though wary of this clinical examination of her face.

'She looks sad.'

'I think she was mostly just angry. My father promised her a fortune, but all she got was his second-hand dreams and some headaches.'

'She was sick?'

'I don't know. But she used to get a lot of them, so when the last one came, we didn't think anything of it. By the time anyone realised it was typhoid, it was too late.'

Mahommed wanted to fold her into his arms. To tell her that he understood the pain of losing a mother, losing a father. That it was something they shared. But the telling had been brittle, and he was afraid she would not welcome his sympathy or his touch.

His offering was tentative. He indicated the room. 'But they are still here, watching over you. Your mother and your father.'

'If they are, I can't feel them. I used to try to summon them. Not pray, exactly, but wish them into some sort of presence. But they never came.' She shrugged. 'How could they? They're dead.'

She turned towards the bookshelf, dismissing the subject. 'Anyway,' she said, 'you're here for the books, not all that.'

He let the moment go. Alice was concentrating on the books. Free from scrutiny, he was able to properly absorb his surroundings. The chairs, the dishes, the sideboard, the sampler on the wall asking God to bless this humble home.

He felt momentary indignation that anyone, let alone God, might see it as humble. How could anyone think that when the parlour was the most beautiful parlour he had ever seen? When the things inside it were treasures? He wanted to touch each piece, hold them all in his hands, feel them in a way that Alice must have so often felt them.

It was the first time since he had set foot in Australia that he had been in someone's home. He had been in Abdullah's shack, he had been in the boarding house; but this was more than a place where someone lived, it was a home, a proper house with rooms, rooms where doyleys were the right size; rooms where meals were prepared not by lardy cooks, but by Alice. Alice who was here with him, who had invited him inside, who right now had her back to him while she looked through a shelf full of real books; who was wearing a pale-green blouse with frills, tucked into a long green skirt cinched tight at the waist, her bottom pushing out invitingly while she leaned forward to examine the contents of the shelf. Alice, who filled his dreaming with joy and dread, who was turning to him with green-brown eyes, saying, 'Would you like to look at this?'

She was holding out an atlas. 'I like to look at it. To think about places I've never been.' She opened it up to the world map, and traced a hand over the pink areas. 'I haven't even been to the parts that England owns.'

He took the atlas from her, using his forefinger to search for Kandahar; then moving further right across the map. 'There, you see? I am Afghan Afridi.'

Alice peered at where his finger rested. A place with strange names she'd never heard of. She could conjure camels and Arabs, but that was all. Another empty space in her head, waiting to be filled.

He was conscious of her physical closeness. He
wanted to kiss her, to bridge the sliver of air keeping
them apart.

'We are warriors.'

She looked up from the page. 'Are *you* a warrior?'

He nodded. 'I have been in the Turkish army.'

'Why there?'

'Their sultan is our sultan.' He could see she didn't
quite understand, and explained further. 'As the English
king is your king.'

'Oh.' She nodded. 'You must be brave.'

'When I have to be.' He kept the details spare,
omitting the daily acts of cowardice he had performed
to stay alive; the cold blotchy nights spent holding the
wood of his rifle tight, pressing his cheek against the
metal like he had once pressed it against a bar of soap;
praying he would not be called upon to use it, or if he
was, that his hands wouldn't shake. If he had killed
anyone, it was from a distance, so he could never know
for sure.

Alice put the atlas back on the shelf and pulled
out its neighbour. A picture book titled *Major Lochs of
Scotland.*

Mahommed struggled with the title. 'Lotches?'

'Loch. It's a Scottish word for lake.' She flicked it
open to reveal a photograph of Loch Lomond, dark,

deep and invitingly bleak. 'See? Loch Lomond. I was born near there.'

'In Scotland?'

'Yes. My mother was Scottish.'

'Not English?'

'No. But my father was.'

Mahommed ignored the last detail. She was Scottish! He didn't know where Scotland was, or why it mattered so much to him that it wasn't England, but nonetheless he felt a surge of warmth towards it.

He took the book from her and drank in the photograph, drank in Loch Lomond, drank in Aliceland. He read the description underneath. 'Loch Lomond. The largest lake in Scotland and the largest str ...'

'Stretch.'

'Stretch of water in the United Kingdom.' Mahommed concentrated on the photo, searching for Alice.

Alice said, 'You know what I imagine?'

He shook his head.

'Going back there and diving in, as deep as I can go, till my lungs are nearly bursting, till I can't last a second more. Then, at the last moment before I get frightened, when I'd have to try to go back up to the air, just then, exactly then, it all starts to make sense, and it doesn't matter being down there without air because I don't need it any more, all I need is to drift wherever the water wants to take me and that's enough.'

She stopped, as though feeling foolish about the words tumbling out. She said, 'I was a baby. I can't even remember it.'

'But your heart remembers.'

Her eyes met his. 'What if it's lying?'

'It isn't.'

His own heart told him that if he reached out to kiss her she wouldn't resist. But memory can as easily move forward as backward and he already saw the awkwardness that would follow. He said, 'I have no job.'

'You'll find another one soon. I know you will.'

'When I do, may I call on you again?'

'You don't have to wait till then.'

'Your brother would not allow it.'

She hesitated. 'I won't tell him.'

Mahommed could see her struggling with this, and knew he had to leave quickly. Stealing moments with Alice in darkened corners would not be an honourable way to proceed, but he could feel that resolve collapsing. He said, 'So. It is decided. I will visit again when I have employment.'

She said, 'Lewis has been very good to me.'

'I understand.'

She seemed relieved not to be pressed on the matter. She pushed the book onto him, telling him he could keep it until she saw him again. He promised he would take good care of it; that he would see her again, soon.

'How soon?'

'Almost instantly.' Sensing her doubt, he added, 'And then together we shall dive into deep, deep water and when the light above us almost disappears from view …'

'We'll drift?'

'No, we will swim! Deeper and deeper until we reach the other side of the world!'

Alice was by now caught up in this fancy. 'Scotland!'

'Yes, in Loch Lomond! The largest lake in Scotland and the largest stretch of water in the United Kingdom!'

He left her, carrying a vision of how events might unfold. Humiliations large and small, the accident, the barely hidden sneers, the failure to find work, Abdullah's apparent defection – all these were swept away, leaving a future once again budding with infinite promise. Everyone would see him as the man he knew he could be: a man with a job, a parlour – and a Scottish wife. He had learned enough from the English; enough to know he no longer wished to be like them. It was time to see what Scotland had to offer.

17

There was no parlour in Alice's vision. Only a jumble of feverish hope that something would surely happen to make things right. She had been brave in going to see Mahommed. She had invited him into her home, and she hadn't been struck down. She could be brave again. Life could be danced into, even if you didn't know all the right steps.

Lewis came home from work that night, awkward and tight. Alice didn't notice. She was feeling happy – the kind of happiness that comes from dwelling on the possible rather than the probable.

'You're in a good mood,' said Eileen.

'Aren't I always?'

'No.' Eileen looked at Alice, suspicious. 'Has something happened?'

'No.' Alice smiled, teasing, ignoring Eileen's frown. 'But it'd be lovely if it did.'

Her good cheer lasted until after dinner. Lewis finally said what he had been trying to say for days. He told her while Eileen was with them, so Alice couldn't protest too much.

'I've decided,' he announced. 'I'm enlisting.'

Alice said nothing.

Eileen said, 'What about us?'

Lewis told her about the two shillings a day for dependants. He told her about the poor frightened women of Belgium and France who needed protecting by Australian men. He told her what the British government man had said about lamps going out all over Europe; how they weren't going to be lit again if they didn't do something about it. He said he didn't want to leave, but it was a question of doing what was right; that other men were throwing their hats into the ring; that he couldn't hold his head up if he wasn't prepared to do the same. He told her about duty.

Alice finally spoke, matter-of-factly, as though it were a perfectly natural thing to say. 'They'll be needing nurses. If it's our duty, then I'll go too.'

'Alice, you can't.'

'But you can?'

Eileen started to cry.

Lewis assured her that Alice didn't mean it, that she wasn't going anywhere.

'Alright then,' said Alice. 'Go, if that's what you want. But don't say it's for duty. Don't say it's for Belgium. Say it's because you *want* to go. Because that's the truth.'

'You really think I want to go to war?'

'I do. So don't say one more word about sacrifice, because it isn't true.'

She thought of the trip to Adelaide he had given her. It had been presented as a gift; now she understood it had been part of a bargain, one she hadn't agreed to. He wanted a new life, one that didn't include her or Eileen. A life of excitement and danger and the knowledge that each day would bring something new and unexpected. It didn't matter to him that she might want those things too. It didn't matter to him *what* she wanted.

He said, 'I'm supposed to be a shopkeeper all my life, a glorified servant, is that what you want for me?'

Alice answered him, uncertain, 'You do alright there. You've always liked it well enough.'

But Lewis wasn't listening. 'And I will say sacrifice. You think it's been easy for me, do you? All these years, Alice, I've paid, I've bloody paid. I kept my promise, I didn't go to the mine, I did what was expected. So don't you tell me what words I can use or I might find ones you'll like even less.'

He scraped his chair across the floor boards, and headed out into the night.

Alice thought he'd gone to the yard to smoke his temper away but when she looked out he wasn't there. She guessed he'd gone to a hotel, where a man's loyalty to the Empire would be applauded, not scorned.

Eileen wasn't speaking to her so Alice let her be. It wouldn't be fair to make her take sides, and anyway Alice would lose; she knew that without trying. Eileen went to bed but Alice stayed up, thinking if Lewis came home she would find a way to make peace with him. While she waited she took out the atlas and looked at Belgium, trying to feel sorry for it. She widened the scope of her sorrow to include France as well. When her eyes strayed to Afghanistan, she put it away.

She pushed open the door to Lewis's bedroom. It had changed little since their father died. He had built the bed himself from timber scavenged from the house leftovers, but the oak bedside cupboards had been bought from a repossession auction. The coverlet had been made by their mother from hoarded scraps of material. After she died, their father slept alone, hunched on his side of the bed, and when he also died, Lewis moved in from the sleep-out. When Lewis left it would be empty again, although it would still be his room.

On one of the cupboards was a photograph of their father with Lewis, taken outside Lenard's Pictureland on a Saturday afternoon, a year after their mother died. Lewis was fourteen; it was his birthday, and for a treat he had been taken to the moving pictures. There had been no money for her or Eileen to go, so she didn't know how her father had been cajoled into paying for the photograph, but she was glad he was. They both looked so serious, but for all that she knew, Lewis had been proud to be with his father, the two men of the family, out on the town together.

She hoped he remembered that time more than the others. The times when he had to help his father onto his bed and ease his boots off, because he wasn't capable of doing it himself. The first time it happened she had followed them into the bedroom and tried to help, but Lewis barely looked at her.

'It's alright,' he'd said, as he struggled with the bootlaces. 'It's my job.'

His hands had been clumsy. Even then they were large. They were hands made for shovelling, for swinging an axe or a pick, for cradling a rifle. Man's work. He wanted to do man's work.

When the accident happened it was Lewis who took control. Lewis who climbed down into the shaft and held their father, whose head was at an angle that wasn't right. Lewis who organised the funeral, went through the papers, signed what had to be signed; who went to work at Millers without a word of complaint.

He had been hardly more than a boy, although she hadn't realised it at the time. She hadn't realised anything much. Only that everything was different. She hadn't known how to respond to the well-wishers who came with cakes and kind words.

One woman, a neighbour, said to her, 'God must have wanted your father for better things.'

Alice looked at her, deliberately stupid. 'What use is a dead man to God?'

The kind words she didn't know what to do with; the cakes she ate with Eileen and Lewis, eating them for a week until they put out what was left for the chickens. She supposed she said thank you for them; she couldn't remember. But now, tonight, it occurred to her that Lewis may have felt as lost as she had. She wished she had asked him.

It was late. He was still not home.

Lying in her bed with her back to her, Eileen was either asleep or feigning sleep. Alice was thinking how strange it was that you could be so wrapped up in your own bits of pain that you couldn't see past them to what other people were feeling. And Lewis had been right in front of her.

She was thinking this, and of how selfish she'd been, when it occurred to her that if Lewis was away, there would be no-one to object to her seeing Mahommed. She didn't want this thought. She wanted to make her peace with Lewis out of love for him. But the thought refused to budge and she gave in, playing with it for a while.

It was no good. She couldn't have two lots of thoughts in her head, fighting over the same space. They intersected where they weren't supposed to and conclusions that rightly belonged in one place insisted on sticking their noses into another.

She turned on her side to look at the huddled lump that was Eileen. The quilt pulled up around her left only her hair, roughly pulled out from its plaits, showing. She heard a muffled sob from inside the quilt. She got up and went over to Eileen's bed, lifted up the covers and curled in next to her.

'Can you breathe under there?'

'Yes,' came the indistinct reply.

Alice said, 'When Lewis goes, we'll wave him off. We'll wear our best dresses and our best smiles. We'll give him a present for luck and tell him how proud we are of him. We'll tell him that even if there aren't any lamps left in Europe, we'll keep one burning here for him. And we won't cry until we get home.'

Eileen, still under the quilt, said, 'Belgium's only little. Can't the Germans keep it?'

Alice had wondered this herself. 'No. It wouldn't be right.'

Eileen was quiet now and Alice snuggled in closer to her. She had grown so much. There wasn't really room any more for two of them in the one bed. When she was younger they had slept together every night. Eileen's hot little body had been softer than a bed-warmer and unlike a bed-warmer had kept its heat till dawn. Alice wondered what it might be like to snuggle up to Mahommed in the same way. The thought made her limbs ache.

Eileen came out from under the cover and turned her head. Her eyelids were red and swollen. She said, 'Everybody leaves me.'

Alice thought of their father, who smelt of cigarettes and whisky and toothpaste. Who loved them, but left them a long time before he died.

'But Lewis is coming back,' Alice said. 'By the time he gets there it will all be over.' She buried her head in Eileen's shoulder, not wanting her to see her doubt.

Alice was still awake two hours later when Lewis came home. She heard him move around in the kitchen before going to his room. In the morning she would put her resentment aside. She would tell him she was proud of him.

When Mahommed parted from Alice, he was floating on dreams. He hurried back towards his room, clutching her precious book to his chest, wanting to put it where it would be safe. He reached the boarding house, tightening his arms around the book as he pushed through the men milling at the front desk. Normally he politely acknowledged everyone he saw – a nod of the head, a good morning, a good afternoon – but now he had a book of lochs to protect, and courtesy would have to wait. He made it to his room and went in, locking the door behind him. He sat on the bed, and gave himself to the book, taking care not to bend the pages.

He found the photograph of Loch Lomond, and touched it, feeling the paper where Alice's hand had touched. She had freely lent it to him, something that wasn't possible. He laughed. If this miracle could happen, then perhaps a shipping empire was not such a flight of fancy. Perhaps one day after work his Scottish wife might hand him his mail, addressed to Gool Mahommed, Esq.

If he couldn't get work in the mines, well, he would find it elsewhere. Alice had given him a gift, welcomed him into her home. He could not return until he was a man of substance, a man with employment. The situation with her brother would be difficult, he saw that much already, but if he had something to offer, the way would be eased.

He looked at Loch Lomond again, drawing strength from its depths. He was a good worker. He was clean, honest, reliable, and spoke English well. He was, by any reasonable assessment, extremely employable. If anyone deserved a job, he did.

It was too late to do so now, but tomorrow he would approach the task methodically. He would go downstairs, head to Chloride Street and turn right into Argent Street. From there he would make his way around the block, turning left into Delamore, along Blende, then left into Bromide until it met Argent Street at the other end. He would enquire at each business he saw along the way. If offered a position, he would thank the man politely. He would not immediately accept, but tell him he would let them know by close of day. Then he would move on to the next business. After he had completed his circuit of the block, he would carefully consider the merits of the various offers. Then he would make his considered decision.

He looked out his window and saw the day was nearly gone. He closed the book and went to his cupboard, where he found his turban cloth. He laid it on the bed, opening it out, and placed the book on one end. He wrapped it tightly, to keep it free from dust, and put it in the cupboard.

He washed his hands and face, unrolled his carpet for *Maghrib*, and performed his three *rakas*, keeping his private prayer general, feeling Allah didn't need to be bothered with intimate details of his longing for Alice.

He put the carpet away, but was still too churned up by the encounter with Alice to eat whatever version of mutton was on offer, so he ate three spoonsful of Sanatogen instead. As before, it tasted horrible, but he didn't approve of waste and, having bought it, felt he should eat it. It didn't calm his stomach as much as he hoped, so he went to the cupboard again, unwrapped the book, and spent the next hour poring over photographs of grey Scottish water. After that he realised he needed to be fit for tomorrow. He went downstairs and ate, not with relish but with the understanding it was much needed fuel. When he finally found sleep, the night was filled with half-remembered visions of Alice, camels, naked female loins, and mine accidents occurring in the centre of Loch Lomond.

He woke feeling sluggish and drained. He climbed out of bed and washed, taking care to dress neatly, reminding himself of his purpose. He straightened the doyley and washed his hands once more. When he couldn't put it off any longer, he headed outside.

*

The man in the yard at Martin's store barely looked at him. 'We're not hiring.'

'Will you be hiring again in the near future?'

'Might do. If the war ends tomorrow.'

The rest of the shops along Argent Street yielded similar results. He tried them all except the hotels (the alcohol), the butchers (the pork), Millers General Store (Alice's brother) and the Workingman's Club (alcohol again). Some of the men he spoke to were pleasant, some rude; none showed any interest in hiring him despite his honesty and reliability. He turned into Delamore Street, reminding himself that he had so far enquired of less than a quarter of the possible employers. He must not allow himself to become downcast.

The bakery manager was frank with him. Broken Hill was falling apart now that Germany had stopped buying its zinc, because no zinc meant fewer miners with money. No-one was hiring. Not Englishmen, and definitely not foreigners.

'But I tell you where you might get a job.'

Mahommed perked up, interested.

'Have you tried the armed forces?' The bakery manager started laughing halfway through his own question. Apparently it was a joke.

★

It was a little after ten by the time he reached the corner of Blende Street. The day was already hot, the air heavy and still. His shirt stuck to a damp patch on his back. His shoes had kicked up dust and were no longer as shiny as he would have liked. He was about to turn left when he heard a horse whinny in nearby Iodide Street. He turned to watch. The horse, hardly more than a pony, was pulling a cart loaded with sheets of corrugated iron, destined to become the walls of someone's new house. The load was heavy, and the horse was protesting. The driver managed to get the horse under control and continued on his way.

All this had taken less than thirty seconds, long enough for Mahommed to think about the fact that with one more turn, Iodide Street would lead to the camel camp.

If Jemadar had been telling the truth, Abdullah would be back by now. Whatever the reasons for their present estrangement, it could not be allowed to continue indefinitely. Abdullah was his friend. If the gulf between them was not bridged soon it would grow. Mahommed reasoned that, as the younger man, it was his duty to re-establish relations. Although his preference was to spend the day continuing his search for employment, it was nonetheless his duty to leave this search until he had fulfilled his obligations towards Abdullah.

He turned towards Iodide Street and started walking towards the camp. There he found Abdullah, selecting a goat for slaughter. He offered to help with the goat. The offer was coolly accepted.

18

Abdullah followed with his knife as Mahommed dragged the goat through the scrub, keeping hold of the rope around its neck as it tried to pull away. It could smell the blood in the dust around the stake, the space around it bare from the hooves of other goats.

It nearly got away from him but he held it firm and lashed it to the stake as its eyes rolled in panic. Mahommed avoided looking at them. It was only an animal, but the Prophet (peace be upon him) had said that being kind to animals was being kind to yourself. Mahommed hadn't had much kindness directed at himself recently, and didn't want any to slip away. He was glad Abdullah was the butcher. Abdullah would say the words as he slit its throat and that would make it alright.

Abdullah was watching him as he tied the knots, making them secure. He said, 'I have a contract for Milparinka.'

Milparinka was a gold- and silver-mining outpost, north of Broken Hill. Mahommed had travelled there in the past with Abdullah, working a camel string, delivering supplies to Heuzenroeder's General Store. There was nothing much to remember about it; there was nothing much there. Mr Heuzenroeder. A courthouse. A couple of hotels. Dust.

'Oh yes?'

'I will be leaving in two weeks.'

He had come back only yesterday from a shorter trip to Wilcannia. This was the trip he had not told Mahommed he was taking; Mahommed had not asked him anything about it. He was only with Abdullah now because he had nowhere else to be.

Abdullah whipped his knife across the grindstone five or six times before turning it to sharpen the other side. 'I'll be taking ten camels,' he said. 'I'll need someone to go with me.'

Mahommed struggled to keep the goat under control. Had it come to this? Camels stank. The bull camels bit. They could reef their necks with enough force to pull a man's shoulder out of its socket. They had to be unloaded every night and hobbled, then reloaded again in the morning, *hooshta* twice a day. Eight hundred pounds of goods loaded and unloaded every day. No break from the searing midday sun because they wouldn't stand still with their loads and there was no time to unload them. And for what? Abdullah would be fair, but the money earned would be less than half what he made in the mine.

But it wasn't only a matter of money, nor his dislike of camels. It would be tantamount to admitting defeat. For the first time in months he thought of his mother. She had believed in him. She had bought him soap.

He said, 'Abdullah, I'm seeking other employment.'

'And have you found it?'

Mahommed ignored the tone. 'I'm looking at a number of possibilities.' He thought this a reasonable response. He'd only covered half of Argent Street and none of Blende Street. He might have found a job by now if he hadn't decided to do the right thing by Abdullah.

Abdullah said, 'But are they looking at you?'

Mahommed looked up from the goat. 'Why do you want me to fail?'

'Because what you are striving for is nothing. They are nothing, and they think the same of you.'

'You're wrong!' Alice had invited him into her home, entrusted him with her book, allowed him to stroke her heart. 'I won't be like Jemadar, sliding into death still telling his lies about making *Hajj*. I won't be like you, Abdullah, hating it here but lacking the courage to leave! If you have made these bargains, then that is your choice, but I want more and I will have more!'

'Then you should hurry. All those possibilities must be wondering where you are.'

Abdullah moved to the goat, pushing past him. Mahommed knew he had hurt him, but the words were out and couldn't be called back. He could stay and make things worse, or leave and make things worse. It required no real decision, so he stayed.

'Abdullah, I have no right to say those words. But what is so wrong about wanting a better life?'

'Everything, if you think it can only be had among the English.'

'I don't think that!'

'You don't think.'

Abdullah concentrated on his task. He grabbed the goat and put his left hand around its chin, forcing its head up. As he had done a thousand times before, he called *Bismillah Allahu Akbar,* and with his other hand he took the knife and plunged it deep into its throat, dragging the blade down. The words mingled with the blood that spurted, pumping out bright-red life until there was no life left.

'Stop!'

There was a rustle from some nearby bushes. Mahommed turned to see a man emerge from behind the bushes and hurry towards them, holding an empty hessian sack. It was the Sanitary Inspector.

'Abdullah, no!' Mahommed grabbed the knife Abdullah was holding up, and pushed himself between the two men, dropping the knife to the ground. Whatever was going on, killing the Inspector wouldn't help.

He turned to him. 'What do you want from us?'

The Inspector ignored him, looking past him to Abdullah.

'As Chief Sanitary Inspector, I'm summonsing you to appear in court on Tuesday on a charge of slaughtering meat away from the abattoir.' He reached into his coat pocket to produce a summons, and handed it to him.

Abdullah let it drop, refusing to be part of the exchange.

The Inspector shrugged as he stuffed the goat into the sack. 'Appear or be arrested. It's up to you.'

Mahommed picked up the knife as the Sanitary Inspector dragged the bulging sack away. Using a handful of dried grass, he wiped it as clean as he could. 'If you tell the magistrate it is *haram* for us to use the abattoir ...'

'I told him before. He didn't listen then, and he won't listen now.'

'Did you tell him it's your duty to slaughter, that if you are not allowed, the camp will have no meat?'

'The magistrate doesn't care about what is right. He only cares about everyone belonging to the butchers' union.' He took the knife back from Mahommed. 'And why do you think that is, that a powerful man would want to force people into a butchers' union with a disgusting abattoir holding carcasses full of blood?'

'Because … they pay him?'

'Can you see a different reason?'

Mahommed let the question go. He went with Abdullah back to his shack, where they sat together in silence. He wanted to tell him they were not all like the Sanitary Inspector. That Scotland wasn't England. That he had a book of lochs to prove it. That Abdullah was beaten down because he allowed himself to be so; that hearts must be kept open because once closed they would stay that way; that if a man shut his eyes to hope, hope would shut its eyes to him. He said none of these things.

After a time he said, 'I will talk to Adrian Kadran. He understands them. He will speak for you.'

Abdullah shrugged. 'It will make no difference.'

Mahommed didn't argue. He looked at Abdullah – head drooped, shoulders bowed – and wondered at the steps that had brought him to this. A fine was nothing, it could be dealt with. Goats could be slaughtered away from prying eyes if that is what it took. A younger Abdullah would have brushed it aside, feeling nothing more than contempt.

'Wadud is leaving,' Abdullah said. 'He is planning to join the Turkish army.'

'They won't want him. Not with his eye.'

'He feels it is his duty.'

Mahommed knew Wadud had had difficulty finding contracts of late. He owned only two camels, and the new trucks had taken some of his business. Duty, he thought, might not have been uppermost in Wadud's mind.

'Abdullah, I have done my time.'

'Did I say you hadn't?'

'No.'

Abdullah's meaning was clear but debating it wouldn't achieve anything. He stayed respectfully quiet until the old man spoke again.

He said, 'Go home.'

19

When Mahommed entered his room, he was disturbed by the notion that something had changed, although a quick investigation proved everything was as he had left it. He realised the only change was the feeling he had when he opened the door. It didn't feel like home any more. He hoped it was simply a reaction to a difficult day; that by tomorrow the room would again embrace him. Because if this wasn't his home, where was it?

He poured himself a glass of water and drank it, then sat on his chair to think about what was in his heart. He thought about Alice, and what he had to do to win her respect. He thought about Abdullah, and what he had to do to win his. He thought long and hard about whether both things were possible.

He took out a piece of paper and began to write a letter to the Turkish Minister of War. He asked to be accepted as a member of the Turkish army, which, he wrote, he would serve by the will of Allah, and be true to His Majesty the Sultan of Turkey. He would, he continued, fight to the best of his ability.

Having finished the letter, he began to feel at peace. Tomorrow he would give it to Wadud and ask him to take it with him when he went. He had no intention of joining the army again, but he didn't believe that Turkey would enter another war. It had been in too many wars; it was exhausted by them. The War Minister would surely not expect him to cross the ocean to fight a war that didn't exist. And even if he did, he would hardly reach out from Turkey to pluck Mahommed all the way from Australia. The letter was a gesture, nothing more, but at least he could tell Abdullah he had done it. It would go some way in restoring Abdullah's feelings for him, without interfering with his intentions for Alice.

It was time for *Asr*. He put the letter aside and opened his case, taking out his prayer rug. He decided to perform five *rakas*, not the customary four. He would tell that to Abdullah as well.

Mahommed watched as Mr Kadran poured a cup of straw-coloured tea and passed it to him over the desk. 'Camomile, soothing for the nerves. I've been thinking of offering a parcel of it to our boys in the A.I.F.'

Mahommed didn't know what he was referring to. Maybe the army, he wasn't sure. He left his tea untouched. Mr Kadran still hadn't responded to his request.

'About Abdullah?' he prompted.

He was answered with an expansive shrug. 'Well, the law's the law, and unfortunately, going by what you've told me, he's guilty.'

'If you could just speak for him. Tell them he is a good man.'

Abdullah had told him Mr Kadran occasionally made use of his services, sending and receiving consignments from Adelaide. All Mr Kadran was being asked to say was that Abdullah had been honest and reliable. Surely that wasn't too much to ask?

Mr Kadran had a sip of tea, savouring the taste before putting his cup down. 'The magistrate will be fair. I don't think you'll find any problems.'

Mahommed leaned forward, trying to make him understand the seriousness of the problem. 'He was fined before. And you are a gentleman much admired. Your words will be listened to.'

Mahommed waited, hoping the flattery would have some effect. Mr Kadran looked away.

He said, 'No promises. But I'll see what I can do.'

Mahommed thanked him. He was uncomfortable with the situation and wanted to leave. But for once

Mr Kadran seemed in no hurry to dismiss him. He picked up a copy of the *Barrier Daily Truth* and opened it out. 'Have you read today's?'

Mahommed shook his head.

Turning back to the paper, Mr Kadran found what he was looking for. 'Here we are. It's good news.' He read it aloud to Mahommed. 'The plucky French have sent the Germans back over the Marne with their tails between their legs.' He put the paper aside. 'It's important to show we support them, don't you agree?'

Mahommed moved his head perfunctorily – neither a nod nor a shake.

Mr Kadran continued. 'We have to pull together, you see. Now that a war has broken out, I feel morally obliged to do what I can for the war effort, but if I'm not making money ...'

Mahommed finally realised what this was all about. He said, 'I'll pay. As soon as I find work.'

'Well, there's the thing ...' Mr Kadran sighed, oozing sympathy. After a deliberately long pause, he said, 'You could always think about moving back to the camp. They'd make room for you. Only as a temporary measure, of course.'

There was his doyley, his prayer rug, his Sanatogen tin. There were his four soap wrappers pinned to the wall.

There was his bar of Puritol. There was a change of clothing. There was Alice's book.

He unrolled his prayer rug, then re-rolled it tightly, securing it with a piece of string. He took Alice's book and held it up to his face, hoping for some lingering scent. Her hands had held it; her fingers had traced its patterns. But there was nothing. He took the doyley and put it on top of the book, then carefully wrapped both of them in the clothing before putting them in his case. He took the soap wrappers off the wall, placed them one on top of the other, and put them in his case. He put the bar of Puritol in the case and closed it.

He moved to the window and looked out. The outside of the pane was grimy with mine dust, softening the view of neighbouring boarding houses. He went back and picked up the case. As he opened the door he tried not to think of anything at all. He went out and shut the door, leaving nothing but his dreams of a mighty shipping empire and a half-empty tin of Sanatogen. The few dreams he took with him were scattered and shapeless. He would try to reform them later. He wasn't up to it now.

Three sheets of scavenged corrugated iron were enough for three walls. Another for the roof. Sherdil had commandeered the materials from Wadud's shack for himself, but donated some hessian from it; enough to cover the last wall. Abdullah offered to help Mahommed find another piece of iron for the wall, but he declined the offer. He didn't intend to make a permanent home in the camp. A flimsy structure would do as well as a strong one.

20

Irma, already bored by the proceedings, watched as Mr Kadran moved to the box beside Mr Evelyn Butler, the attending magistrate. Her face, nonetheless, was a picture of rapt attentiveness. Robert had suggested she come to see the fruits of his work. He wouldn't have done so if he didn't have definite intentions towards her; the least she could do was feign interest. She wouldn't tell him so, but it seemed an awful lot of carry-on over who killed a goat and where and how. The Afghans were the ones who were going to eat the thing, so who cared if they got sick? One of the men was that Afghan who had been on the train. He had nodded towards her when he saw her, as though she was someone he knew. She'd done the right thing, ignored him and looked away. But it had given her an unpleasant sensation, a nasty shiver that went right through her.

She was glad Alice wasn't here. She might have engaged him in conversation like she had at Millers store. It wasn't her fault that she'd never had a mother to guide her, but Irma had come to the conclusion that she was slightly common. She had distanced herself a little from her of late. Once she was Mrs Robert Brosnan, she would have a certain standing. It wouldn't be right to compromise that by having unsuitable friends. She wouldn't desert her, because that would be unkind. She would simply give less of herself.

Robert's health had improved. There had been no more upsetting episodes, thanks to her and Mr Kadran's vigilance. She understood it was important for him to have his medicine regularly if his catarrh were to remain under control; that occasionally there could be flare-ups necessitating a larger dose, but that these would become less frequent as the catarrh finally dissolved.

Now that she'd consulted him on a number of occasions, she knew she had misjudged Mr Kadran. This was understandable given he was an Indian, but she had come to realise that he was not an Indian like the Afghans were Indians; that he was, in his own way, quite a superior person. Although he was modest about it, it seemed his family were nabobs or sultans or whatever the Indian words were for minor royal family members. Not royal like the King and Queen, but certainly respectable.

He was well educated. He had been to universities, proper English ones. He didn't make a fuss about it, but she had seen the certificates on his wall and had been very impressed.

As for his diagnosis of her, he couldn't have been more accurate if he had tried. When last she had consulted him about Robert's ongoing treatment, he had broken off their discussion to look at her intently.

'Miss Cowie,' he said, 'now that I have met you again, I am even more struck by the disparity between your divisions.'

She thought he was being discourteous, but he quickly explained. A person was like a triangle, the mental, emotional and physical parts being the corners. When everything was in balance these three lived in harmony, making for perfect health. But Irma was possessed of mental maturity beyond her years, which meant that the mental corner tugged at the other two. The emotional corner also tugged, due to the distress she felt about Robert's illness. All this tugging meant that her physical corner had become weakened, unable to withstand the pulling. It was being dragged along, cruelly battered.

He said, 'Your burdens are more than a young woman of your delicacy should be asked to bear. Sometimes you feel faint with their heaviness, yes?'

She nodded, feeling teary.

'Accompanied by palpitations of the head?'

'I don't like to complain.'

'Of course you don't. Which is a mark of your refinement. But there is no need for you to continue to suffer. There are remedies for conditions such as yours.'

'There are?'

He nodded, allowing her a moment to grasp the import of what he had just told her. 'If you will put your trust in me, I will help you become the woman you deserve to be.'

Irma almost swooned, drawn in by his kind brown eyes. Why hadn't she noticed them before?

Mahommed, sitting next to Abdullah, felt him stiffen as Mr Kadran went through the preliminaries, explaining to Mr Butler who he was and the nature of his acquaintance with Abdullah. Abdullah had been unimpressed when Mahommed told him Mr Kadran would speak for him. He had thought Abdullah was being ungrateful. But Abdullah wasn't; he was being perceptive. Already Mr Kadran was distancing himself, claiming his dealings with Abdullah had been minimal, that the best he could say of them was that they had been satisfactory.

Worse was to come. On being questioned about Abdullah's method of slaughter, Mr Kadran apologetically professed ignorance. 'You have to understand,' he said, 'that as an Anglican, my knowledge of such things is purely academic.'

He paused to share a one-Protestant-to-another smile with Mr Butler before continuing. 'But to my mind the practice seems extremely unhygienic, and if Mr Brosnan, whom I know to be a very honest gentleman, says that the lamb was maggot ridden, then I'm sure that is the truth.'

There were more knives to come.

'But we have to bear in mind that the Mullah Abdullah is considered to be a touch on the feeble side, and may well have not understood that what he was doing was, by our standards …'

Mahommed glanced at Abdullah, sitting rigidly next to him. He wanted to reach out and touch him, but knew he would not welcome a public acknowledgment of his humiliation.

'… completely unacceptable. And as someone suffering from mental impairment to an unspecified degree, he deserves our sympathy rather than our condemnation.'

Mahommed's outrage became too much. He stood up to shout at Mr Kadran. 'He is not feeble! He has no mental impairment!'

He was dimly aware of hands grabbing at him as Mr Butler brought down his gavel and called for order.

He continued to protest, trying to make them see the truth. 'He leads us in prayer, he is authorised to provide us with meat!'

Mr Butler ignored him and called for him to be removed. As Mahommed was dragged out by a court official, he saw Abdullah staring straight ahead, refusing to be part of it.

He raised his voice one last time. 'And it was a goat, not a lamb!'

Abdullah was found guilty and fined. There would have been little profit from the trip to Milparinka. Now, with the fine to pay, there would be none. Mahommed had waited outside the courthouse for him. He briefly moved away to buy a newspaper, but otherwise kept vigil near the door until Abdullah came out. He knew Abdullah was burning, that words would only fuel the flames. He walked him home in silence.

There was no woman to do it, so he made him tea. Jemadar joined them. He quickly understood what had happened, and for once held back. The three of them sat quietly, washing in hurt and anger. When he felt the circumstances allowed, Jemadar asked Mahommed about the news in the paper.

Mahommed told him what was said about Turkey. He read, 'Turkey's attack on Russia, without any declaration of war, has made an immense impression. It is reported that German officers used threats and trained the guns of their ships against the Turkish Sultan's palace.'

'Why did they do that?'

'I don't know.'

'Did they use their guns?'

'I don't think so. Only threats.'

'So far.'

'It might not go any further.'

Jemadar snorted. He gave Mahommed a sly look. 'You were one of their bravest fighters. The Turkish army must be wondering where you are.'

Mahommed bridled. 'The War Minister will tell me if my services are required. Until then, I don't have money for the voyage.'

It was his own fault, he shouldn't have made such a show of giving Wadud the enlistment letter. If Abdullah had been impressed by the gesture, he'd given no sign of it.

'Anyway, Turkey won't be part of their war. There's no reason for them to be in it.'

He put the paper aside. He didn't want to argue with Jemadar, not today. He wanted only to comfort the old man by his side.

A wind began to blow, disturbing the layers of dry red dust at their feet. Abdullah used this as an excuse to go inside his shack. Mahommed knew better than to attempt to join him.

He didn't come out again until the morning.

Mahommed sat behind the safety of a wall, watching as people went in and out of the hospital. He saw one man being carried in, his foot a bloody stump. Perhaps he had stepped in a trap, laid for an animal, maybe a dingo. People did all sorts of careless things out in the desert. The heat did strange things to a man's mind, causing him to misjudge dangers.

He had been there for two hours. He wasn't certain Alice was in there or if she would be arriving at all, but he wasn't prepared to knock on the door of her house. Nor did he want to be found loitering outside it. He had with him her book, carefully wrapped in muslin. It had once been his turban, but it was a long time since he had worn it.

He looked up at the sun and judged it to be about eleven o'clock. He was in no hurry to go back to the camp. He would wait as long as he needed to.

Flies buzzed round his head. He was an easy target, for without the turban his hair was exposed, and they liked dark colours. He should have bought a hat while he still had money, but those days were gone. He shook his head and swatted the flies away.

As he did so, he saw her. She was coming down the steps of the hospital, wearing the pale-green blouse with the frills, her hair pinned up, a little squashed from where she had been wearing her cap. She squinted as she came into the sunlight. He thought about his work in the mine and how he always had to make the mental transition from the dank underworld of the mine to the almost overwhelming brightness above. He wondered if she felt the same thing.

He had not counted on the effect of seeing her. He was almost too afraid to show himself. But he had to get it over with. He climbed over the wall and stopped in front of her. An awkward silence was broken by formal greetings that said nothing about what he felt.

Alice said, 'I thought you'd forgotten me.'

Mahommed shook his head. 'I can never do that.' It was more of a declaration than he had meant to make. Embarrassed, he held the book out towards her, retreating again into the safety of formality. 'I've come to return this.'

'Have you finished with it?'

Finished with it? Of course not. He had pored over every picture. He knew more about Scottish lochs than any child in Scotland had a right to know. He knew that Loch Morar was the deepest loch in Scotland. He knew that Alice had held this book. He wanted to keep it forever.

He said, 'I won't be able to look after it as I promised. I am going away on business.'

'You've found work?'

'Unfortunately not in Broken Hill. I am going to … to Adelaide.' He didn't want to tell her about the camels. He couldn't.

Alice frowned. 'Why there?'

He was struggling. 'Because I have negotiated some trade. There are some goods there that have to be transferred and … I have involvement with this.'

'But you'll come back?'

'Yes, of course. I'll only be away for two, maybe three weeks.'

'Then keep it. I know you'll take good care of it.'

'But it is precious to you.'

'That's why I know you'll take care of it.'

It wasn't going as he had planned. He had wanted to give her back the book; have one last brief conversation with her; behave with dignity, then leave, taking no trace of her with him. He would grieve, but she would never know.

'It is better you take it.'

'Mahommed, please. I trust you.'

He gave up. It was the music of his name coming from her mouth. It was the impossibility of wrestling with her in the street over a book; of parting from her and believing he would never see her again. He accepted the book.

He wanted to leave before his lies grew so large that she saw them for what they were. But she was still standing there, making no move to go. He noticed tiny beads of sweat glistening above her upper lip.

She said, 'Lewis is coming home for lunch.'

He understood. Walking her home was out of the question.

'He's leaving in a few days. He's enlisting, going to war.'

'Oh.'

'So once he's gone it'll only be Eileen and me. At least for a while.' Her voice had risen in pitch.

'He is leaving you alone?'

'Yes.'

He had shut the door to possibilities, yet here they were again, demanding to be let in. But what was the point? He had nothing to give her. Even worse, she would discover he had lied about his work.

She said, 'Will you kiss me?'

He skirted the question, appalled by the forwardness of her request. 'I must go.'

'There's no-one here to see.'

There was no-one out in the street, that much was true. But behind doors and windows a hundred pairs of eyes could be watching. It was wrong of her to do this to him. He had planned to farewell her, give her back the book, shut down the engine of his heart until no longing remained. This was why he had been sitting for hours in the sun, waiting for her.

'No,' he said.

'Then I'll kiss you.'

Before he could step back she leaned forward and brushed her lips against his.

She said, 'I hope your trip goes well.'

He nodded, incapable of speaking. He felt that something was expected of him but he didn't know what.

She said, 'I'll be late.'

'Yes.'

'Well ...'

And that was it. She turned and hurried away. He watched until she was gone from sight, leaving him with her book and the memory of her skin touching his.

That night, in his shack, he opened his bag. He took out the soap wrappers he had taken off the wall in his room at the boarding house. He flattened them out with his palm. The top one was a Rexona wrapper. He stood, and fixed it to the wall.

When he had put all the wrappers up, he moved aside the hessian flap and looked out into the night. It was late, the embers from the night's fire glowing dully through their coat of ash. Everything was still. He could see a faint lamp glow from inside two of the shacks, but these would be extinguished soon. Day turned to night so quickly here. There were no long twilights; no slow dawns, either. The light would come again, without warning. He turned back inside, holding onto that thought.

21

There was no breeze, but the brass *zungwalla* around the neck of the lead camel tinkled as her body swayed. Behind her the other camels, in a string joined tail to nosepeg, tinkled their songs to the surrounding desert. Abdullah was riding the lead camel, Mahommed the last. He had walked alongside for the first few hours, because the extra weight of a man slowed the camels down. He would ride for a few hours, then walk again. Whether he walked or rode, there would be no stopping, not until the lead camel stopped. He knew this would not happen till well after sunset. Abdullah's cartage agreement with Mr Heuzenroeder stipulated that the goods had to arrive within a certain time. If they were late, money would be deducted from the fee.

He had Alice's book in his saddle bag, carefully protected from the elements. He had wrapped newspaper around the muslin and tied it firmly with string. He hadn't wanted to bring it with him, but could think of no safe way to leave it behind.

Its presence was worrying him. A load could be dislodged, a camel might bolt, a dust storm swirl up with no notice. It could be damaged in many ways, no matter how much care he took. Worrying about it made him think of Alice. He didn't want to think of her lips brushing his. He didn't want to think of decisions being made and unmade; of hopes being dashed, then raised again. He tried to think of nothing but the rhythmic swaying of the camel beneath him. He listened to the bells and wondered at the song being sung for no-one.

Abdullah had wanted to leave at dawn, but this had not been possible. The camels had to be loaded with provisions from Millers General Store, which meant waiting in the yard until Lewis Mercer arrived to check them. Alf, the young assistant, was already there because he slept there under the counter, but he didn't have the authority to check the goods as they were loaded.

The camels were lying on the ground in a circle. Alf had dragged out nearly all of the goods, already parcelled. Dry goods mostly – oats, flour, peas and the like.

Lewis arrived at seven o'clock, and gave no sign of recognising Mahommed. He gave no sign of recognising Abdullah either, although Mahommed knew they must have had dealings before. He began ticking off the parcels. As he did so, Abdullah and Mahommed loaded, working as quickly as possible, wanting to leave before the camels were sapped by the heat of the day. Lewis and Alf made no move to help them; it was not their job. Mahommed thought of Lewis going to fight in the European war. Perhaps he would die there. He was soft; he would not be a good fighter. Thinking about this made the work more bearable.

Half the camels were loaded when the Sanitary Inspector entered the yard. Mahommed didn't know why he was there; as far as he knew, he had nothing to do with this contract. He knew he was an acquaintance of Lewis, because he had been there that day at the store. Perhaps he and Lewis had some private dealings. He glanced at Abdullah, and saw that he had closed his face.

They were laughing at some private joke. Mahommed hoped the Sanitary Inspector would also enlist and die. Both men dying was probably too much to hope for, but that didn't stop him wanting it. He saw Lewis's face blown off, leaving only a pulpy mess. He liked what he saw and replayed the moment. The surprise, bewilderment, the realisation that it had all been for nothing. Then the face, gone; the body thrashing around, hands scrabbling to hold together what was left.

They finished loading at eight-thirty. *Hooshta.*

*

He was walking again. Abdullah, too, walking beside the lead camel. They were too far apart for conversation; there was none Mahommed wanted to make. When he finally told Abdullah he had changed his mind and would make the trip with him, Abdullah had responded with a curt nod. There was no need for either man to discuss it.

The camels had been walking now for over six hours. They would walk for another two, maybe three. The loads were heavy; the camels could travel at no more than three miles an hour. They had stopped briefly at a well, lowering a bucket to capture the brackish water for the camels. It was the only stop they made. Mahommed knew Abdullah would want to push the camels as long as possible each day. He didn't want to arrive late at Milparinka.

Up ahead, he saw Abdullah stumble, then right himself. There were holes everywhere on the track. Burrows of one sort or another. Stones, rocks, snakes, all manner of things that could hurt an unwary man. If there was an accident there would be no-one to help them. Mahommed saw him limp for a few yards, favouring his left leg, then was relieved to see him put his weight fully on it again.

He knew Abdullah had aged. He could see the hunch of his shoulders, holding his body in place against the jarring ground. He would not be able to make these trips for much longer. Mahommed didn't know what would happen to him then. He could sell his camels, but the money would not last forever. Jemadar had his women, his children. Abdullah would have only his gall.

It was a little after five-thirty when Abdullah finally called a halt. The sun was no more than a red glow on the horizon; to press on in the dark would be foolish. They wasted no time. With the camels on their knees, they loosened the cords, allowing the bales to fall.

They worked quickly and quietly, working towards the centre. When the camels were unloaded and hobbled for the night they would attend to their own needs. They would pray, *Salat ul Maghrib* – the sunset prayer – then eat a simple meal. Bread had been packed, a little cooked meat. After today there would be no meat because it would go off, but there was enough for tonight. They would make a fire, for warmth against the cold, and for tea. Mahommed hoped they would talk. He hoped the quiet of the desert night would allow them to find each other again; that he could be more open about the confusion he felt, that Abdullah would be more understanding about this confusion than he had so far been.

He fumbled with the cords on one of the loads. Only two more to go, and he would be done. He glanced across at Abdullah, working two camels away from him; saw him loosen the cords and stand back as the loads fell to each side; saw him stop to stare at one of them.

He called Mahommed over and pointed. 'Open it.'

Mahommed didn't move.

'Open it,' he repeated.

Mahommed stared at the greasy stain showing through one of the sacks. He knew what it was; knew why Robert Brosnan had been at the yard; knew why he and Lewis had been laughing. He said, 'It could be anything. It's late. The light is playing tricks on us.' He didn't want to meet Abdullah's eyes. 'Wait till morning. We can see better then.'

'Open it!'

He stopped arguing and moved to the sack. He began to open it, using only his fingertips, keeping his shirtsleeves pulled up, making as little contact as possible. He could smell it already.

He dragged out a bag of flour, some sugar, some rice. Underneath was a shapeless parcel wrapped in white paper, stained with grease. His stomach lurching, he took the bottom corners of the sack and used them to shake the parcel on to the ground.

He took his mind elsewhere. To a photograph of dark water; to the words underneath telling him the most mysterious of all Scottish lochs was Loch Ness, home of the Loch Ness Monster, a monster believed by many to inhabit the murky deep. Took it to a girl from Loch Lomond; to the soft feel of a mouth touching his.

He found a stick and poked gingerly at the paper surrounding the parcel. There was another layer of paper underneath, stained a watery pink. It was damp, what was left of it easily pulled away by the end of the stick.

A black pig's eye stared at Mahommed. The other eye was white and moving, crawling with the fat bodies of a thousand maggots. He turned and retched, bringing up nothing but bile and revulsion.

Abdullah hurried to one of the still-loaded camels. He worked at the knots, clumsy with agitation. 'They have tainted it! It has to go! All of it must go!'

Mahommed knew it was pointless to argue, but he had to try. He said, 'Abdullah, it was only one camel.'

'All of it!'

They dragged the supplies into a rough heap. They removed the camels' saddles and bridles, the *zungwalla* and nosepegs, hobbles, everything. These too they dragged towards the heap, building it ever higher.

Abdullah was exhausted to the point where he could hardly stand. Only his anger held him up. He moved to the lead camel and began to beat it. 'Go! Go now!'

Mahommed hit the next camel, using the stick to beat its flanks, screaming *go go go go!* until they finally began to understand what was being asked of them. The lead camel moved off, and the others followed, slowly at first, unsure of what to do with their unexpected freedom. Then the lead camel started to gallop, and the others went with it, becoming a herd, then no more than a cloud of red dust between Mahommed and the darkening sky.

Abdullah had already turned his attention to the heaped supplies. Using his knife to tear at one of the saddles, he exposed the straw inside. Some spilled. The rest he roughly pulled out, pushing clumps underneath the supplies wherever he found a gap.

He turned to Mahommed and held out his hand, impassive.

Mahommed said, 'No.'

Abdullah squatted on the ground, prepared to wait it out. He had lost everything but time. He would wait as long as he needed to.

Mahommed covered his torso with his hand, feeling the outline of the book beneath his shirt. 'It's not tainted.'

How did Abdullah know he had it? Had he seen him in the fury of tearing apart the loads? Seen him take out the one thing that mattered to him, the one thing he would not, could not throw away?

'It is wrapped. Nothing has touched it, nothing.' This dance had only one end but he owed it to Alice to perform all the steps. He ran his fingers protectively along its spine. 'It does not belong to me. It has great value.'

He would perform ten *rakas*. Twenty. Fifty *rakas*. He would pray so much that a *zabiba* would grow on his forehead from all the times it had touched the ground. Even Abdullah would remark on his piety.

'It has been entrusted to me. You can't ask me to break that trust. Please, Abdullah, don't ask this of me.' He exhausted all his words, pleading to a man with no ears.

Abdullah continued to squat in silence until he was done.

Mahommed reached inside his shirt to where the book was pressed against his skin. Fingers trembling, he pulled it out, untying the string around the paper. He pulled the paper off and unwound the muslin. He held the book in his hands and looked at it. He opened it until he found the picture of Loch Lomond. She had told him she was born near there. He pictured a village with small, neat pressed-metal houses, sitting in the hills above the Loch. He opened the door of the house that was hers. She was there, smiling, waiting for him. When he had held the picture long enough in his mind to remember it, he shut the book.

He took it to the heaped pile and placed it carefully on top. Abdullah took out a match, struck it, and set fire to a clump of straw near the bottom of the pile. It was dry, and the flames took hold instantly. Mahommed watched as the heat made the book open, its pages fluttering in the hot air before beginning to burn. They became red, then black, then white powdery flakes mingling with the sky.

They prayed. The sun had set hours ago. It was too late for *Maghrib* although Mahommed knew that Abdullah had performed it privately, despite the circumstances. They performed *Isha*. There was no water for ablutions so they used dust. Four *rakas*, not fifty. The book was worth fifty, but the book was gone.

There was nothing to eat or drink. They gathered pieces of wood and placed them away from the main fire. Abdullah lit this smaller fire. Once it was alight he took the matches that were left and threw them into the larger fire before moving back to Mahommed.

Mahommed searched for words that might comfort him, but found none. All he had was anger and bewilderment that men could find such actions amusing. He couldn't share it; he knew Abdullah considered him a fool for ever having higher expectations of their behaviour.

They sat in silence, huddled close to the small warmth of the fire. Eventually Abdullah looked up at him. 'I did not ask to be Mullah. I did not ask for it or want it.'

'You were the most learned.'

Abdullah shook his head, dismissive. 'Before me, there was Zarif Khan, who understood not only the words of the Qur'an, but the river that flows beneath. But when he returned to Peshawar, there was no-one.'

'There was you.'

'*No-one.* No-one wanted to lead the prayers or do the slaughter. No-one was knowledgeable enough. But I didn't see the flattery for what it was, and I let it persuade me.'

Mahommed wanted to tell him that there could have been no better choice, but he held back. Abdullah had never told him these things. If Mahommed spoke, Abdullah might stop.

'Those years before, in the Chaman market, when the air began to shake. My son should have been with me, but my wife had been ill, and had kept him with her. I knew instantly what the shaking meant. I left my stall, I began to run home, but the earth was groaning, shifting, and I fell to my knees. And after …'

He faded off, and poked at the fire before continuing. 'After, through the stench and rubble and wailing, there was only one child I wanted to find, but when I found him I wished I hadn't.'

When he stopped, Mahommed found the silence unbearable. He had known nothing about a son. 'Your wife …?'

'She lived. And a daughter. But when we buried my son, my wife and I could no longer look at each other. After our divorce, I waited to see her marry a cousin, and then I searched for a land where I thought memory would not exist.' He looked out past the shadows thrown by the remnant fire. 'But there is no such place. Not even here.'

'… I never knew …'

Abdullah turned back to him, refusing to accept his sympathy.

'When I became Mullah, I studied the Qur'an, not only for words, as I had done before, but for meaning. I had failed my family; I couldn't now fail the men who had put their trust in me. And slowly I began to understand that this burden I had been given was a gift, that within the laws of the Qur'an was everything I needed to find my way out from the blackness.'

Mahommed squirmed, hearing the accusation in what Abdullah was saying. But the book had been Alice's, not his. To give it up lightly would have been impossible. 'Abdullah, I respect the laws …'

'Respect is not enough! The laws are everything. Without them we are lost!'

Abdullah stood and went in search of more wood, not waiting for Mahommed to argue. As he foraged, Mahommed saw that he was limping again, his ankle still troubling him. Mahommed's bones were already aching from the cold. He was a young man; the night would be harder for Abdullah.

Abdullah found only a few twigs. The flames died, becoming embers. There would be no more talking tonight.

Mahommed lay still, looking up at the stars, which were where they shouldn't be. At home they had meaning, but not here. He didn't know how to read them. He didn't know how to read anything in this country, apart from Mr Kadran's testimonials. If even the stars were different here, then who could know for sure that the laws weren't different too? It was a question that troubled him, but not one he planned to put to Abdullah.

Sharp stones pressed against his flesh. He had scraped a hollow as best he could but it was not deep enough to cradle his hip bone. He thought Abdullah might also be awake, but if he wasn't he didn't want his movements to wake him. He thought of the camels, running free. They would be three, four miles away by now. They would have stopped running. Unlike him and Abdullah, they would be asleep. In the morning there would be a moment when they realised they were no longer hobbled. They would graze, and move on. Within days they would find a larger herd and join it. They would accept all of this without question. Their *zungwalla* songs would be silent.

22

His shirt tied loosely around his shoulders, he pushed his fingers into a crevice in the rock face, digging deep. Though the well was narrow, making it hard to manoeuvre, it allowed him to use both hands against the sides. If he was careful, he could get to the bottom without mishap. He looked up at the circle of light above him. It had grown smaller; he was nearly there.

He had found a place near the well for Abdullah to rest, a low boulder, offering a little shade. The old man had protested, claiming he was not tired, that they should press on. But Mahommed was watching the sun. He knew they had taken five hours to cover what yesterday had only taken three. They had started before dawn. There was no sleep to be had and they needed to get going before the worst of the day sapped their strength. Already the heat haze had obliterated the distance, throwing a shimmering silvery line in front of them. Abdullah's ankle had swollen. Each step would be sending knives up his leg. Mahommed insisted he was thirsty. They had had nothing to drink since yesterday. Abdullah could go on if he wished but he, Mahommed, needed to drink. Abdullah made a show of irritation at having to waste time in this way; then, his pride salvaged, sat down to wait.

Mahommed reached the bottom of the well. Yesterday they had stopped here, using the well bucket. He knew it held less than a foot of water. It was brackish; alright for camels. Today it would have to be alright for him and Abdullah. He scooped it up in his hand and drank deeply. He soaked his shirt in the water, taking care not to disturb it more than necessary. It would squeeze out no more than a cup of water for Abdullah but he had no other way of carrying it. He put the shirt around his shoulders again and looked up at the light, lingering in the coolness. The silence of the narrow well called him to close his eyes and stay. He thought of the old man waiting for him and began to climb.

'How much money do you owe?' Mahommed asked.

'Including the fine?'

Mahommed nodded.

'Seventy, eighty pounds. Maybe more.' Abdullah shrugged.

Mahommed's eyes widened at the thought. After a certain point the numbers were meaningless. 'I've never seen so much money.'

'How much do you owe Kadran?'

'For the room? Only one pound ten.'

'Well then. Only eighty-one pounds and ten shillings. They are kind people, your Englishmen. I'm sure they will be more than happy to wait.'

They were sitting in the shade of the boulder. It was time to move.

Mahommed said, 'Abdullah, what will we do?'

Abdullah looked around him. 'I don't know.' He dragged himself to his feet. 'I'm ready.'

They continued on their way. Abdullah lasted for an hour before he allowed Mahommed to take his arm and drape it over his shoulder. If he had been on his own Mahommed would have kept walking. There were no more wells or waterholes of any kind before they got back. But he judged that Abdullah would not be able to continue. He needed water but he also needed rest. He found some shade and told Abdullah they would stay there until after the sun went down. They would gather their strength, then continue walking through the cool of the night. They would make Broken Hill by morning.

He expected Abdullah to argue, but he didn't.

Mahommed didn't sleep. He kept watch over Abdullah while the curlews, scratching for insects in the night, keened, joining him in his vigil. He knew when their keening stopped it would be dawn, and if they wanted to avoid the sun they couldn't wait till then; they had to move before the dawn coloured the sky. He gently shook Abdullah awake.

They walked for four hours before Mahommed saw the slag heap. He had stopped to let Abdullah rest. Abdullah had long ago given up any attempt to talk, his tongue so swollen in his mouth he could barely swallow, let alone speak. He took shallow breaths, avoiding the in-rush of searing air that accompanied deep ones.

The sun was already high; the day would soon become hotter. Mahommed was worried about Abdullah's ability to keep going. Holding out a hand to him to help him up, he told him they were nearly there. He wasn't sure it was true. Travelling by himself, maybe one or two hours. But Abdullah was exhausted. He would have to force him along. He pulled Abdullah's arm around his shoulder. He put his free arm around his waist. He felt the weight of him leaning against him, both heavy and papery light.

They had gone no more than thirty or forty feet

when he realised Abdullah had nothing left. He stopped and hoisted him onto his back. He was heavy, but Mahommed knew he could do it. His heart was strong. It was fed by outrage.

He stopped twice more along the way, needing to rest and catch his breath. After the second time it had been almost impossible to lift Abdullah onto his back and he knew he wouldn't be able to stop again. He kept walking, keeping his head down so as not to see the slag heap. If he couldn't see it, he couldn't be disappointed about how far away it still was.

He counted the stones as they passed beneath his feet. The growing numbers kept the thirst out of his mind and allowed him to keep walking. When the numbers grew too high to remember, he put them aside and started again at one. When the sun became too hot for thinking in numbers, he counted the stones in colours, then cities, then months.

When he reached the camp, he carried Abdullah into his shack and placed him on his bed. Curious, the children followed him to the doorway. Mahommed told Zainie to fetch water and food. He took off Abdullah's shoes, easing them from his swollen feet, making him comfortable. When Zainie returned with a jug of water, Mahommed gave it to Abdullah, holding his head so as to let the water trickle in slowly.

Only then did he drink himself. He told Abdullah he would be back soon.

Alice thought how odd it was that you could think one thing, and something completely opposite, at exactly the same time. You could think the war was nothing important at all, and still weep when you read about Antwerp and Ypres, even when they were nothing more than dots on a map to you. You could love and admire Lewis's patriotism, and also resent him for the adventure you couldn't have. You could be frightened for his safety and want him to stay, and at the same time be glad for the moments you'd be able to have without him. You could be counting the days before you saw him again, while you were counting up different days for Mahommed.

Sometimes she wasn't sure what she thought about anything. If she tried to think it through logically, she got into a worse mess because it wasn't really about thinking, it was about feeling, and that was something else entirely. It was feeling that had made her kiss Mahommed, right out in a public street. A sense that their hold on each other was tenuous, that he might give up his memory of her to more pressing memories. She was glad she had done it. He had her book and a kiss. They would bring him back.

'How long now?' Eileen looked up at her, pressed against her despite the heat. She was wearing her best dress for Lewis's send off. She wanted to look nice for him.

'Soon,' answered Alice. She shrugged, and gave her a sympathetic smile. 'Too soon.'

The night of her argument with Lewis, she heard him come in, late. She was still awake, partly because she was troubled, and partly because Eileen's bones were poking into her.

She heard him stumble and she knew he'd been drinking, something he hardly ever did. A schooner or two on a Friday, sometimes not even that. She couldn't blame him for drinking tonight, not after the things she'd said. Or maybe it wasn't that; maybe he was simply toasting freedom.

He slept in late; Eileen had gone to school by the time he was up. Alice made him breakfast. They skirted around the night before. After he had finished she drew up a chair and told him that the things she had said were because she was afraid of losing him. England was lucky there were brave men like him prepared to fight. Eileen was proud of him. 'And so am I.'

Lewis looked at her, puzzled by the change in her. 'You don't mind?'

'I mind terribly. But I'm hoping your courage is contagious.'

'Maybe I haven't got any. They haven't even accepted me yet.'

'They will.' She was working hard at sounding cheerful. 'They're going to take one look at you and sign you up on the spot.'

'They're doing that to just about everyone. As long as you're tall enough, and you've got two arms and legs.'

'Well, I won't tell them if you don't.'

He returned her smile. They were friends again.

He said, 'You and me, we've done alright with the cards we were dealt. No-one could say we haven't.'

'Has it been so hard for you?'

He shrugged. 'I don't have anything to compare it with.'

'What do you think you would have done? If you hadn't had to look after Eileen and me?'

'I never thought about it. It's just the way it was.'

'You might've gone somewhere else. Done something different.'

Lewis was puzzling over it. She could see he didn't understand.

'But I wouldn't've had a reason, not without you two. You need reasons; otherwise you just get in a mess and do things every which way.'

She let it go at that. If she pushed him further it might make him uncomfortable; might cause him to ask if she had her reasons. She didn't want to have to answer that. Once she started she wouldn't know how to stop.

The band played 'Rule Britannia', then 'Sons of the Sea'. Then they played them both again. They were saving 'Auld Lang Syne' for when the men started boarding the train.

Alice watched Lewis talking to Keith. She knew he had asked him to keep an eye out for her and Eileen. She didn't want him to, but she could hardly make a fuss. If Keith took that to mean more than it did, then she would have to put him right. But today was Lewis's day, and she wasn't going to do anything to spoil it.

Another half-hour and he'd be gone. Adelaide first, then Morphettville, where he would do the training. He might not even leave Australia, not if the war was finished by then. The training was for about a month; he promised to write and tell them exactly when they were shipping out. She could see the light in his eyes. He was excited, eager to get going, ready to be carried away by a wave of adventure. He hadn't said so, but Alice knew he was hoping the war would last long enough for him to be part of it. Most of the others had that same look about them. There were some who didn't. They were older. Alice thought they probably didn't want excitement in their lives, only the full stomach that an army pay packet would bring.

She couldn't stop looking at him. The thought that he might not return was weighing on her, crowding out everything else. The papers were full of war now. She tried not to read too much because knowing about it wouldn't help him stay alive, but from the sound of things, all Europe was involved. She began to shake, and briefly shut her eyes to regain control. *Not Lewis. Please, not Lewis.* He had done nothing wrong. He had already sacrificed himself once for her and Eileen. *Please don't make him do it again. It wouldn't be fair.*

'Alice? What's wrong?'

She looked down at Eileen, reassuring her. Nothing was wrong. Only the sun in her eyes. She would keep Eileen safe. And in return the Germans would let Lewis live.

He came back to them. Eileen gave him her locket and a hug and began to cry. She told him if he didn't come back she'd never forgive him. He kissed her. 'I'll be back. And if you're not waiting right here for me, I'll never forgive *you.*'

Irma and Robert joined them, late; Irma protectively close to Robert. Alice wondered why Robert hadn't enlisted. Irma had said defensively it was because he had an important job.

The band was playing the final chorus of 'Rule Britannia'. Alice wanted it to be over, wanted him gone. She had said everything. All that was left was a forced heartiness that would have to last until the train pulled out. She looked away from Lewis, feeling a surge of protectiveness towards him that she didn't want him to see. He needed to leave them with an easy heart; she owed him that, and more.

Mahommed did not find Lewis at the store. Alf, cowardly under duress, told him where he was. As he ran towards the railway station, he heard the band playing the last bars of 'Rule Britannia'.

He pushed past milling family groups. He didn't care that he was dirty, that he stank. He cared only about finding Lewis before he boarded. He searched for his face among the other men.

He saw him, speaking to the policeman and the Sanitary Inspector. The band had started 'Auld Lang Syne'. He pushed through the crowd and came to a halt in front of Lewis and his companions. He said, 'I wish to speak with you.'

Lewis regarded him warily. 'You can't. I'm busy.'

Mahommed refused to be intimidated. 'I will speak with you now!'

He caught sight of Alice, moving closer, but he had started now, and could not stop. He could not let this man board the train without people knowing him for what he was.

Others were watching, torn between their farewells and curiosity at this unexpected entertainment.

Mahommed continued, 'I need to understand how you can consider it amusing to destroy an old man's livelihood? Please tell me how this is funny because I cannot find why I should laugh!'

The policeman took hold of his arm, but Mahommed shrugged him off.

Lewis said, 'I don't know what he's talking about.'

Mahommed slipped free of the hands trying to grab him. He lost the words he wanted to say, but others kept coming. He said, 'Maybe this is a fault in me that I cannot laugh, and if so I am eager to be instructed. You will find that I have been most eager to be instructed in British matters and up until now I have not found difficulties in learning, but here …' He felt faint. He could barely stand, let alone hold his thoughts together. '… here is a door with no key …'

He saw Alice put an arm around Eileen, heard Lewis say, 'Get him out of here.'

Mahommed moved away. Why was everyone trying to stop him? He had to make them understand, *had* to.

'But if you would lend me that key, then the door would open and we could laugh together ... but ... Abdullah is a good man! What right have you to destroy him? What right!'

The policeman got hold of him, keeping a firm grip. 'Come on, that's enough.'

Alice looked at him, bewildered. 'Mahommed, why are you here?'

Lewis said, 'Don't speak to him, Alice.'

Mahommed turned to Alice. 'I am sorry; I have broken your trust. I have destroyed your book. Loch Lomond is no more.'

Lewis looked at her sharply. 'What's he on about?'

She held Mahommed's look, as though asking him for an answer. But hadn't he just given it? Hadn't she, at least, heard what he was trying to say?

She turned her back to him, and answered her brother.

She said, 'I have no idea.'

23

There was the Puritol. There was a sliver of Rexona and a sliver of Lifebuoy. He chose the Rexona. He went to the ablution pool by the mosque and began to scrub the filth away. The red dust had caked into sweat lines on his body. The soap could deal with this, it was only surface dirt.

As he scrubbed, Ibram, Jemadar's son, came over to watch, squatting on the ground nearby. Mahommed asked after Abdullah. Ibram said he was resting.

It was less than two hours since Mahommed had returned to the camp, carrying the barely conscious Abdullah on his back. He had achieved nothing at the train station. He had not shamed Lewis. He had not shamed Robert Brosnan. He had wanted to show them dignified anger. Instead he gave them incoherent babblings, spouting from the mouth of a wild-eyed

Afghan scarecrow, hands waving in the air, jabbing at points that hadn't been made. The policeman had bundled him through the crowd and told him to be on his way. He had been flotsam, easily pushed away. The crowd had turned its back on him, eager to dismiss him.

Alice had seen him, heard what he said. She had also turned her back.

He continued to wash, rinsing away all remnants of the last two days. He cleaned his body. He cleaned his mind.

He watched Abdullah while he slept. The frail body, half hidden by the loose shirt; the chest barely rising with each breath. The face etched with sorrow. He thought of his father's face, which was lost to him. His mother's he still knew better than his own, but his father's was a sliding puzzle with fragments refusing to join together. He was no longer sure if these fragments were of his father, or if he had merely conjured them into being.

When night fell, and Abdullah was still sleeping, he left his side. What he needed to say wasn't important. What he needed to do, was.

The horse was a glue-ready nag; the ice-cream cart held together with rust and rotting wood. Both were in a paddock with a sign announcing they were for sale.

He bought them with money he didn't have, borrowed from Jemadar. Jemadar was making him pay twice. Once, when he asked for the money, and twice, when he paid it back. Mahommed swallowed what was left of his pride. He flattered Jemadar, praising his wisdom, his piety, his business acumen. He explained to him in detail how one could make money by selling ice-cream. The cart could be taken to cricket matches, could wait outside churches, be taken up and down Argent Street. Mahommed would ring a bell, letting everyone know what he was selling. It was almost December. It was hot. People would line up for ice-cream. For every shilling's worth he sold, one penny would be his.

He could see Jemadar was not yet convinced. He told him he was only asking for the money because if the Sultan commanded him to fight, it would be his duty to go, not just to the Sultan, but to Allah. As yet he had received no reply to his offer of enlistment, but when it came, he wanted to be prepared.

He reminded Jemadar that the Prophet (peace be upon him) said it was more lovely for Allah that a man sits for an hour thinking and weighing his actions, than if he prays for seventy years. Given that Jemadar may not have seventy years, although it would be a most wondrous and happy thing if he did, would he perhaps like to think about it for an hour before making up his mind?

Jemadar made Mahommed plead for another ten minutes, then gave him the money on the understanding he would have to be repaid before Mahommed booked his passage. From what he had read, he told him, many people were being killed in this war. Repayment would be problematical if Mahommed were no longer alive.

Abdullah tried to concentrate on what Mahommed was telling him. He sucked on the *narghile* they were sharing and tried again. 'How can you fight for the Sultan if you are here?'

'I will earn money from the horse.'

Abdullah passed him the *narghile*. 'Enough for a passage?'

'If I work hard.'

'And you have not worked hard already?'

Mahommed sucked on the pipe, floating with the *bhang*. It gave him more pleasure than taking Abdullah's bait.

Yes, he had worked hard enough, but he had done it for the wrong reasons. He had been shallow, easily swayed. He had come perilously close to selling his soul for little more than a soap wrapper and a flash of green-brown eyes.

He passed the pipe back to Abdullah. 'I will work even harder now. I will save all my money. When I have enough for my passage I will leave; I will join the Turkish army, and I will fight.'

'And if there is no reply to the letter you sent?'

'I will go anyway.'

'Is this what you want? Or are you saying it for me?'

'I am saying it for Allah.'

Wasn't it Allah's hand that had led him to write the letter, offering his services to the Sultan? At the time he hadn't really meant what he wrote; it was done to impress Abdullah. But wasn't it Allah showing him the way?

'And you are my witness.' There, he'd said it. And he was glad he had. Every word joined him closer to the only real friend he had. He thought he had others, but they were an illusion.

Abdullah seemed to weigh all this up before nodding, accepting his statement. Mahommed was grateful. There was a peace between them since they had come back from the desert. He didn't want to disturb it.

'So.' Abdullah smiled mischievously. 'You are going to win the war for the Sultan?'

'Yes, if that is his wish!' Mahommed laughed at the absurdity of such a statement. He had failed to win Libya for the Sultan. It was, he conceded, just remotely possible he could also fail to win the European war. Abdullah laughed too, then began to choke on the smoke. Mahommed waited until he had coughed himself out.

'I will win the war single-handedly! All by myself! I will gallop in on my ice-cream horse and shoot all the English!'

'And the French?'

'Yes, if you like!'

'And Inspector Brosnan?'

'Of course! I will shoot him twice! And all the good people in the world will praise me, and say, thank you, Gool Mahommed! You have saved us, Gool Mahommed!' He laughed louder, his stomach cramping with the pain of it.

He finished the *narghile* with Abdullah. After some time the smoke cleared and so did his mind and none of it seemed funny any more.

It was a friendly cricket match, between St James and Nicholls Street. A sort of no-hard-feelings gesture about not being Anglican from St James, and a generous understanding that not everyone could be Methodist from Nicholls Street. Eileen had wanted to go. Keith had come calling while Alice was at the hospital and by the time she arrived home, Eileen had already told him yes.

Alice told herself it didn't mean anything, he was only doing what Lewis had asked him to do. It would be unkind not to let him accompany her and Eileen.

Lewis had written to them, telling them about his training.

> *Reveille sounds at six o'clock. You'd laugh to see me scramble with the other chaps to get to the latrines and ablution sheds and then get back again before the inspection parade at seven-thirty. They're exercising us jolly hard; the way my muscles are aching they'll have to carry me to the war on a stretcher. But I'm getting stronger, and like the other fellows here I'm champing at the bit to do my part.*

The rest of the letter had continued in the same cheerful vein. Alice was sure he wasn't faking it for her and Eileen's benefit. She had seen the look in his eyes. If it made him feel even happier to think Keith was looking after them, well, there was nothing to be gained in letting him think otherwise.

She wouldn't encourage Keith, though. She didn't want him, she didn't want anyone any more. Her nightmares had started again. All she wanted was sleep.

She had denied Mahommed. If she could only sleep

she could forget her betrayal of him. But what choice did she have? She had made promises: to herself, to Eileen, to Lewis. She had acknowledged the sacrifices Lewis had already made; the ones he was about to make. And he had been about to leave them; the train was there, the music, the people singing the words as if they were their own.

We'll take a cup o'kindness yet, for Auld Lang Syne.

There had been no choice, none. But when she had turned from Mahommed she had been filled with the thought: *What a small cold heart I have.*

The memory of this kept her awake during the nights, but the pointlessness of everything made her want to sleep through the days. There seemed no reason for doing anything. Working, eating, combing her hair, even. She would stop halfway through and wonder why she was doing it. 'I might as well' was the best answer she could come up with.

Eileen had arrived home from school the week before to find her curled up in bed. She had asked her why, and Alice had claimed a headache. She couldn't say, 'Because I don't know what else to do.' It was the truth, but she couldn't say it.

Alice was sitting next to Irma; Eileen some way off, with some school friends. She tried to concentrate on the game. Nicholls Street was batting. She didn't know who was winning. She didn't care.

She glanced at Irma. She hadn't seen much of her lately; she had been mysteriously absent.

'Where's Robert?' Alice said.

'Working at home. He's going to try and come later, but he's extremely busy.'

'But it's Saturday.'

'His work's important. He takes it seriously.'

Irma's manner was strange, Alice thought, as if she were hiding something.

'Is something wrong?'

'Of course not. Why would there be?'

'I don't know.'

'Well there isn't. He's simply working very, very hard.'

Alice could hear the strain in Irma's voice and did her best to sound soothing. 'I'm sure he is.'

'He *is*. You have no idea what pressure he's under, and he gets very little help at work, and none at all from that Mary Hamilton, and … and …'

Alice put an arm around her. 'It's alright, Irma, you don't have to tell me.'

'I can't because it's a secret, and … he doesn't want anyone to know because he's so brave, but … oh, Alice, he's very sick.'

'Robert is?' Alice hadn't paid much attention to Robert, although she had recently thought he had become rather unkempt for someone in his position.

'He's got … you won't tell anyone, will you?'

'Not if you don't want me to.'

'He's got … a catarrh of the stomach.'

'A what?'

'An extremely acute one.'

'Irma … are you sure it isn't in his nose?'

Irma looked at her, alarmed. 'Are you saying it could spread?'

'You don't get catarrh in the stomach. Only in the nose.'

Irma bridled at her tone. 'Robert has it in the stomach. It's extremely rare.'

Alice should have left it there, but by now she was curious. 'Is that what the doctor told him? That it was catarrh?'

'Yes.'

'Which doctor?'

'You don't know everything, Alice.' Irma looked away, cross. 'Just because you empty bedpans in the hospital.'

Alice let the slight go. If she reacted to it, Irma would cry and apologise, and Alice would have to respond in kind, and it would all take too much effort.

'You're right. I'm sorry he's ill. I hope he gets better soon.'

The batsman from Nicholls Street hit a ball to the boundary, which required clapping and cheering. By the time that was done with, Irma was back to her normal self. When they heard the bell from the ice-cream vendor, she even suggested they go together to buy some.

It was Irma who recognised him first, selling ice-creams from the back of a cart. Zainie, the girl who had brought his meals to the hospital, was helping him, as were two other smaller Afghan children. Irma was scandalised that he would dare come to a church event, after the awful commotion he had created.

Alice wasn't listening. She was looking at him; as she did so, he lifted his head and saw her.

Eileen hurried up and asked her if she was getting ice-creams. Alice fumbled for some coins and gave them to her. Told her she'd changed her mind, but Eileen could buy one if she wanted.

Alice hurried away, with Irma struggling to keep up. She wanted to get away from him, stop thinking about him; wanted to sleep and have everything go away. Her lungs choked her; she had to stop to drag air in.

'Alice? Is it about that awful man?'

Alice shook her head.

'All that carry-on at the station. Honestly, it was only a joke. They take things so seriously.'

Alice looked at her sharply. 'What things?'

In return Irma gave her a wide-eyed stare. 'Didn't you know?'

Alice grabbed her, giving her a shake. '*What things?*'

24

Jemadar had been feeling unsteady. In the mornings when he rose from his bed, he had to hold something to keep himself up until his legs were ready to do the job. Walking with Edith, he would occasionally have to reach out and put a hand on her shoulder. Only last week, out in the camel paddock, he had felt so faint he had to sit down suddenly on the ground, right next to a fresh camel turd. He'd had to sit there for a full ten minutes breathing turd fumes before he found the strength to stand again.

Apart from the shakiness there was the vice that squeezed the blood from his heart. It was happening more frequently now. Sometimes the pain would start after exertion; sometimes for no reason at all. It could be short and sharp, enough to make him wince, or it could be drawn out, requiring him to lie down until it was over.

He wasn't sure how old he was. About seventy, he thought. However old he was, he had begun to face up to the fact he wasn't going to go on forever. His body was letting him down. He couldn't remember when he'd last had, or even wanted to have, sex with Edith. Since Partimah was born, probably only half-a-dozen times. He'd been proud of his virility. But now, what a tired old piece of flesh he was.

He knew he was running out of time to perform acts of righteousness and faith. *Hajj* was out, given his physical frailty. He wished he hadn't lied about making it, but he wasn't up to untangling that one in public. He went through the rest of his balance sheet, and ended up unsure of the result. He thought it was mostly in his favour, but it was hard to know for sure.

He prayed regularly, nearly always five times a day. Not on camel runs, but that was the same with all the men. He had recently lent Gool Mahommed money, which was surely in his favour. It was an act of charity, and he felt he had performed it in a generous spirit.

The Prophet (peace be upon him) said that after a man died there were three things that could benefit his chances after death; charity given and which continues to help, was one of them. So he was glad he had lent the money to Mahommed, even though the ice-cream cart was a stupid idea.

The second was knowledge from which people continued to benefit. Surely he was safe there. After seventy-something years on earth he must have imparted something worth imparting, something that would continue to resonate in the lives of others.

The last of the three was uncertain. He needed a pious child to pray over him. He had a child; in fact he had three, but none of them was particularly pious. He had given Zainie instruction for a while, so she at least had some knowledge of the Qur'an. But he had become lazy by the time Ibram was old enough to learn. Ibram's mother, Nita, had kept filling his head with Aboriginal nonsense when Jemadar was out of earshot. He had tried to counteract it once she'd gone, but had to admit he hadn't tried as hard as he should have. Edith was slightly more tractable than Nita, but Partimah was little more than a baby. He could hardly expect her to pray over him.

It had to be Ibram; it would count more from a boy than a girl. There was still time for some basic instruction. He could at least give him the words of the prayers he wanted said, and trust that the piety would take care of itself.

He hoped he would be allowed some small foreknowledge of his death. Enough time to say what should be said. *Ash'hadu laa ilaaha illallaah.* I bear witness that there is no god but Allah. That was all he had to say, surely he would be given time for that?

Time wasn't the only issue. Lately he'd had trouble marshalling his thoughts. He would be thinking about one thing, and someone would mention another, and by the time he got back to thinking about whatever had been on his mind in the first place, it had gone. So he had to be sure to remember to say it. *Ash'hadu laa ilaaha illallaah.* He had already told Ibram to prompt him when the time came. He would have to tell him again, make sure he understood how important it was.

He was tending to his camels. When he was younger he had occasionally leased more than the six he now had, taking his camel train up to Tibooburra and as far as Dig Tree. But those days were gone. He had to be honest with himself, he was unlikely to take another trip. When was the last one? May? February? He had been on one this year, he was sure of it.

He probably should sell them. If he died in the next couple of years, Ibram would still be too young to take over. But if he sold them now, there would be the problem of what to do with the money. He didn't trust Edith. Her lazy relatives would pounce and she wouldn't know how to fend them off. She might not even try. But if he kept the camels, they had to be looked after, and that was becoming a chore.

Never mind, the solution could wait for another day. He was feeling tired. It might be a good idea to lie down for a half-hour or so. There was nothing pressing he needed to do. He would rest until *Salat ul Asr*.

He looked at the sun, guessing the time. He had performed *Zuhr*, hadn't he? He must have, he did so at noon every day. If he didn't there was always a good reason. Had that been the case today?

The problem troubled him. Given the state of his health, now was not a good time for diminishing righteousness. He decided to put off the rest. He would go to the mosque, perform four *rakas*, then rest until it was time for *Asr*. If it turned out he had already performed *Zuhr*, then those extra four *rakas* could be added to his life's balance sheet.

He knelt by the ablution pool, grateful for the chance to sink down. He leaned over the water. In its mirrored surface he could see his reflection. He stared at it. Was that really him? Where was the dignity, the wisdom shining through?

Enough. Goodness was within. Allah would not criticise him for his wrinkles. He plunged his hands in, once, twice, three times, washing them to the wrist. He scooped water into his mouth and rinsed it three times.

Now the nostrils. He leaned over to scoop a handful of water and as he did so he saw his face again. No. Not his, surely. The panic in the eyes, the mouth, opening to a silent scream as a vice squeezed his heart, pushing out every drop of blood.

As he fell forward, he remembered there were words he had to say. He couldn't remember what they were. He was still puzzling over them when he slid under the water, causing barely a ripple.

Mahommed, Abdullah and Sherdil washed him, waiting until the freshly boiled water had cooled. Mahommed provided the soap. He thought hard over which was his favourite. He had not liked Jemadar, but did not wish to compound the ill feeling by using a second-best soap. He finally chose what was left of the Lifebuoy, because it had been his first love.

They washed his head first. Then his upper right side and upper left side; his lower right and lower left sides. They did it again, five times in all, before shrouding him in three winding sheets of calico. Mahommed felt humbled by the respect Abdullah showed towards Jemadar's body. Abdullah had not liked Jemadar any more than Mahommed had, but he was able to put that aside so that tenderness and love could be Jemadar's companions on his final journey.

They held *Salatul Janazah* by the side of the mosque, out of sight of the ablution pool. There were thirty men in the camp at the time; Mahommed counted thirty heads bobbing in prayer and wondered how many would pray for him when he died.

After *Salatul Janazah* they carried Jemadar's shrouded body to the cemetery and said more prayers for his soul's peace before lowering him into the burial chamber, Mahommed and Sherdil making sure his head was correctly aligned. They placed boards over the chamber and covered it with earth.

They made *du'a* while Jemadar was being questioned by the angels, and then they went home. Mahommed was glad it wasn't yet his own turn to be questioned. He wasn't sure what answers he could give.

The horse, about eighteen years old, didn't have a name. Her teeth, long and yellow, reminded Mahommed of Jemadar's. Her eyes were her own: large, gentle and rheumy. She had a bald patch on one brown flank, the result of a past infestation of mites. She was sway-backed, partly due to age, partly to years of poor nutrition, and partly to the heavy loads she had been expected to carry most of her life. She had a placid, stoic nature.

Mahommed didn't love her, but he respected her. She performed her part without complaint. It was not her fault he would be an old man before he would earn enough money for his passage to Turkey.

He had overestimated how much money he would be able to make from selling ice-cream. He had been doing it for more than two weeks now. On the weekdays people were busy, and he sold only enough for the most minuscule profit. The weekends were better, but, thanks to the war, money was draining out of Broken Hill. Ice-cream was not an everyday treat.

He had hoped to sell a lot at the cricket match. It was hot, people were in a relaxed mood. But then he saw her. One minute he had been handing change to a woman who had bought two ice-creams for her children. The next, he was looking straight across at Alice. He should have looked away, but he didn't. He couldn't. He watched as she hurried away with her friend.

He couldn't risk meeting her again. He put the money and the ice-cream away. He got the horse moving and left, despite a queue of people still wanting ice-cream; despite Zainie and Ibram's confusion about what was happening.

He despised himself for his weakness. I am Afridi, we are warriors, he had told her in that moment of boastfulness.

He would be a warrior again, somehow. He would find the money for his passage. He would keep his promise to Abdullah. He would help Turkey fight the

English. If, Allah willing, he came face to face with Alice's brother, he would be glad of it. He would splatter his face with bullets and show him the same mercy Lewis had shown him and Abdullah. He would think of her face when they told her the news.

He heard the music from the camp and shut it out. He didn't want to be part of it. There was nothing to celebrate. Jemadar was dead and Abdullah was dying; had been since they came back from the aborted trip. Mahommed could see it in the eyes that had flickered with hate, but now held only hopelessness; that had believed Mahommed would avenge him, but now no longer did.

Abdullah still led the prayers, but his sermons were hollow and uninspiring. He kept more and more to himself. Mahommed knew he was fretting about the fine he could not pay; the discarded goods he could not replace. Mahommed had no way of helping; he was barely earning enough money to feed himself. Abdullah had given the little he had left of himself to Jemadar's last journey. Now he and Mahommed had nothing to give each other.

Mahommed moved his horse a little further from the camels, tethered her to a rail and brought feed to her. He became aware that someone was watching him.

He looked up to see Alice, standing a little way off. He saw that she had become thin. She was no longer a goddess. Flushed and unlovely, her face was all bones and angles.

He looked away, turning his back to her. He had closed off from her, taken a new path, made promises to himself, to Allah, to Abdullah, promises he meant to keep.

He didn't want to see her. He wanted to hate her, but he had forgotten her eyes.

25

Alice hadn't meant to come. When Eileen asked if she could go to the funeral feast, Alice told her she couldn't.

'But why not?' asked Eileen.

'Because people dying is private.'

'Not for them. They want people to go.'

Alice knew it was true. She remembered the other funeral feast, when she and Lewis had been given fruit and lollies. They had been made welcome. If her mother had been alive they would not have been allowed to go, but her father, who was less concerned with propriety, had not even noticed their absence.

'My friends are allowed.'

'No.'

Eileen looked at her, deeply resentful. 'What's the real reason?'

Shame; remorse; pride; fear. How could she explain these things to an eleven-year-old when she couldn't explain them to herself?

Eileen pressured her further, and she let herself be persuaded. She told herself it was for Eileen, although it wasn't, and the closer they came to the camp, the more she knew it.

She loitered at the edges of the feast, trying not to look for him. She saw the old man, Abdullah, but he didn't acknowledge her, something she was glad of. Eileen had gone home with her friends. After accepting fruit and listening to some music, they had drifted away when the novelty of the occasion wore off, but Alice lingered, conspicuously alone. She knew she should leave, but if she did, how could she ever come back?

An Aboriginal woman stared at her from the doorway of a shack. She recognised her as Edith, the woman she had questioned in the street, all those months ago. She smiled uncertainly at her, aware that on this occasion, it was she who was out of place. Edith's eyes were swollen; she looked like she'd been crying. 'Are you alright?'

'Yes thank you, missus.' She picked at the skin of an orange she was holding, gouging another crater to join the others.

'Was the man who died a friend of yours?'

'Yes, missus.'

Edith concentrated on the orange. Alice could see her presence was making Edith uncomfortable. And she had no reason to stay, none she could explain.

'He's not here,' Edith said.

'Who isn't?'

'Gool Mahommed. He's not here.'

'Oh.' Alice watched as Edith continued to pick at the orange. There didn't seem any reason for what she was doing; she was just doing it.

Edith saw her looking at it, and held it out to her. 'Do you want it? It's just the outside bits, the inside's alright.'

'No. No, thank you.'

She was trying to find an acceptable way to leave when Edith lifted her hand to indicate a dusty track leading towards the camel paddock. 'He's down there. That way there.'

Before she had time to either thank her or deny her interest, Edith withdrew inside the shack. Alice started walking down the track. A scrawny dog followed her for a while but when she turned it slinked away. She was glad it didn't know how afraid she was.

He heard someone approach and looked around. When he saw it was her he looked away.

Despite the heat, she trembled. She said, 'I'm sorry about the man who died.'

He kept his back to her and shrugged. 'He was old.'

She persisted. 'He's probably already bossing them around in heaven.'

She knew it was a stupid remark. It didn't mean anything, but it was enough to make him turn. He looked at her with disdain.

'No. He will lie in his grave until judgement day, when he will be called and judged. If he is found to be a good man, he will never die again.'

She could see he wanted nothing to do with her, but she had to keep going. 'And if he's found not to be a good man?'

'If he fails the judgement test, he will be cast into the outer darkness for all time.' He turned back to the horse. 'Please go away. I don't wish to cause you embarrassment, and if you are seen in my presence this will follow.'

'No, it won't.'

'I have seen that it does.'

'I didn't know the truth then, but I do now. I know what happened.' Not Lewis. It was Robert's idea, Irma was proudly sure of that. Lewis was part of it; he must have been, but only a small part, surely. 'I know what they did and I'm sorry.'

She told him she knew she had behaved badly; that she was ashamed. She told him that from now on she would be brave. She had only one more thing to offer.

'I love you, Mahommed.'

'Don't say that! Don't think it, don't feel it, don't say it!'

She faltered, stung by the ferocity of his tone. 'But what if it's true?' She edged closer and told him again what was in her heart. She said, 'Tell me you don't love me, and I'll go away.'

She was close enough now to touch him. She reached out and put a hand on his sleeve. She said, 'Please, Mahommed, tell me you don't.'

She waited for him to push her away, but he didn't.

They were quiet, aware that people might be passing outside, might hear them over the *santur* and the drums. They were clumsy, clutching at each other, fumbling to undress.

Alice didn't know what was expected, but when he lifted her skirts she pushed her body against his and when he laid her down she clung to him, wanting no space between them. She heard her own breathing, shallow and uncontrolled. She pressed her face against the sweat of his neck to quieten herself. She thought, I am done for now, there is nowhere left for me. She stopped thinking, and gave in to the rhythms of his body, keeping time with her own.

When it was over, he lay still on her, his eyes shut. She didn't know if she should say anything. He opened his eyes and looked at her. He kissed her mouth. He took his weight off her and lay to one side. She wanted him to speak to her, but he didn't.

She had been aware of nothing but his touch; now she took in her surroundings. She saw how he lived. She didn't care.

The newspapers on the walls drew her attention. She saw a recent headline announcing yet another British success. Not only had they taken Basra, but now Qurma, another place she had never heard of. The war, she thought, was improving her knowledge of geography.

She didn't know how to talk of what they had done together, so she talked of the war. 'We're winning, aren't we?' she said, drawing his attention to the headline.

He said, 'There are conflicting reports.'

'As long as we win in the end. And as long as the end is before Lewis gets there.'

Mahommed didn't tell her he dreamed of killing Lewis. He pulled her towards him again, gentler now. He stroked her hair, traced her face; undid her blouse and kissed the hollow of her neck; caressed her breasts, feeling their weight in his hands. Felt the rib bones sharp beneath her skin.

He was less hurried this time. He took care with her. He tried to remember her as she was on the train. He tried to remember how he had felt. A boy, awkward in her presence. He did all this because he wanted to shut out the word drumming in his ear; an unwelcome, accusing word that refused to go away.

He came out from the shack first. To protect her, he said, although he knew it was only part of the truth. The music was still playing; he could see no-one close-by. He called her out and led her at a distance towards the road. They lingered, saying awkward goodbyes in the daylight. They made no declarations but as she left they touched hands and he felt the unspoken promises they were making.

He knew he should join the feast; instead he went back to his shack and sat outside, letting the distant music wash over him, calming his turmoil. He was almost ready to rejoin the others when Ibram approached him, carrying a letter.

There were many stamps on it. It had come a long way. He opened it and saw it was from an official of the Turkish army. It was a reply to the letter he had almost not written.

The official wrote:

We have accepted your request to be a member of the
Turkish army, and the will of Allah will help you to
be a true member, and to fight only for the Sultan.

Ibram watched as he read it. He asked if it was an important letter.

Mahommed refolded it and put it back in the envelope. He told Ibram it was from his family, sending news and good wishes. He took the envelope into his shack and put it safely away. Then he walked with Ibram towards the music.

Sherdil was playing, nodding his head to the drum beat as he plucked the *santur*'s strings. The other men were clapping in time. Mahommed could see Abdullah on the edge of the circle, and took care to stand away from him, pretending not to see him.

He began to clap, louder and louder, but nothing, not the clapping, not the *santur*, not the drumming, could drown out the sound of that accusing word.

He did not show Abdullah the letter that day. Nor the next day. He did not tell him he had been with Alice, although Abdullah didn't need to say anything for Mahommed to know how he felt about it. All his fine words; the hatred he claimed to be nourishing, the courage he swore to show, the army he had so glibly joined, the money he would earn for his passage. Abdullah silently spat these out and laid them in front of him.

But there were dark rooms where a light still shone; where a gap in a door or window frame allowed a ray of sunshine through. Enough to let a man warm his cold heart to the hope that outside the darkness, life was still waiting.

Mahommed had lived his life in hope. He couldn't throw it away; it was part of him. It was a sickly faded thing, but without it life would be beyond contemplation. Without it, Alice would surely not have come to him. Without it there would be only the dark room.

But still that word.

Coward.

26

Alice sat up two nights in a row, making a dress from the blue brocade she had bought for Eileen. When Eileen saw what she was doing, she protested. Alice laughed and told her not to worry; she was making it for herself. Eileen sat up with her, knitting woollen squares, a school project for the war effort. For every square she knitted for school, she knitted another one, which she put aside in a growing pile. She was making a rug for Lewis.

Another letter came from him, and they read it together. He was still enjoying his training. He thought it probable they would be shipped out in another two weeks, after the New Year. The prospect clearly made him happy. Alice thought how strange it was that happiness could come from such different directions.

Lewis's came from doing something everyone approved of, while hers came from something that would be condemned if it were public knowledge. Killing was alright, but what she had done with Mahommed was a sin.

She had known, both from schoolyard gossip and from the hospital, something of what to expect, but no-one had told her how utterly consumed she would feel: not only by the act but by the physical closeness it forced upon them, so that his breath became her breath; his skin, her skin; his mouth, her mouth.

When she parted from him, she expected to feel shame. She waited for it to envelop her but she reached home without it, enveloped by nothing but happiness. What was even more surprising was that happiness had been joined by relief. She had done the worst thing a decent woman could do, she had stepped on the crack, and whatever the consequences there was no way of pretending she hadn't done it, but despite all that, she felt no fear at all. There had been a closed door, waiting for her. She had opened it. As yet the earth hadn't stopped turning.

If she felt shame later, then so be it. She wanted to sin again.

Irma looked at her in disbelief. 'You're not thinking about asking children from the camel camp?'

Alice brazened it out. 'Yes. Why?'

She was making a list for Eileen's twelfth birthday party. She had already cleared the inclusion of Zainie, Ibram and Partimah with Eileen, casually mentioning their names along with others. She had reminded Eileen how welcoming they had been to her at the funeral. Anticipating a protest, she had mentioned them in almost the same breath as a proposed trip to Adelaide to wave Lewis's ship off.

Irma was not so easily fobbed off. 'You can't possibly ask them.'

'Why not?'

'You know why not.'

'Actually, I don't.'

'What you do to your reputation is your own business, but you ought to at least think about what you're doing to other people's.' She picked up the tea tray Alice had prepared, and hurried out to the garden.

Irma knew, Alice thought. How much she knew, she wasn't sure, but this display of moral rectitude was not coming solely from the inclusion of three Afghan children in Eileen's birthday list.

Irma had dropped in unexpectedly. In the past this would not have been unusual, but they had seen little of each other recently. She seemed ill at ease; as if there were something difficult she needed to talk about. Alice had assumed it was something about Robert; she knew the much awaited proposal of marriage had not yet materialised.

Alice followed Irma out. Someone must have seen her walking alone from the camp; a neighbour, a friend of Irma's. She thought they had been discreet. He had walked with her to the edge of the camp. They had touched fingertips on parting, nothing more.

Irma was sitting at the garden table. 'I don't know how you could lower yourself,' she said, looking away.

Alice refused to help her out. 'Irma, you're my friend. The least you could do is be a little more open about what you're saying.'

'You haven't been open to me. Or to Lewis. How do you think he'd feel, going off to war, knowing you were fraternising with the enemy?'

'With the Germans?'

'You know who I mean.'

'Not yet.'

'With that horrible man.'

Alice gave her a puzzled look. 'Are you talking about Mahommed?'

'Don't pretend. You know exactly who.'

'If you are talking about him, he's not the enemy. He's as loyal as any of us, probably more so.'

Irma scoffed. 'How could he be?'

'Easily. Some of the men are Indian, and British subjects to boot. I think you've got a nerve suggesting any of them are traitors.'

'Lots of people think they are.'

'Then they're wrong. Mahommed's never said a single word against England.' She was sure it was true. But it occurred to her that she had never heard him say a word in favour of England, either.

Irma said, 'Whatever he is, he's still a dirty Afghan.'

'What am I, then? A miner's daughter and a nurse's help, which makes me no better than a drudge. Why shouldn't I care about him?'

'Because he's beneath you.'

'Oh, well, you'd know. You spend your time with a man who occupies himself by rubbing his nose in other people's poo!'

Irma looked at her as though she'd been struck. 'He does not, he's the Sanitary Inspector!'

'There's a difference?'

'Of course there is.'

Alice could feel her crumbling. She knew she should stop, but she wanted to punish her for saying what she had said. For putting thoughts in her mind that had no place there.

She could see Irma's lower lip trembling, working up to something. 'There's a huge difference.'

'What?'

'A really big one.'

'Then what *is* it?'

'I don't know!' She started to cry, overwhelmed by her ignorance, and Alice's attack. 'I ... don't ... know ...'

Alice moved to her and gave her a comforting hug. 'Never mind,' she said. 'It's often better not to.'

She moved quietly and pulled the hessian flap closed behind her. She would have a little time, she thought, before the children alerted anyone to her presence.

Zainie, delighted by the invitation, had shyly accepted. She had never been asked to a party in the town before; none of the children had. Alice had to repeat the invitation a number of times before the reality of it sank in. She told her where the house was, and suggested Gool Mahommed could bring them. Zainie nodded in agreement with this, and ran off to find the other children, to tell them what good fortune had come their way.

She hadn't meant to spy. She simply wanted to see Mahommed again and she thought he might be inside. It was only once she was there that she acknowledged something else was tugging her.

She knelt down to look at the newspaper headlines. There were no new ones. The latest one was from

November, claiming that the Russians had overthrown the Turkish front in the Erzerum district. She had seen it on her earlier visit. It meant nothing.

She held her breath to listen. There was a hum of distant voices; nothing close by. The only voice she could hear was the one in her head.

She knelt on the rug and pulled up the edge. There was only soil underneath. She should go. This was wrong. She should go and never think these thoughts again.

She felt under his bedding; looked in his case. Clean clothes, a length of muslin, a book – the Qur'an, his bible. Her shame grew.

She would leave. Now. He did not deserve this. She looked under his pillow. The cushion by the bed. She lifted it, and was about to let it drop again, when she saw the letter. It was addressed to Mahommed. She had gone too far to stop. She opened it. It was some form of official communication, the writing full of curls and loops that meant nothing to her. She looked at the postmark on the envelope and saw that it was recent. It was a letter, nothing more. Why shouldn't he receive one?

'What are you doing?'

She scrunched the letter in her hand, balling it up, and turned to face Mahommed, standing in the doorway. He wasn't accusing, merely puzzled.

She told him about the birthday party, the invitation for the children. She made the letter even smaller, holding her hand behind her back as she embellished the details of the invitation, trying to cover her crime with words.

He moved to her and kissed her. He drowned the sound of her lies. He found the hand clenched around the letter and gripped it, dragging it between them. He prised open her fingers and pulled the letter out.

She watched in silence as he smoothed it out and put it to one side.

He turned back to her. She was silent, ashamed.

'Why?'

The room was filled with her anxiety. There was nowhere she could hide it.

She thought of Lewis, kneeling down to pull off their father's boots. Lewis, tenderly putting him to bed. Saying, with no hint of resentment, 'It's my job.'

She said, 'Lewis is going overseas to fight, and it's possible he'll be hurt or even die. And if that happens I don't think I could live with myself if I was, if I'd been … fraternising … with someone who might think that his dying was a good thing.'

He said nothing so she kept going, her voice shaking. 'I know you've got no reason to like him, but that's not the same as … Well, we're all cheering for our troops, and England too because … because they're fighting for us, so we have to.'

She was getting muddled. She thought of Belgium. The papers never mentioned Belgium any more. She couldn't remember what had happened to it. Maybe it had drowned, stamped under the ocean by the march of German feet.

She wished he wouldn't keep looking at her like that. She only knew she couldn't leave without knowing. She said, 'Mahommed? Are you loyal?'

He looked at her directly. 'Yes. Always.'

'Who to?'

'To those who have a right to my loyalty.'

'Does that include England?' She didn't care about England, she cared about Lewis. But that was the same, wasn't it?

He dodged the question. 'It includes you. It includes Scotland, which was your first home.'

'And England?'

Mahommed turned from her to look at the soap wrappers on his wall. He said, 'England has produced some very fine soap.'

Her face tightened. He had insulted her. 'Who is the letter from?'

He turned to face her. 'The Turkish army.'

She struggled to understand things she didn't want to understand. 'You *are* a traitor ...'

'No. Never. That is what I am not.'

'Then say it, say you're loyal to England! Please say it, say it for me, I need to hear it!' She could feel her bones pushing against her skin. She thought, I am ugly, you have made me ugly.

He said, 'My feelings for England are ... that it has put a great deal of pink on maps and ... many people say it is a very fine colour ...'

She began to cry. 'How can you do this to me? You know I can't have anything to do with you now, not any more.'

He said, 'There are many motor cars in England and it is a land of green rolling hills.'

'Say it!'

He wouldn't.

She avoided his eyes as she pushed past him. He made no attempt to stop her.

27

She lay curled in her bed, her quilt pulled over her. Outside it must have been nearly a hundred degrees. When she had gone out earlier, the day was already shimmering through a liquid heat haze. It was only slightly better inside. The white-painted metal walls reflected some of the heat, but most of it seeped through. Even with the doors thrown open it would stay, thick and unwelcome, long after midnight.

She was cold under the quilt; shivering. She knew it couldn't be coming from outside. It must be from her, cold all the way inside. Was that how her mother had felt? She had been trapped by her husband's dreams in a desert country she hated. Going to bed with a headache might have been a release for her. It was time that didn't have to be lived through.

Alice drifted, trying not to think. She had called him a traitor. But what was she? She'd never been to England, she didn't love it, so why should he? She didn't know how a war could start from an archduke being shot. She didn't even know what an archduke was. She knew he wasn't English, and neither was the man who shot him, so why did England need Lewis to go and fight?

Thinking didn't help. Thinking just left you with a mass of untidy information. She loved Lewis, and always would. She loved Eileen, and always would. She loved Mahommed, but had to find a way of stopping that love.

She wished the word *traitor* held more power over her. It would be easier then.

'Alice? Are you alright?'

It was Eileen, home from school. Alice hadn't heard her come in. She came out from under the quilt and sat up. Alice saw the concern in her sister's eyes. Eileen expected Alice to be at work, at the hospital. Not lying in bed, shivering under a hot quilt.

'Yes.' She forced a brightness into her voice. 'I was a little unwell before, but I'm alright now.'

She made herself get up. She asked Eileen to go to the hospital to make her excuses to Matron Guthrie. By the time she was back, there would be a pot of tea ready.

When she had gone, Alice looked at the bed, wanting to crawl back in. It wasn't warmth she craved, but blackness. In the light she could see herself; she didn't like what she saw.

She went into the kitchen to make the pot of tea.

Alice came out from Millers, carrying a neatly wrapped parcel. Inside was a cotton blouse with a white sailor collar, discounted on price, on account of Lewis. She had taken time choosing it. It was pretty, it would suit Eileen. Most of her clothes were home-made or hand-me-downs, and Alice wanted her to have something new. With Lewis away, their family had shrunk to two and she didn't want Eileen to dwell on it. There was also two shillings Lewis had given to Alice before he left. Enough to make a birthday. She didn't feel like celebrating, but Eileen didn't need to know that.

She was just about to turn out of Argent Street when her eye was caught by a blue uniform. She tried to pretend she hadn't seen it, but it was too late.

Keith hurried to greet her. 'Alice … how lovely to see you.'

He seemed genuinely pleased to see her. She had avoided him since the cricket match, but she couldn't ignore him now. She replied as best she could to his pleasantries about the weather, about Christmas, about Lewis. When the conversation looked like drying up, he indicated the parcel. 'You've been shopping.'

'A blouse. For Eileen's birthday. She's having a party on Saturday afternoon.'

'Really, a party? Then you'll need help.'

'No, I can manage. It's only a handful of children … they can entertain themselves.'

'But without Lewis there …'

She could see he had already made the decision. That what she wanted would make no difference. She made one last try, knowing it would achieve nothing.

'You're busy. I don't want to trouble you.'

'It's no trouble. It'll be my pleasure.'

After ascertaining the time of the party, he took his leave, and Alice was at last free to go home. Once there she unwrapped the blouse and spread it on Eileen's bed while she looked at it. It lay there, limp and unappealing. She no longer thought it was pretty.

Zainie fidgeted, unused to the attention she was receiving. Edith took firm hold of her chin. 'Sit still, or you'll end up with berry stain all over your dress instead of on your mouth.'

Zainie stole a look at Ibram and Partimah, sitting on the bench next to her. They were already in their finest; Edith had dressed them first.

Edith gave her a pinch. 'Did you hear what I just said?'

She frowned as she concentrated on the now compliant Zainie. She wasn't going to muck this job up, not for anything, because apart from anything else, she loved Zainie.

She wasn't her blood daughter. She didn't know what had happened to Nita, Zainie's mother, although there were rumours she'd gone drinking with some of the miners; when she returned a week later with her tail between her legs, she was no longer welcome. Edith didn't know if that was true, nor how the separation between Nita and her children had been effected, but when she arrived at the camp six years ago, Nita was no longer there.

She hadn't planned to stay either. Only long enough to work out where to go next. But Jemadar, finding her on the outskirts of the camp, had brought the children to her, making it clear that looking after them would be the price of a meal.

Ibram, barely two at the time, was crying; Zainie, four, was silent, her eyes planted firmly on the ground. But when Jemadar left, Zainie had lifted her eyes to Edith, and surprised her with a great big smile, one that she interpreted as, 'You'll do.' She decided Zainie would do, too, and, once Partimah was born, she decided the same about Jemadar.

Although she hadn't admitted it to anyone, in many ways life was easier now he was dead. She wasn't interested in studying the Qur'an and now it could remain shut, casually tossed into a corner of their home. Ibram had made a brief show of disapproving of this disrespect, but when no-one paid him any attention he quickly forgot about it.

Another thing, there was no more marriage talk. She had not been included in the discussions but she knew Jemadar had talked to Sherdil and two of the other men about Zainie's bride price. They had no wives; they would pay well for a half-Afghan girl. Zainie wasn't averse to the idea of marriage, mainly because she had no idea what it entailed, but Edith knew, and had shooed the men away.

She had become bossy without Jemadar. She was now the sole owner of his money tin. There wasn't a lot in there, but enough to counter the temptations of a bride price. She told the men she was in charge now and the girl wasn't marrying anyone, not for at least a couple of years, thank you all the same.

Mahommed had gone to get the horse ready, which was just as well. He had a nerve trying to tell her the children shouldn't go; that things had changed. Edith thought something was going on between Mahommed and that lady, but that didn't give him the right to upset the children. She didn't care why they'd been asked, only that they had been.

She finished with Zainie's mouth and began to outline her eyes with Jemadar's leftover kohl. She wasn't going to have anyone say these children weren't beautiful. She'd gone to town earlier and bought a cake of soap. She'd bought paper, too; had wrapped the soap up nicely. They didn't go to parties every day; they were going to do it right. She'd also bought some tinsel. She thought she would hang it up while the children were out. Blow Jemadar; he was dead. If she wanted to celebrate Christmas, she would.

She moved on to the other eye. Zainie was beautiful, no doubt about it. No wonder they all wanted to marry her.

Their chatter died down as the horse pulled the ice-cream cart into Cobalt Lane. Mahommed could feel their nervousness. He had tried to dissuade them from going, but had been no match for Edith.

He stopped the horse three doors from Alice's house. He did not want to be seen. He moved to the back of the cart and jumped off, reaching up to help Partimah down, and straightened her dress as Ibram and Zainie clambered down after her.

He looked over at the house. He knew by the children's silence that it would take little to change their minds about going in. It angered him that they were so afraid. At the camp Partimah never stopped talking, even when admonished to do so. Zainie was fearless, Ibram bold.

He pointed at Alice's house. 'It's that one.'

Zainie nodded, too frozen to answer him.

Mahommed transferred Partimah's hot hand from his own to Zainie's, and indicated the present she carried in her other. 'You give that to Eileen.'

'I need to do a wee.'

Mahommed looked around him. If Zainie did it in the open, someone might see her and chase her off.

'Can you wait?'

She nodded again.

Mahommed fought the urge to gather them up again and drive off. It was a party. They had nothing to fear from a party. He gave them an encouraging push. 'Go on. They're expecting you.'

He watched as they walked slowly to the closed front door. It was only small, but it loomed over them, dwarfing them. Zainie looked back. Mahommed nodded at her from behind the cart and mimed with his fist, indicating she should knock.

★

Keith had arrived early, and made a fuss over Eileen. Alice could see he would have rather made a fuss over her but she held herself apart from him. She didn't want to be rude but she didn't want to give him the chance to broach the subject of romance.

She wasn't even sure why he wanted her to like him. Possibly it was something to do with the fact that there weren't many available young women in Broken Hill. There were prostitutes – Cobalt Street was full of them – but she could hardly tell him to look there. And of course she knew Lewis had extracted a promise from him to look after her and Eileen, so that was mixed into it as well.

She began buttering scones, putting them on a plate while he hovered. Eileen had left them alone; she was in the bedroom, getting ready.

'I'll put them on the table for you.' He was already reaching for them, wanting something to do.

'Alright. Thank you.'

As he took the plate from her she saw him glance at the cuffs of her blouse. Well, good. If he noticed they were dirty he would realise she wouldn't be much use looking after him.

She looked around the kitchen, trying to think what else needed to be done. She was already exhausted from the morning's baking, although she hadn't done much – some scones and pikelets, and the icing for the cake that she had baked yesterday. A few months ago it would have been nothing to her.

She wished the party were over. She wanted everyone gone before they were here; she wanted to lie in bed with her mind empty. Instead she was in the kitchen, thinking about Mahommed.

She went out to the parlour, where Keith praised her for the festive appearance of the table. She thanked him. Along these lines they managed to keep some sort of conversation going for a few minutes. Then he asked her about the party. Who was coming?

She went through the list of Eileen's friends. 'There might be two or three others,' she added vaguely, trying to make it sound of no importance.

'What others?'

'It's possible that some of the children from the camp might come.'

'Why would they do that?'

'Because we asked them.' *Because I asked them,* thought Alice. *Because I wanted an excuse to see Mahommed. Because I didn't know then what I know now.*

'Was that a good idea?'

Alice, busying herself with the table, explained they

had been generous to Eileen and her friends after the funeral. 'But I don't think they'll come.'

She hoped that was true, that Mahommed would have disallowed it. If they came they might mention him, and she didn't want that. Ever since she had made the invitation she had searched for ways to unmake it, but they had all involved a no longer possible journey out to the camp.

'Alice … they could just be rumours, but …'

She interrupted him. 'I don't listen to rumours, do you?'

'Do you know what side the Afghans are on?'

'No. How would I?'

'Do you think Lewis would be happy about them being in his house?'

She hesitated. 'I don't know. He's not here to ask.'

'But if he were?'

'He's not!' She heard the shrillness in her voice. But what did he want her to answer? The truth? That Lewis would be appalled?

'I'm only saying what I've heard.'

'Does it matter? They're just children.'

'It matters if they're traitors.'

'In that case, when they arrive you can interrogate them.'

'Alice, this isn't a simple matter.'

'Then make it simple, do what you like!'

Eileen came out from the bedroom, wearing her new blouse.

'That looks lovely on you,' said Keith.

Eileen looked at Alice, ignoring the compliment. 'Who are you talking about?'

'No-one.'

'You must have been talking about someone.'

Keith answered for her. 'We were talking about Lewis. About how he would have liked to be here today.'

There was a knock at the front door, soft, hardly a knock at all. Keith looked at her, and when he moved to the door, she didn't protest.

As he opened the door, she caught a glimpse of them. Zainie, in the middle, with the two younger ones pressed against her, doing their best to be invisible. The little girl with her face pushed into Zainie's dress, too afraid to even look at Keith. The three of them, beautiful and terrified. It would only take one step. She could join Keith at the door, smile at the children, calm their fears, invite them in.

Eileen, next to her, plucked at her sleeve, wanting answers. Alice put an arm around her and shepherded her away from the door. 'Later,' she said.

28

Mahommed watched from behind the ice-cream cart, to make sure the children were safely inside. He also hoped for a glimpse of Alice, though he knew it would cause him pain. He saw the door open, saw the policeman emerge and talk to the children. Alice had told him the policeman meant nothing to her. But now he was in her house. Mahommed was outside it.

Mahommed struggled to hear what was being said, but the policeman's voice reached him as meaningless sound. He felt an all too familiar anxiety. It should have been a simple sequence of events – the door opening, the children being welcomed and ushered inside – so why were they still on the doorstep?

He crept forward, not wanting to be seen. He could have misunderstood the situation, in which case advertising his presence would do no-one any good. But the children were in his care; Edith would rightly hold him responsible for any harm that might befall them. There were bushes in front of the house next door; they would do to screen him.

Partimah had her head still buried in Zainie's dress as the policeman, smiling, leaned towards them. He said, 'I'm afraid there's been a bit of a mistake. It's not your fault, but the party's only for children from the neighbourhood.'

Mahommed saw Zainie pull back as the policeman reached into his pocket. He wasn't wearing his uniform, but she would have known who he was; Edith had pointed him out as someone who could put them in gaol.

'It's alright,' he said. 'I've got something for you.'

He brought out three pennies and pressed one into each of their hands. 'One for you, one for you, and one for you because you're so pretty.' This last comment was addressed to Partimah. He had to prise her fingers open.

'Go on, then. Off you go.'

The children stayed where they were, immobilised by fear. Mahommed did the same. He had all the information he needed about what was going on, but he wasn't ready to assemble it in the right order. He continued to watch as Zainie held the present out to the policeman.

He said, 'No, you keep it. It wouldn't be fair otherwise.'

She lowered it, holding it awkwardly in front of her. The policeman's smile had become a grimace, as though it were hurting him. He said, 'I've got to get back inside, so you've got to go, alright?' He spoke carefully and slowly, as if he wasn't sure they understood.

Zainie stayed where she was, as did Ibram and Partimah.

The policeman stopped smiling. He shouted at them. 'Go away! *Now!*' He shut the door in their faces.

Mahommed gave up his hiding place and began to run towards them. He was too late to stop Zainie from taking two steps back, lifting the present, and hurling it at the door as hard as she could. It made contact with a loud crack, and the soap inside tore through the wrapping paper, leaving a pink wax dent on the door before bouncing off and falling to the dirt below. In his hurry, Mahommed barely noticed it, stepping on it as he reached the children, grinding it further into the ground.

He picked Partimah up under one arm and hustled Ibram back towards the ice-cream cart, but Zainie shrugged him off. She marched ahead of them, refusing to meet Mahommed's eyes, refusing to acknowledge her moment of triumph had dissolved before she'd even had time to taste it.

★

Halfway home, Mahommed pulled the horse to a halt, wanting to check on the children. They each had a hand tightly wrapped around the penny they'd been given. Zainie's eyes were stone. Mahommed reached out, wanting to give her comfort, but she drew into herself.

He said, gently, 'It was a misunderstanding. Nothing more.'

Zainie was not fooled by the lie. She held her clenched hand over the side of the cart, and let the penny drop onto the dust below. She turned to Ibram, who tightened his grip on his penny, resentful of what she was trying to make him do. He held out as long as he could.

Mahommed said, 'No, it is yours, you must keep it, please keep it.'

A penny for what had been done to them. They could at least have a penny, couldn't they?

Ibram opened his hand. The penny fell, joining Zainie's in the dust.

A penny would buy nothing. Some sweets, pencils, a ribbon for Partimah's hair. A brief moment when the hurt could be forgotten. Couldn't they have a penny?

Zainie and Ibram turned to Partimah. They began to wrestle the coin from her grasp.

She shut her eyes and gripped it tight.

'No no!'

As Ibram prised her fingers open, Mahommed turned his head away, not wanting them to see the tears welling in his eyes. He began to weep openly. He wept for children who were worth only a penny. He wept for Abdullah's dignity; for the letter he had kept secret from him, for his own lack of faith, for his cowardice. He wept for the workmates who never once spoke his name; for his failure to learn the meaning of coagulation; for the disdain in Lewis's eyes. The shipping empire without ships, the department stores never built, the ice-creams never sold. He wept for the memory of Alice's body next to his. He wept for hope. He wept for himself.

'Noooo!'

He looked up at Partimah's scream; saw through his tears her fingers opening one by one. It was her penny; the policeman gave it to her, why should she give it up? Her mouth was already open from the scream; she closed it on her brother's shoulder, biting down hard.

Ibram yelped in pain and pulled back, falling against the side of the cart. He turned to Zainie to complain but she had lost interest. She was looking at Mahommed, his shoulders still heaving.

Partimah and Ibram watched as Zainie moved towards him, the penny forgotten. 'Gool Mahommed?'

He continued to weep.

He heard Ibram say, 'He's crying.'

'Why?' asked Partimah.

Zainie jumped off the cart and began to scrabble in the dust for her coin. She found it and ran to the front of the cart, holding it out for Mahommed to see. 'Look, here it is.'

Mahommed stared at it, seeing nothing, seeing only his dreams dying.

Partimah plucked at his shirt, opening her fist to show him her penny. 'It's alright. I've still got mine.'

Mahommed kept crying.

Partimah looked at the coin in her hand. She hurled the penny to the road. 'No, I haven't. See?'

As she realised what she had done, she began to wail, already in mourning for the only penny she had ever owned.

He couldn't let Partimah keep crying. He controlled his own tears and soothed hers into some sort of quiet. He took her and the other two children home, and put them back in Edith's care. Abdullah was nowhere to be seen. He didn't look for him. He unhitched the cart, setting the horse free in the paddock, and went back to his shack.

He wept again.

What sort of people were they? Their rules, their laws, their show of civilisation, their fine clothes, their money – they had everything already. What pleasure could be had from wounding the hearts of children? And Alice, *her*, she had called him a traitor when the only treachery was hers. She had been with him here in this shack, clinging to him, whispering *I love you I love you I love you* with the words flowing from her *I love you* and through him, binding them together *I love you*. She was nothing but a whore, speaking whore's lies. Was she thinking of the policeman then, were the words meant for him, was she lying with him now?

He calmed himself. She was nothing, why weep for nothing? She was no different from the rest of them.

They are all the same, he thought. They start wars and they kill us without question. They think we are nothing, and that we deserve less. And we let them think that, which is why we are powerless, forced to live like this, like the camels, like animals, they want to kick us and we let them, I let them, I almost begged them to do it, I could see the knives in their hands but still I begged them.

He felt the tears begin to prick again. The hard ball of anger he'd been growing had somehow got sidetracked into self-flagellation, which was leading to self-pity – not somewhere he cared to go.

He looked around him, wanting to take his mind off his own faults. There was nothing much to see beyond the corrugations of the iron walls. Only the newspaper headlines and the soap wrappers.

He stared at the Lifebuoy wrapper. Even that was a lie, in what way could it be a lifebuoy? He narrowed his eyes, giving the wrapper the full force of his contempt, and spat, sending a gob of saliva towards it. It hit its mark and splattered before starting to dribble down off the paper.

In between the spitting and the dribbling down, Mahommed found what he was looking for.

Treachery. He would show them treachery.

He began to call for Abdullah.

Abdullah stood, reading the letter.

'Well?' said Mahommed.

Abdullah didn't seem to be sharing his excitement. He refolded the letter and handed it back to him. 'You received this weeks ago. And you are only showing it to me now?'

'Yes, yes, I know, it was an error, an inexcusable one, and I ask your forgiveness, but Abdullah, did you read it?'

Abdullah shrugged. 'The Sultan called you … *weeks* ago … to fight. But you have no money and I have no money. How does the letter change anything?'

'It obliges me to fight. To avenge the injustices done to us.'

'But without money, how can you go there? The war is many miles over the ocean.'

Mahommed could barely contain himself. He said, 'No, Abdullah. It isn't.'

Abdullah frowned. 'Then where is it?'

Mahommed leaned forward, his eyes shining. He made the words wait until he was sure Abdullah was ready for them. 'It's here. We will bring it here.'

The fire was crackling, burning high from the extra logs Mahommed had dragged onto it. Zainie threw a soap wrapper towards it. 'Goodbye, Mr Rexona!'

Ibram threw another. 'Goodbye, Mr Alpine!'

Partimah jumped up and down, clutching a soap wrapper, waiting for her turn. She threw it on the fire. 'Goodbye, Mr ...'

Mahommed helped her out. 'Goodbye, Mr Cuticura!'

He watched with her as the chemicals in the wrapper burned bright yellow and green.

It was Zainie's turn again. She didn't know why they were doing it, but she liked it. 'Goodbye, Mr Lifebuoy!'

Sherdil was watching from outside his shack. He moved over to Abdullah and asked him what Mahommed was doing. Abdullah told him he had discovered fire.

Ibram threw the last wrapper. 'Goodbye, Mr Puritol!'

They looked at Mahommed, excited. Burning things made up for the party. They wanted to keep doing it. He told them there was nothing more.

Then he remembered something. He told them to watch the fire and hurried inside. He found his case and pulled out the muslin. His second shirt. His Qur'an. Beneath them all was what he was looking for.

He grabbed it and ran back to the children. He hurled it onto the flames and shouted, 'Goodbye, Mr Doyley!'

The children watched as the little white disc hovered above the flames. It buckled in on itself and burst into a bright ball of fire, sending a Catherine wheel of sparks scattering into the air around it. And then it was gone.

Later that night, when Abdullah was asleep, Mahommed went to the paddock to check on his horse. She was silhouetted against the moonlight, dozing, her head drooping low. At his approach she raised her head to look at him, as though wondering if something was now required of her. He stroked the long muscle under her jaw, soothing that thought from her head. He whispered in her ear that the time was not now. But it would come soon. When it came, she must be ready.

As he stroked her, he looked up at the sky. He remembered another night long ago when he had come from below deck and looked up at the stars. He had been struck by the vastness of the universe and had vowed he would grow to meet it. He understood now that he had been wrong. It was not his place to meet it.

He must serve it.

29

Adrian felt the tightness in Irma's neck and shoulders under his gently kneading hands. 'Please relax, Miss Cowie.'

Irma leaned her head back, trying to do as instructed.

'You are on an island of calm. Around you, the seas are rough, with white caps blown wild by the cruel wind. The sky is dark, threatening. Thunder roars, lightning cracks. The storm rages overhead. The trees beneath are battered by the onslaught. But you, Miss Cowie, are safe. Safely enveloped in the warm embracing arms of Mother Earth. What are you?'

'Safe …'

'Of course you are. Safe and secure in the knowledge that no harm will befall you.'

As her head lolled back, Adrian felt a familiar warmth spreading in his groin. He would have liked to push her head down on to it.

She had come to his rooms, flustered, her plump cheeks rosy red. Her weekly appointment was not due for two more days but she was hoping he might be able to find time for her. It was the disparity between her divisions; they were overwhelming her even more than usual. She wondered if perhaps she needed another dose of his wonderful tonic?

Life, she said, was troubling her greatly. She was even more worried for Robert than before, if that were possible. There would be days when he was almost the man he was before his illness, but they were inevitably followed by a relapse. She was concerned that no-one at his office knew the nature of his illness. She would never betray his confidence, but twice last week he had been so sick he was unable to go to work. It was courageous of him to suffer so silently, but she was afraid his illness might not be understood, especially when his workload was so heavy.

She studied him, building up to a difficult question. 'Mr Kadran, Chief Sanitary Inspector is a very important job, is it not?'

Adrian had forgotten how stupid she was. 'Yes, Miss Cowie. Extremely important.'

'It doesn't have anything to do with' – she looked down delicately – 'lavatories?'

'Certainly not.' This was obviously the required answer, so he gave it. He assured her that it was a very high government post. It was in many ways akin to his own calling, in that both professions dealt with the higher echelons of scientific enquiry.

She was pleased with the explanation. It was, she said, as she had thought. It was largely why she was so concerned for him.

She opened her bag and took out a small blue bottle. 'I hope you don't think I was snooping, but I found three of these in Robert's briefcase. All empty.'

Adrian made a show of examining what he already knew to be a chlorodyne bottle. Chlorodyne was cheap – the Afghans sometimes used it when they ran out of *bhang.* Not that he was about to share that with Irma.

'It's a worrying development.'

'Is it medicine?'

'Of an inferior kind. And not prescribed by me.'

'Then why would Robert take it?'

'Because he's a very brave man. His pain is clearly much greater than he has admitted.' He went on to tell her such courage was admirable, but the prescription of medicine was an exact science, and Robert was possibly complicating the problem.

He praised her for her efforts, assuring her that her information would help him cure Robert faster. He told her that what she was doing was not snooping. It was a pure expression of love.

Encouraged by this, Irma informed him of a new symptom, possibly also related to Robert's illness. He had become incapable of making decisions. There was one big decision she knew he wanted to make, one that would please them both, but for some reason it seemed beyond him to make it, even though it was nearly Christmas and the year was practically over. She would be twenty soon. She couldn't be expected to wait forever. She felt so alone. Even her closest friend had turned against her, revealing herself to be of lesser character than Irma had previously thought.

Adrian stopped himself from smiling as the misery tumbled out. Not that she amused him; he thought her complaints tedious. But the more tedious she became, the more attractive he found her. Her lower lip was swollen where she'd been worrying it with her teeth. He noticed that her mouth hid a small overbite. His mind wandered, imagining the uses that overbite could be put to.

He had no intention of letting it go too far; experience had taught him the dangers of that. But a chaste therapeutic massage could do no harm. Unlike

Robert Brosnan, he understood the importance of discipline.

Irma needed little persuasion. She agreed that her nervous pathways needed clearing. If Mr Kadran could clear them, she would be grateful.

He could feel her dozing off, partly due to the massage and partly the measured dose of tonic he had administered, as requested. He continued to work her neck and shoulders, careful not to let his hands stray any lower, despite the inviting softness of the flesh beneath her blouse. But her head lolling against him lowered his defences. He moved his body closer to her chair, rhythmically matching the movements of the massage. He shut his eyes, conjuring another plump-limbed girl from Melbourne, long ago. That experience could not be repeated, not with Irma. Under no circumstances, definitely not. But oh, it would be nice, oh yes oh yes …

'Mr Kadran? I think that would be enough for now.'

What on earth was he doing? He gave a couple of extra hard kneads to signal the end of the massage and moved back round the desk to the safety of his own chair. Had she noticed anything? He studied her manner. It seemed unchanged.

She thanked him for clearing her pathways. She wished him a happy Christmas and he did the same to her. They made polite small talk for a few minutes and then she left.

Adrian locked the door after her. He moved back to his chair and sat. He was feeling tense. He undid the buttons of his fly and began to think of Irma's small pointed teeth.

Robert lay in bed, trying to bat away thoughts of Irma. She had been particularly tiresome lately. At first he had thought it a good idea that she consult Adrian, that it might quiet her. Initially she had been full of praise for him. Apparently Adrian mixed her a tonic each week. Nothing like his own, of course, simply – as Adrian explained to him – a mixture of health essences suitable for clearing the hysteria that young women were prone to.

For a while she seemed to improve, so much so that he even began to reconsider their relationship. Instead of complaining about his lack of attentiveness, as she had been wont to do, she became thoughtful and solicitous.

It wasn't until the last week that her conversation began to be peppered with vague criticisms of Adrian. Nothing specific, but she was apparently troubled by a feeling that all was not as it should be. When Robert tried to pin her down the best she could come up with was that to her mind Adrian was a little too, well, *Indian*.

This irritated Robert. He needed Adrian Kadran. He was the only medical man who had any idea how to treat his ailment, and if Irma thought her ill-considered misgivings were going to persuade him otherwise, she could think again.

The more he thought about it, the more he came to the conclusion that Irma had to go. Not because of her ongoing refusal to allow him more than the chastest of kisses, but because he was finding the idea of remaining a bachelor more and more appealing. He had made an inventory, weighing up the evenings spent in Irma's company against the evenings spent on his own. Evenings with Irma had a depressing sameness about them, and usually ended with a coy reference to their future. On the other hand, his solitary evenings, with only a pen and paper for company, were a source of intense pleasure.

He sat up. He couldn't go back to sleep, not with those Christmas bells clanging. Anyway, despite Reverend Piercey not being the most inspirational speaker, he had to go to morning service. Apart from Irma and her family, there would be others there he knew. Due to his illness and the pressures of work he had neglected his social obligations. It would be a chance to wish everyone a merry Christmas.

He forced himself out of bed, and showered and shaved. He dressed, putting on his last clean shirt. He was about to head off when he remembered he had not yet wrapped Irma's present. He had bought her a linen handkerchief and one almost the same for her mother. Irma's handkerchief had an 'I' worked in one corner and her mother's a 'D'. He knew the handkerchief would not meet Irma's expectations but he didn't want to encourage her hopes with anything grander.

Once he found the handkerchiefs he realised he had forgotten to purchase paper with which to wrap them. There were no shops open so buying some was out of the question. The whole thing was a damned nuisance. Then he remembered he had some used paper in a drawer. Irma had wrapped his birthday manicure set in it. It was blue, probably not appropriate for Christmas, but if he was lucky she wouldn't notice.

The paper was not large, but if he was careful he could make it stretch to two handkerchiefs. He took the scissors from the manicure set – the first time he had used them – put the paper on a table and began to cut it into equal halves. The scissors were small and curved; cutting with them required more manual dexterity than he had assumed. He was holding the paper with one hand and cutting with the other when his two hands met and he stabbed himself.

He yelped and pulled his hand away, tearing the paper in the process, leaving a ragged edge.

He examined the wounded finger. No serious damage, but it was beginning to bleed. He was deciding what to do about it when a drop of blood rolled over the side of his finger and fell onto the paper below.

He stared at it in dismay, sucking his finger to stop any more blood falling. The droplet hadn't spread yet; if he mopped it up straight away he could stop it from soaking into the paper. It might not even leave a stain. He didn't want to leave it to find a cloth; in the time he took to do that the blood would soak in. He pulled out his shirt tail and, using one end, tried to blot it up. Under pressure from the shirt tail the blood droplet, until now a perfect sphere, collapsed and spread out over the paper.

He pulled the shirt tail away and surveyed the damage. This was all Irma's fault; he hadn't wanted to buy her a present in the first place. He wiped his hand over his shirt front, leaving a streak of blood behind. He turned back to the blood on the paper. There was still time to limit the damage. He leaned down to lick the blood off, doing his best not to spread it any further, and was hit by a sharp pain in his abdomen.

He doubled over, clutching himself until the pain subsided to a manageable level. He hoped he wasn't going to have a bout of his illness today; that was the last thing he needed. He shook the thought off; it was probably just some chemical in the paper.

He looked at it again. The worst of the bloodstain was off, but now there was a pale brown circle taking its place. He calmed himself. If he scraped off the top part of the paper it would be dry underneath and no-one would be any the wiser.

Using the nail of his forefinger, he began to scrape off the top layer. He worked slowly, scraping from the outside of the circle towards the centre. The scraped area wasn't as smooth as the rest but at least it was clean and white. One last little bit to do. Just a little scraping there and …

He felt his fingernail scrape wood before he realised what he was doing. He lifted the finger and saw a circle of timber showing through the paper where he'd completely scraped it away. Fuck it. And fuck Irma too – not that there had ever been any chance of that.

Well, it would have to do. If he held his finger over the hole in the paper as he handed it over it would probably go unnoticed. And if it didn't, too bad. There was a limit to the amount of effort he was prepared to go to. All he had to do now was wrap the handkerchiefs in the two pieces of paper and glue the ends down.

He had no glue. He thought about it for a moment, refusing to let it add to his distress. He had flour. He could make a paste of flour and water and use that to glue the paper, then wait till it dried, and … fuck it, fuck it, fuck it. What he really needed was a small dose of tonic. He usually tried not to do that so early in the day, but it wasn't his fault all this was happening.

He took out his watch. Ten minutes to ten. He didn't have time for the tonic, not if he was to get to the church in time for the service.

He thought of what the Reverend Piercey might say in his sermon. The usual about mangers and no room at the inn and how they could all draw lessons from that. Something about the gifts from the three wise men and how the monetary value of those gifts was not the point. Well, exactly. It was the thought that counted. Everyone knew that.

There was no point in going, feeling the way he was. The sensible thing would be to take some tonic; just enough to calm him. He'd have time to glue the paper and let it dry properly. He'd go straight from home to Irma's and arrive in a comfortable and relaxed frame of mind. Yes, that was the best plan.

He unscrewed the top from the tonic bottle. He thought about finding his measuring glass but decided that was unnecessary. He lifted the bottle to his lips and took a sip, holding the precious liquid in his mouth before allowing it to float sweetly down his throat.

★

'Irma, love, sulking won't help.'

Irma looked up from fiddling with the Christmas decorations. 'I'm not sulking.'

Irma's mother looked at her husband, trying to soften his irritation. 'It won't hurt to wait a few minutes more.' She put a friendly arm around Eileen. 'How about you give me some help in the kitchen?'

Irma turned her attention back to the decorations. It was a bit much, her mother inviting Alice and Eileen. Irma hadn't wanted them there; she wanted it to be just family: her parents and Robert. Her mother had insisted, so Irma had no choice but to give in. She understood about being charitable and Alice and Eileen not having anyone else, but Alice had become peculiar lately and Irma didn't see why she should have her Christmas ruined by her presence.

Irma glanced at her, sitting in a chair by the window, looking out. She was wearing that dress, the one she'd made out of that horrible blue foreign material. Irma had told her it was common when she bought it in Adelaide, and had tried to steer her towards something more suitable, but as usual Alice had ignored her advice. The dress was completely inappropriate and Irma felt embarrassed at having to sit next to her in church. Not that Alice seemed to care. She hardly said a word, just sat there, and only spoke when she was asked a direct question. After the service, when everyone was talking about the beautiful sermon Reverend Piercey had given about the joy of giving, Alice just stood and looked off into the distance.

It wouldn't have bothered Irma so much if Robert had been there. He'd said he would be, and while she was waiting outside the church for the service to begin she'd told a number of people he'd be arriving shortly.

He didn't. She'd had to go into church without him, pretending nothing was amiss. Halfway through the service her mother had given her a sympathetic pat, which made her feel worse. Then she'd had to make excuses for him after the service, and even more once they'd gone home for Christmas lunch.

She'd felt sick inside. They were all pretending that Robert was unavoidably delayed; that he would soon arrive carrying a perfectly good reason for his lateness. Only Alice didn't pretend, but that, Irma thought, was because she hadn't even noticed he wasn't there. If she'd been a true friend, she would have done something to soothe the situation. Instead she continued to behave as she had at church.

Irma's father moved to the head of the table and pulled out his chair. 'Right, that's it. We're not waiting any longer.'

He sat, and when Irma's mother and Eileen were

back, he continued with his announcement. 'It's Christmas. We've got roast pork and corned lamb and plum pudding waiting, and I'm ready to carve. Robert needs to examine his behaviour, and if and when he deigns to join us, I'm going to tell him so.'

Irma didn't argue, meekly joining the others at the table. She bit her lip, trying not to cry in front of Alice. She had almost lost the battle when there was a knock at the door.

Her mother looked at her, encouraging, 'Go on. You answer it.'

Irma didn't need to be told twice. She pushed her chair back. Between that and the shut door she had a moment of pure happiness. It was Christmas. Robert was here. He was sick but now was well. He would make peace with her father. He would tell her father he loved her.

She opened the door.

Robert was on the step, swaying. He said, 'Happy Christmas.'

Irma stared at him. His shirt was hanging out. There were bloodstains down the front of it. There were other marks she couldn't identify, white and floury. His eyes were glassy. He held two crumpled blue parcels in his hand. The paper, stained with the same floury white marks, looked vaguely familiar.

He held one of the parcels out. 'This is for you.'

As she took it he leaned forward, attempting to kiss her cheek. She flinched, moving sideways to avoid him. His momentum carried him forward, and he tumbled into the living room and fell on his face in front of the others.

Irma looked at him for a moment. Then she stepped over him, walked into her bedroom, shut the door and began to cry. Despite her mother's entreaties, she stayed there, refusing to emerge for the rest of the day. She heard voices from the living room and, after an interval, Robert leaving. She opened the present he'd given her and saw it was a cheap handkerchief. She took the nail file from her manicure set – from Bebarfalds, the same make as the handsome set she'd given Robert – and stabbed the handkerchief with it a number of times, studding it with jagged holes. After an hour or two, she heard Alice and Eileen leave.

Her mother tapped gently at her door, and she allowed her to come in. She was carrying a handkerchief similar to the one Irma had stabbed. It had an 'I' embroidered on it. She said, 'I think this one's yours.'

30

All that noise, just to announce a birth.

Mahommed looked up from Alice's gun cabinet, distracted by the constant clamour. The church bells could clang all day if they wished, but their message would remain a lie. Although Jesus was an important prophet, to call him the son of Allah was nothing but blasphemy. He had been weak enough to be swayed by many of the ways of the English, but never that one. It was beyond his comprehension.

He thought about that for a while, doing his best to grow a sense of superiority. All the things they believed in … they were based on nothing but silly ideas. Whereas his beliefs …

He frowned. The soap. He had believed in the power of soap. But that was different. He'd been a child, a small boy in need of something to sustain him. On the other hand, the Holy Qur'an had been revealed as the true word of Allah by Gabriel, his Messenger, so …

He jiggled up and down, trying to find an explanation that would fit. It was being in the house, Alice's house. It was doing things to him. He didn't want to be here, he'd been afraid of the effect it would have on him. This morning when he woke, he felt sick, knowing he had to come here. He could have asked Abdullah to do it, but Abdullah didn't know where things were. He might have thought the request meant Mahommed was having second thoughts.

So … the Christians were wrong because the prophet Jesus had not had the Bible revealed to him, and had in fact written nothing, whereas the Prophet (peace be upon him) wrote down the words exactly as they were spoken by the Messenger, and therefore the words must be the truth.

He thought about it. There, that sounded right. But, how could he tell for sure? If everything was done through belief, how could he be absolutely sure what Allah was guiding him to do?

He jiggled again. Enough. It was only because he was inside the house. It was complicating things. Once he was outside things would be clear again.

He turned back to the gun cabinet. There was only one rifle in the cabinet and he recognised it instantly. It was a breech-loading Martini-Henry, similar to one he had used in the Turkish army. Although not as old as Abdullah's Snider, it had not been maintained; he would need to clean it. But it would do.

He meant to leave straight away; put the key back above the doorway, as he had seen Alice do, and go. She would not be back from church for hours, but there was no reason to stay. He took the gun and shut the cabinet. He was moving out when he noticed the door to her room was slightly ajar. He had been in the house only once before. He had not seen her room. *She means nothing to me now.* He repeated that twice to himself, reinforcing it. There was no harm in opening the door.

He saw the two beds. One must have been Eileen's; there was an old rag doll on the quilt. The other was Alice's. He reached out and touched her quilt. The cotton was faded and soft from many washings. Touching it made his heart thump. He put the gun to one side and lay on the bed, his head on her pillow. He pulled the quilt around him until it completely covered him. He breathed in the smell of her body. He turned his head face down on the pillow; breathed in the smell of her hair. Doing these things quietened the thumping of his heart.

He lay there for a long time. When he went back to the camp he did not tell Abdullah what he had done.

That night he dreamed he was a small child, sick with fever. His mother hovered, ministering to him with love. A man joined her. He thought it was his father, but it was Abdullah. He had come over the Khyber Pass from the Peshawar plains to bring him a book. 'These are lotches,' he said. 'They are lakes.'

He dreamed he was on Loch Ness, where the water looked like the ablution pool where Jemadar died. He was in a rowboat, rowing towards a man who was drowning. The man was Mehmed Resad, the Sultan of Turkey. His face belonged to Jemadar's son, Ibram, but that didn't change who he was. Above him were angels, protecting him. On the bank of the loch, Lewis was slitting the throat of a pig. Alice was watching. She had no eyes, but she watched. The blood ran into the water and spread towards the boat.

It was still dark when he woke. He lay quietly, thinking about the dream. After a while it scattered, and he couldn't think about it properly any more. His dreams were becoming more real, even though he still didn't know what they meant. They were also more frequent, leaching into daylight hours. Yesterday he had been grooming his horse when it became a giant bat, darkening the sky with its caped wings. It bared its teeth at the world and spread its wings, causing a wind so strong that it tore the earth. Then it disappeared, leaving only his horse. Mahommed didn't know why it had happened, but he wasn't frightened.

He turned on his side, looking at the sacking of the opposite wall. He had thought this shack a mark of his failure. He had come from the opposite side of the world to improve his life, and he had not done so. But now he understood that what he had suffered was not failure. He was being readied. Whatever the dreams meant, he knew they were being given to him to strengthen his resolve. The reasons could be found later. He pulled out the letter from the army, and read it again. In the gloom he could barely see, but he knew the words by heart. *The will of Allah will help you to be a true member, and to fight only for the Sultan.*

The Sultan was closer than any man to the heart of Allah. He wouldn't ask him to do anything that was wrong, would he?

The letter comforted him. It was the English who were wrong, they had to be. They wanted to destroy Turkey, for no other reason than to show they were powerful. His task was to show them they were not.

He got up from his bed and pulled aside the sacking of the doorway. The air was still, the night empty. Waiting to be filled.

He whispered to it. *Laa ilaaha illallaah.* Allah is great. The silence carried the whisper a long way. Soon it would be heard as a roar.

Laa ilaaha illallaah.

The empty bottle of Clements Tonic stood alone in the desert, resting on a small boulder. From a distance it shimmered in the late December heat, like a small glass bead, jumping from side to side.

Mahommed had found the empty bottle in the street, with some beer bottles he had also collected. Over Christmas the English indulged in even more alcohol than usual. He assumed the Clements Tonic had been drunk as an antidote to that.

There was a loud crack, the sound of a bullet exploding from a rifle. A piece of rock shattered from the side of the boulder. The bead kept jumping from side to side.

Abdullah fell from the kick of the rifle against his shoulder. Mahommed let him sit for a moment before helping him up.

Abdullah peered at the bottle. 'It's no good. It's too far away.'

'And you think a target will obligingly come closer? You think you can say to the Sultan, to Allah, I am sorry, I have failed you because I misjudged a distance?'

The old man cringed. Mahommed resisted the urge to apologise for his disrespect. 'There is no turning.'

Abdullah looked at him, offended. 'I have no wish to turn.' He looked away. 'I only wish there could still be time to make *Hajj*. I've yearned so long to make it.'

Mahommed ignored his plaintive tone. 'Yearning is nothing. Yearning is being sad about something you could have done but didn't do.'

He was dancing now, too agitated to stand still. He had enough regrets seeping into his head. The last thing he needed was Abdullah planting more.

'But this, this is something we *will* do!'

Behind Abdullah he could see Alice. She was no longer thin, but plump and beautiful, the goddess from the train. She was carrying an atlas, open to a map of the world. She smiled at him and said, 'Look at all that pink.'

He saw the pink spread out and cover all the countries of the world.

'*No!*' he shouted.

Abdullah looked behind him. 'Mahommed?'

'*No, no!*'

'Mahommed, I am here! We are here!'

Mahommed felt Abdullah's hands on his shoulders. He forced his eyes away from Alice, trying to make his mind go back to where it should be. It was in pieces, and he didn't know why. He didn't know why Alice was doing this to him *I love you* he needed her to leave him alone, this had nothing to do with her, it was only for Allah *I love you* to leave him alone to do what must be done …

Abdullah kept his hands on his shoulders and looked at him steadily. 'I will aim again.'

Mahommed held his look, not daring to see if she was still there. 'And again and again and again if necessary, because Abdullah, dear Abdullah, I cannot do this without you …' He sank to his knees and wrapped his arms around Abdullah's ankles. 'Without you I don't have the courage … without you I am completely alone.' He stayed on his knees. 'Help me, Abdullah. I have no-one. Only you.'

Abdullah reached out a hand and stroked his hair, and allowed silence to surround them. By the time Abdullah spoke, Mahommed sensed that Alice had gone. His agitation faded.

Abdullah said, 'When my son died, I could not speak his name. Not then, not for many years. But one day another boy came to me from across the sea. I did not ask for him, I did not want him, but he needed me, as I needed him. And finally, because of him, I spoke my son's name. It was Mahommed.'

He raised Mahommed to his feet. 'I will help you. You are not alone.'

31

Irma sobbed as she ran towards Argent Street. The police. She must go to the police station and report it to Constable Fitzpatrick. She'd tell him everything. No, not everything. Only enough to put that wicked man in gaol. She wouldn't tell him she'd been there; only that someone had witnessed him do something, no more than that. She couldn't let her parents know, she couldn't let anyone at the church find out, because people would say she had led him on, that it must have been her fault even though she was a completely innocent victim of a beastly man.

The jolting of her feet turned her sobs into hiccups. She stopped, weeping and hiccupping as reality sank in. She couldn't go to Constable Fitzpatrick. He would know that the someone was her. He would ask her how she knew that the something had happened; one way or another he'd winkle the truth out of her.

It was wrong. Robert had been practically her fiancé; he was supposed to protect her. She never wanted to see him again.

She had moped through Boxing Day. Her mother tried to be kind but Irma had never told her the truth about Robert and now was not the time to start. Her father had simply refused to discuss the situation.

Spinster. She could already feel the word burning into her forehead for all to see. She should be married by now, with children. Instead of which she had wasted a whole year with a man who was not worthy of her affection.

Today she had gone for a walk to free her mind, taking care to avoid seeing anyone to whom she might have to give awkward explanations. Her plan was simply to take the air, but her feet had other ideas. Without making any conscious decision to go there, she found herself near Mr Kadran's rooms.

Perhaps, she thought, she had been hasty in deciding she had no more need of his services. There was something unsettling about her last consultation but she couldn't remember what, so it mustn't have been very important. She felt tense, unwell. She needed to talk to someone about her situation and the more she thought about it, the more she realised there was simply no-one else whose discretion she could trust. He was probably closed for the holidays but there could be no harm in knocking on his door. It would be impossible to feel worse than she was presently feeling.

Mr Kadran welcomed her warmly, instantly divining the depth of her suffering. Robert's illness notwithstanding, he had behaved despicably; Mr Kadran assured her he would leave him in no doubt as to his feelings on the matter. But his concern right now was solely for her.

'Miss Cowie, I am completely at your service. In return I ask only one thing. That you put yourself safely in my hands.'

His kind words made Irma cry. He gave her a clean handkerchief to dry her eyes. She nodded. Whatever he suggested she would do.

He told her she needed another massage. He could ease her pain and send her out into the world much strengthened, but the severity of her blockages meant he would have to perform the massage on his examination bench. For the clearing to work at an optimum level, it was necessary that all her limbs were on the same plane, something not possible in a sitting position.

Irma agreed with this prescription. She needed help, she knew that. She accepted a draught of a new medicine Mr Kadran prepared for her, which, he said, would aid the efficacy of the treatment. He led her to the examination cubicle and withdrew, allowing her privacy while she loosened the buttons of her blouse and skirt.

It felt right to do this. She was only loosening her clothing, not removing it. Mr Kadran was a medical man; his interest was in her wellbeing. She didn't know whether it was the new medicine or Mr Kadran's sympathetic demeanour but she was already feeling positive about the consultation. She was glad she had come.

'Feel the clearing, Miss Cowie. Your pathways are being cleansed of the darkness that has been inhabiting them. Slowly, slowly but surely, you are being bathed in a golden light, a warm, soothing light, banishing that darkness from your life forever. You can feel the warmth now.'

'I think so ...'

'Lapping at the shores of your fingertips.'

'Yes. My fingertips ...'

Irma felt a tingle there, exactly as Mr Kadran described. He was a wonderful man; she should never have doubted him.

'Your eyes are heavy, Miss Cowie. Morpheus beckons, and you answer his call. Though you sleep, still you are awake. You feel the flutter of a hundred angel wings as they lightly touch you. They stroke you gently, soothing your pain.'

Angel wings, yes, of course. She could feel them from a distance, their feathery softness massaging away all the misery she had endured. She did feel sleepy, a lovely calm sleepiness. No thoughts of Robert. No thoughts of anything. Only the compassionate touch of angels holding her as she was taken to a place far away ...

Bang! She heard a sudden loud noise coming from the direction of the street – some collision, altercation, she didn't know what. Startled, she opened her eyes and came face to face with ... with ... a *thing*.

It was Mr Kadran's *thing* and it was outside his trousers and it was stiff and purple and he was holding it and it hadn't been angel wings at all, he'd been using it to ... to ... to ... he'd been *touching* her with it. Touching her, Irma, on her skin, and she could see her skirt had been pulled up and and and and ...

'Miss Cowie, I know this may seem irregular ...'

She tried to scream but all she could manage was a whimper as she climbed off the bench. She held up a hand to ward him off as she fumbled with her skirt, and started backing towards the door.

He started coming towards her. 'Miss Cowie, I assure you ...'

'Leave me alone!'

As she opened the door, she saw that his thing was no longer stiff. It was soft, flopping out of his trousers. She looked away from it and up to his face. It had the oddest expression. If she hadn't known better, she would have described it as frightened.

She didn't wait to examine it closer. She turned away and ran.

Robert had already spent a large part of the day walking. With no particular destination in mind, he headed up Oxide Street towards White Rocks, wandered around there for a while, then returned via Chloride Street. From there he turned left and meandered along the Tibooburra road before doing a circular loop around White Rocks again. He didn't care where he went, although he avoided the district around Talc Street, where Irma lived with her parents.

There was no getting round it: Christmas had not been a success. He had accepted the invitation to join the family for lunch after the morning service – there was no way he could have refused – but the prospect didn't excite him; there was expectation in the air, from Irma and her parents, that an announcement would soon be made. Given the only announcement he wanted to make was not one that would please them, he would have preferred to spend his Christmas elsewhere. He had thought of pleading work pressures, but everyone knew the council offices were shut until after Boxing Day. And if he hadn't been forced into going, none of this mess would have happened.

At first he wasn't sure it was her. He was walking back from White Rocks and instead of looking where he was going, he was looking at the ground. By the time he looked up, he was almost upon her: a young woman, weeping and hiccupping; her clothes in disarray, her hair wild, her eyelids swollen and red.

Irma's clothes were always neat; her hair brushed and pinned. These incongruities were enough to cause his initial confusion. If he had realised earlier it was her, he might have turned and walked away before she had seen him, but it was too late for that. The depth of her misery was such that he had no alternative but to ask her what was wrong.

She poured out a disjointed tale about Adrian Kadran. She told Robert that it was his fault; that he had made her go and see that man; that she would never have gone there if it weren't for him; that both men had abused her most cruelly.

Her complaints were light on specifics, so Robert was fuzzy about what Adrian had actually done. Only that it was beastly enough for Irma to threaten to go to the police about it.

He had a moment of sheer terror. If Adrian were apprehended, who would be left for him to consult? There were doctors in town, but none who understood the nature of his illness. It was unthinkable that he could consult them; only Adrian understood his needs. Only Adrian was prepared to help him the way he needed to be helped. He couldn't possibly let Irma go to the police.

'Well? Aren't you going to say anything?'

He hesitated, desperately searching for a way out. There wasn't one.

He said, 'Will you marry me, Irma?'

32

Alice poured some sherry into a glass. Just a thimbleful, enough to make Eileen think New Year's Eve was special.

Eileen said, 'You could have gone to the party. You didn't have to stay home with me.'

Alice poured sherry into her own glass. 'I bet everyone in Adelaide is drinking champagne.'

'I wouldn't've minded.'

'There's only us now,' Alice said. 'You and me. So the New Year should be for only us.'

'There's Lewis.'

'Yes, but he's not here. And I don't feel like a party.'

'Are you sick again?'

Alice shook her head. 'I wasn't sick before.'

'You're always sick.'

'I am not.'

Feeling the way she did was not sick. When she lay awake in the silence of the night, she thought she could hear her body closing down. Little pieces of her quietly shutting up shop. Sick was different. Sick was feeling bad and then getting better.

Eileen looked at her suspiciously. 'We're still going on the picnic tomorrow, aren't we?'

'Of course. We always do.'

She didn't want to go. The Oddfellows hired a picnic train to Silverton every New Year's Day. Last year over a thousand people went. There was nothing at Silverton apart from what was left of the mines and a few gum trees shading the dry riverbed, but nearly everyone did it. The trip was the thing; everyone packed into open-air carriages, picnic baskets perched on their knees or under their feet. It felt like they were going somewhere where something would happen. Nothing much did. They spread picnic rugs under the trees and ate corned beef sandwiches. The men played cricket and the women watched. Those who had cameras took group photographs. Then they all packed up and went home.

Last year Irma had flirted with Robert. This year they were engaged to be married. Last year Lewis had been with them.

'And next week? We're still going to go and wave Lewis off?'

When had Eileen developed that pinched, anxious whine? When Alice last looked at her, Eileen had seemed happy. Maybe she hadn't looked closely enough.

'Yes. We're going to wave till the boat disappears, even if our arms drop off.'

Alice was determined they would do it. She had a list of things she thought she could still do, and this was one of them.

She couldn't work at the hospital any longer, although she hadn't yet told Eileen. Matron Guthrie had become impatient with her. Alice had been found staring at nothing one too many times. They had both agreed it would be better if she left, at least until after the New Year. She told Eileen she had been given time off to farewell Lewis.

'Where's he going to go when he leaves?'

'Egypt, I think. Or Europe somewhere. They don't know for sure.'

If she had been told, Alice couldn't remember. It made no difference. A gun could kill as easily in France as in Belgium. She no longer read the war news. She sometimes saw the headlines. They said things about 'Johnny Turk' and 'Our Brave Lads'. She didn't want to know more than that.

Eileen drank her sherry, pulling a face. She said she was going to go to bed.

'Aren't you going to stay up?'

'What's going to happen if I do?'

'We'll wish each other Happy New Year.'

'We can do that tomorrow morning. Before we leave for the picnic.' Eileen emphasised the last bit, as if to make sure that they were going.

Alice agreed that that was what they would do, and bid her goodnight. She listened to Eileen moving around in their room. She heard her climb into bed and then she stopped trying to look cheerful.

She sat for a while, her mind empty. Then she stood, picking up the sherry bottle and glass, and moved outside. There was a low stone wall in the garden. Her father had built it before he stopped caring about things like that. She put the bottle and glass on the wall and sat next to them.

She could hear sounds in the distance. The hotels would be full. Away from the hotels there would be parties. Irma and Robert had gone to one at the church hall. Keith was probably there too. He had kept away from her ever since Eileen's party. She was glad of that; it was better that way.

The sounds grew louder. There was cheering. She heard a noise above and looked up. Someone had sent a rocket into the sky. She watched as it burned a trail of light, then disappeared.

It must be midnight, she thought. She would make a toast. Not to herself, but to Lewis and Eileen. That was another thing she could do.

She picked up the bottle and poured more sherry into the glass. She put it down again, but the wall was uneven and she misjudged. The bottle fell, shattering on the stone path below.

She looked at the bottle, seeping sherry into the ground. She would have to pick up the pieces. They were sharp; if Eileen walked out here barefoot she could cut herself.

She picked up a shard of glass and stared at it. She held it tight in her hand and pulled the jagged edge along the skin of her other arm. She watched as a line of blood formed along the shallow cut. It didn't hurt but it stung; she could feel it. The blood pooled near her elbow and dripped onto the ground, mixing with the sherry.

She dragged the shard along a fresh piece of skin, watching as it peeled open, making a channel for a new line of blood.

A second rocket burned into the sky. She looked up at the trail of light, burning fiercely, then dying.

She got down on her knees and began to carefully pick up the pieces of glass. The smaller splinters would need a dustpan and brush. She walked to the kitchen to get them.

★

Edith, with Zainie's help, was sewing white bits onto a red tablecloth. A big white C with a star next to it. Abdullah had shown them how the star had to look. Smaller than the C, with five points all the same size.

It was a funny way to spend New Year's Eve. She didn't know why it was so important. She asked Abdullah but he wouldn't say. She asked Mahommed, but he wouldn't say either, only that it had to be done tonight. From the look in his eyes, she thought it better she didn't know. He had bright eyes. One of Edith's cousins had developed bright eyes. It wasn't a good thing to have.

She could have gone into town, but there would be a lot of drinking. One good thing about living with the Afghans was you didn't get a taste for the drink. Once you started drinking, you'd get bright eyes for sure; at least for a little while until it all dulled over again.

There was drinking at the Aboriginal camps too. She could have gone there. But the nearby ones were mostly Paarkinji people; Willyama, too, what were left of them. She was Bandjigali, or part of her was; her mother part. Her mother had worked on a station, helping with the children, which was where she had met Edith's father. She remembered her mother pointing him out to her, so she knew who he was. Her mother had to tell her not to stare at him. That was her white part, her father part. When the station children were older they were sent to boarding school in Adelaide, and Edith and her mother had to leave.

Anyway, that was long ago. Once things became long ago they were best forgotten.

Now she had an Afghan part. She wished she didn't have so many parts. She wanted to be just one thing properly but it was too late for that now. If you were too many things it was hard to be strong in any one of them.

She looked at the white C, now stitched onto the red material. She knew one thing: whatever this was about, it was a waste of a perfectly good tablecloth.

Mahommed pulled his turban cloth out of the cloudy water, and looked at it critically. He had only a small oil lamp to guide him; it was hard to see if any marks remained. He couldn't see any, but dunked it back into the water for another wash, just in case. He picked up the cracked wedge of yellow soap Abdullah had lent him. He wished he had some Lifebuoy. Rexona, even.

No. He mustn't wish that. He corrected himself: he *didn't* wish that. He dipped the soap into the water and began to scrub. It was nearly midnight; he needed to hang the cloth out to dry before the prayers.

Two of the men joined them in the mosque: Sherdil and Aziz Khan, a Kandahar man who had only recently arrived in the camp. Neither of them knew anything about what was planned; only that Abdullah's *khutba* was inspired. Mahommed watched them. He could see they were moved.

He turned his attention back to Abdullah. The words were pouring out of him in a torrent. Mahommed listened not only to the words, but to Abdullah's heart, beating through them.

He gave praise to Allah. He gave praise to the Prophet (peace be upon him). He spoke of the forces that surrounded them, forces that denied the true word of Allah. He spoke of the need to listen. There would be times when Allah spoke his needs. When he did, their ears must be open. When he did, they must not question. When he did, they must do what was asked. He gave them the example of the prophet Abraham, who offered up his only son. They must know that no sacrifice is too great when it is demanded of them by Allah.

Yes, thought Mahommed, *yes*. Allah has made Abdullah strong again. He has made him strong to keep me strong.

They had to leave early, after the dawn *Fajr*. He meant to use the time resting, but when he lay down, thoughts came into his head so he got up again. He spent the next few hours checking everything, making sure he was prepared. He had kohl for his eyes; he had clean muslin – nearly dry – for his turban. As dawn neared he smoked a little *bhang* to calm his nerves. He didn't think he was afraid, but he needed his hands to be steady; the *bhang* would help. He rolled another cigarette for later. He might need it.

33

Alice stood with Eileen on the platform, looking for Irma. They had a picnic basket with them; Eileen had given instructions on what should be in it. It wouldn't be like last year, not without Lewis, but that was no reason not to make a proper picnic.

There were nearly a thousand people at Sulphide Street Station. Most of them seemed happy; the air was full of 'Happy New Year!', as if by saying it often enough, it could be made to happen.

Some of the open carriages were full; the rest filling up. In less than half an hour the train would leave. The passengers already seated were squashed in on hard plank benches, picnic baskets under their feet or wherever there was room.

Keith passed by and wished them Happy New Year. Alice understood the encounter was awkward for him and helped him out by telling him they mustn't keep him. He made pleasantries for a moment longer, and headed off, grateful to escape.

Eileen saw Irma's mother waving at them. 'They're over there. See? At the end.' She took Alice's hand and pulled her through the crowd towards the end carriage. Mr and Mrs Cowie were there, with Irma and Robert.

Irma smiled. 'Hello, Eileen, you look nice.' She turned to Alice. 'Hello, Alice.'

Alice looked down at the arms of her blouse, ringed with brown stains where she'd made a desultory effort to sponge off the blood. She supposed she could have tried harder, but for what?

Unlike her, Irma had made a big effort. Everything about her told the world she was an engaged woman now, with appearances to keep up. She was wearing a new white blouse, modest, as befitted her newly unavailable status, and expensive. Sitting next to her, Robert looked merely resigned to his fate. Irma had hinted that her father was not as pleased about the engagement as he should have been, so perhaps their present proximity was the cause of Robert's apparent discomfort.

Mrs Cowie patted the space next to her. 'Come on, then. In you hop.'

Mr Cowie took the picnic basket from them and helped them in. He said, 'It's a bit of a squeeze, but we don't mind if you don't.'

Alice liked Mr Cowie. She liked Mrs Cowie, too. She didn't know where Irma had come from; her parents weren't like her at all.

Alf, the assistant at Millers, came from across the tracks, wheeling his bicycle. He told them he had a plan for the day. He was going to start riding now and see if he could beat them there.

'What if you get tired?' asked Eileen.

Alf assured her he wouldn't; if he did he'd wait till the train came by and hang on to the back. He waved goodbye and pedalled off, wanting to give himself a head start.

Alice watched him go. Simple things still made him happy.

Robert, sitting between Alice and Irma, shifted his weight on the hard wooden bench. Did he make Irma happy? Alice wondered. There didn't seem to be any rules about how happiness worked; who was deserving of it and who wasn't.

Mrs Cowie was the first to hear the gasp of steam from the engine. It was time to leave. 'I'm looking forward to this,' she said. 'It's going to be grand.'

★

Mahommed stopped two miles out of town, following the Umberumberka Dam pipeline to where it nestled in a shallow ditch, about forty yards from the railway line. He had been out here on his own, two days ago, selecting a suitable position.

Abdullah helped him unhitch the horse. Once the shafts were free he left Mahommed to finish and went back to the cart. The two rifles were wrapped in a blanket. He picked them up and took them over to the ditch.

Only the bridle was left on the horse. Mahommed took hold of it and led the horse a little way in the direction of town. He stopped and undid the bridle, pulling it off the horse's head. He stroked her neck. Sadness filled him. He buried his head in the horse's coat until the feeling passed.

He lifted his head and moved away. He hoped she would find kindness waiting, though he did not expect that she would. 'Go! Go now! Go!' He hit her on the rump, hard enough to sting his hand. 'Go!'

The horse began to move off, first at a trot and finally at a gallop. Mahommed kept shouting at her until she was out of sight.

They sat in the ditch and waited. Behind them, stretched over the cage of the cart, was the crescent moon and star of the Turkish flag. One of the points of the star was shorter than the others. Edith had carelessly lopped the end off it. It didn't matter. From a distance no-one would know.

They loaded their rifles, checking and rechecking they were ready, then they put them aside, in close reach.

Mahommed's throat was dry. He moved his tongue around his mouth, trying to moisten it. He wished it were done, he wanted it over. He tried to recall the sermons. The midnight one … it had moved him, hadn't it? But *Fajr* … what did Abdullah say during *Fajr*? It was gone, everything was going when he needed it to stay.

He remembered the *bhang* that he'd earlier prepared as a cigarette. He found it and lit it, drawing deeply before passing it to Abdullah.

He focused his mind on *Fajr,* doing his best to bring back Abdullah's words. Other words pushed their way up, he didn't know why. From an advertisement. He frowned. He had read these words so long ago. Why now?

'Abdullah? Do you know what a lounge suit is?'

Abdullah waited until he had exhaled before answering. 'No. Is it important for you to know?'

Mahommed thought about it. A lounge was a sofa, a couch, wasn't it? Or a room, was it a room? But a suit, that was something to wear. Wasn't it? Had he failed to learn even that?

He looked at Abdullah and answered, 'No. Not any more.'

By ten o'clock the few morning wisps of cloud had long disappeared. The day was already January hot. Mahommed wiped his hands on his shirt. He needed a firm hold on the rifle; sweat would loosen his grip.

He looked at Abdullah, rifle beside him, eyes fixed on the train line, waiting. He could see the curve of the old man's spine: bony lumps pushing through the thin cotton of his shirt. He wanted to embrace him, but it was too late for that.

He said, 'You have been my true friend, Abdullah. I have not always been yours, but you have been mine.'

Abdullah reached out and grasped his shoulder, holding it tight. 'We are together. Always.' There was no reproval in his words; only love. Tears welled in his eyes. 'It is time to go home.'

'Will it be there for us?' He needed Abdullah to tell him one more time. Only one more time and it would be true.

'The angels will listen to our hearts. They will tell them all they need to know. They will lead us home.'

'Allah is with us?'

'Yes. Allah is with us.'

Mahommed tightened his hold on the rifle. The effects of the *bhang* had worn off. He wished he had brought more. He wished he didn't feel so sick. He wished his mother were still alive.

He said, 'I am ready.'

Mahommed heard the train before he saw it. A low rumble coming from under the earth. He saw the smoke puffs, then the engine and the long caterpillar line of carriages behind it.

He put the rifle sight to his eye. He panned it along the carriages. A woman was standing in the end one. She was wearing a green skirt and blouse. She seemed to be staring straight at him. He had to look away from her. He hesitated, then turned the rifle away, and trained it on a boy riding a bicycle, pedalling hard to keep ahead of the train.

Mr Cowie saw the ice-cream cart first, above the ridge where the pipeline was. He said he thought it was probably going out to Silverton to meet their train. He leaned towards Eileen with a smile. 'It's a good day for ice-cream,' he said. 'A treat to look forward to at the end of our trip.'

The bit of red cloth fluttering from the cart meant nothing to him. Alice knew exactly what it was. The sight of it filled her with dread.

★

Alice learned the names of the others later, but Alf was the first.

Eileen had been watching out for him since the train pulled out of the station. She was sure he couldn't have gone far, no more than a mile or two. When she saw the dust cloud ahead she leaned out of the carriage to wave and shout, 'Look out, Alf! We're catching you!'

The train pulled alongside and started to overtake him. He took one hand off the handlebars to wave back at Eileen, grinning.

Alice looked towards the ice-cream cart and saw Mahommed take aim. She turned back to Alf, screaming at him. 'Hurry! Alf, hurry!' If Alf could keep up with the train he would be safe.

Alf continued to wave. Before he could put his hand back on the handlebar, something exploded into his chest, knocking him sideways.

Eileen pulled on Mr Cowie's sleeve. 'Tell them to stop the train! Alf's fallen!'

Mr Cowie looked at the receding figure on the ground. He said Alf's bike wheel must have hit a rock. He told Eileen to give it a moment; he was sure he would pick himself up soon. Alice knew he wouldn't.

She didn't know whether William Shawley, in the carriage ahead of her, was second because by now there were screams from other carriages as people began to grasp what was happening. But she saw William, his wife and three children by his side; saw him raise an arm to shield them as a bullet tore into his shoulder, ripping flesh and shattering bone.

She saw Mahommed and Abdullah, no longer bothering to hide behind the wall of the ditch, standing in clear view as they fired, again and again. She felt the judder as the engine driver, alerted to something going on, stopped the train. She heard a voice as a man, recognising the flag, called out, 'It's Turks, it's Johnny Turk!' She heard other voices, hysterical now, screaming over the rifle fire, begging the engine driver to get going again, that they would all be killed; saw Keith climb out from his carriage, and run, head down, on the other side from the attackers, towards the driver's compartment.

When she looked back towards Mahommed and Abdullah, trying to put some sense into what she was seeing and hearing, she saw Abdullah, taking his time, sweeping the rifle barrel slowly along the length of the train, from the front to the back. He seemed to be looking for someone.

Alice grabbed Eileen and pushed her to the floor

of the carriage, ignoring her protests. Mr Cowie had already done the same to Irma and Mrs Cowie, but despite his attempts to calm her, Irma was screaming, set off by the sounds of others around her. Robert made an attempt to join them, but then faltered, as though he had forgotten why he was doing it. He remained in his seat, vacantly detached from what was going on.

Alice moved her head in an attempt to block out Irma's screams and saw the emptiness in Robert's eyes. *He doesn't know where he is*, she thought.

She moved to grab his hand, to pull him down with the others, but before she could do so Irma shrugged off Mr Cowie's attempts to hold her down and jumped up, flinging herself into Robert's arms, begging him to save her.

Mr Cowie tried to calm her: 'Irma, stop it.' As he spoke, Abdullah's bullet smashed into Irma's skull, shearing off the top of her head. Pieces of brain and bone fragments splattered onto Robert's coat. Alice saw his look of disgust as he tried to detach himself from Irma's weight, saw Irma's wretchedness as she finally understood the truth, speaking her last words to him through pink bubbles of blood. 'You don't love me.'

★

The bullets kept coming.

Mrs Cowie cradled the body of her only child, refusing to accept what Mr Cowie already knew. 'A doctor! She needs a doctor!'

Mr Cowie tried to put an arm around his wife, to comfort himself as much as her, but she pushed him away. 'She needs a doctor!'

Robert, pressed against a corner of the carriage, wouldn't touch Irma, wouldn't go near her. He kept his head down, away from the bullets still being fired, away from Mrs Cowie's accusing eyes. Alice saw him glance at the pieces of Irma's brain, which still clung, glistening, to his clothes; he didn't dare brush them off. He was afraid of what Mrs Cowie might do to him if she saw.

There was a release of steam from the engine. They were going to move; Keith must have reached the driver, told him to start up again. Alice kept her arms tight around Eileen, needing some way to keep herself from shaking.

Eileen struggled against her. 'What about Alf?'

Mr Cowie stood. 'Eileen's right. We can't just leave him.'

He already had one leg over the edge of the carriage, ignoring Mrs Cowie's protests. His hands, streaked with

Irma's blood, left their mark on the edge as he hauled himself over. Before he went he looked at Mrs Cowie, as if willing her to understand, *If I can't look at Alf's parents, how can I ever again look at myself?*

A fellow passenger, a man Alice didn't know, stood, and followed Mr Cowie's lead.

Robert shrank further into his seat, lost in a deep and nameless place.

Alice couldn't see what was happening, but she could see the fear in Mrs Cowie's face. She had already lost Irma; she couldn't lose her husband as well, not now, not here, not like this.

Alice released Eileen, and, using the side of the carriage to support herself, climbed to her knees until she could see over the edge. She saw Mahommed aim his rifle in Mr Cowie's direction as he and the other man ran low towards Alf's body.

She stood, holding both arms up, waving so he would see her, shouting so he would hear her. 'Don't take them! Please don't take any more!'

They had reached Alf and were now dragging him back towards the carriage.

Alice kept waving and shouting, forcing Mahommed to look at her. He aimed his rifle straight at her.

Don't take them, Mahommed, take me instead.

The train began to move. Hands reached over the edge of the carriage to help Mr Cowie and the other man with Alf.

She saw him lower the rifle and watch as the train began to move faster. She wanted to see his face, but he was too far away.

34

Irma was among the dead. Alice covered Irma's head, leaving her face, still perfect and unblemished, visible. Mrs Cowie sat by her daughter and held her hand. It was heavy, and becoming cold, but she held onto it tightly. Alice thought that part of Mrs Cowie still believed Irma would open her eyes and tell her not to worry; it was all just a silly mistake.

Alice was one of the few with knowledge of first aid. There were no medicines; only cloths to hold against wounds in an attempt to staunch the blood flow. She knew the little they could do was largely a waste of time, but kept it to herself. The wounded didn't need to be told; they were grateful for a kind touch and comforting words. She was glad to be busy. There were many who were sitting on the ground in the shade thrown by the carriages, staring vacantly at nothing. She didn't want to be among them.

Mr Cowie was helping her; she could see he was in shock. She thought he should be lying down. Should be having a picnic with his wife and daughter. Instead he was on his knees, tearing up strips of someone's shirt to pack the wound in William Shawley's shoulder.

'What do you believe in, Alice?'

She couldn't bear the look in Mr Cowie's eyes. He wanted her to give him something she didn't have; not even for herself.

'Doreen believes we're here for a reason,' he went on. 'She says it doesn't matter that we don't always know it. She says the important thing is that God knows it.' His voice broke. 'Doreen's wrong. There's no reason for this. There's no reason for anything.'

He put his head down and wept. After a time Alice helped him to his feet. She led him to some shade and gave him tea from her flask. She had to hold the cup to his mouth; Mr Cowie's hands were shaking too much to hold it himself.

'It was Turks!'

Alice entered the makeshift office as Keith, on the telephone, tried to explain the situation to the junior constable at the other end. She wondered if the constable had resented his New Year's Day roster. Probably. He wouldn't once he knew.

'For Christ's sake, people are wounded, people are dying … we need help!'

She heard the edge in Keith's voice; saw him force himself to pause before continuing. There was enough hysteria outside the office; it was his job to contain it, not spread it.

She said, 'Tell him to ring the hospital. Tell Matron Guthrie. She'll know what to send.' She heard her own voice; it sounded calm. She didn't know where it came from, but she was grateful for it.

Keith turned back to the telephone and conveyed Alice's message. He said the train was stopped at the Silverton Tramway reservoir, alongside the office. There were dead laid out next to the track; those badly wounded, too. They would have to be put back on the train along with the less badly wounded and shunted back to Broken Hill. A relief train was needed; reinforcements, guns … whatever and whoever was available. When he had done all he could to impress the urgency of the situation, he hung up. As Alice turned to go back outside, he said, 'I wish I had something to drink.'

*

The train went, taking with it the wounded and dead. Mr and Mrs Cowie were on it, keeping Irma safe on her last journey. Alice had insisted Eileen leave, too.

She probably should have gone with them herself. There was nothing here for her to do, but she couldn't bear the thought of going home.

She sat in the shade next to the office, trying to erect a wall between what had happened and what her mind could accept. *It was only two hours ago, she thought. If those two hours can be stitched out of the day, then none of this will exist.*

She looked over at the men, wondering if Robert was with them. A lot had stayed; some of them had already gone after Mahommed and Abdullah, others were still here, milling, outraged, waiting for guns to be brought.

The rumours began, growing with each repetition. They were Turks. There were two men, there were three, there were ten. They had killed four, six, twelve, wounded many more. They were enemy fiends. They would die.

Alice heard these words. She had seen what Mahommed had done. Was it the war, was it Abdullah, had he somehow persuaded Mahommed, forced him to do it? Mahommed had been gentle, he had been kind, he had given her hope that her life might change. How could he now have done this? The more she thought about it, the more the reasons slipped away from her.

Now the men were shouting louder, now even more determined that Mahommed and Abdullah would die. But maybe they wouldn't. Maybe they would go deep into the desert where no-one would find them. And maybe, if Mahommed could live, he would one day tell her why.

She pulled herself further into the shade and watched as two cars arrived, carrying police and volunteers. She saw the relief train come with more volunteers on board; saw Keith meet them and hand out rifles. She saw the eager faces of the men; heard them shouting over each other. The Turks had been seen heading towards White Rocks. They were going to be taught a lesson by men who knew how to do it. This was better than a picnic. It was a hunting party.

Anger, grief; these she could understand. But she could not allow their enthusiasm. She stood and moved to Keith.

'No more. Please, Keith, no more guns.' She put her hand onto the barrel of the gun he was holding. 'How many do you need?'

He pushed her hand from the gun. 'Alice, keep away.'

She grabbed the gun again.

'There are only two of them, you don't need this, you don't need to do this!'

'Alice, be quiet!' Keith pulled the gun from her grasp, thrust it at a volunteer, and grabbed hold of Alice's wrist. He dragged her, still protesting, towards the office. She fought him but he held her firm, pushing her inside. 'Alf is dead! Irma is dead! What is the matter with you?'

He turned from her, shutting the door as he went out. She rushed to get a hold on the door before it closed, but was too late. She heard the bolt being rammed home from the other side.

35

Mahommed and Abdullah left the flag-draped ice-cream cart behind, and headed towards White Rocks. They didn't talk about what they had done. Abdullah was in front of Mahommed, carrying his rifle. Blood had been spilt, but Abdullah's was flowing again. *I must be like him*, Mahommed thought. *I must become like him.*

He stopped and looked back. There was nothing but desert behind them. He saw no-one, heard no-one. He knew they would come.

'Mahommed!'

They would have to come. He was monstrous; they would come to destroy him, leave nothing behind, not even his name …

Abdullah grabbed his arm, dragging him around to face him. 'Hurry!'

He couldn't move. It was the rifle; was it the rifle? He took it from his shoulder, and let it fall to the ground.

Abdullah grabbed Mahommed again, made him look at him. 'When you were in the Turkish army, you killed many people.'

Mahommed tried to pull away. 'No-one, Abdullah, until today no-one.'

Abdullah held him tighter, ignoring his confession. 'Because until today, it was not Allah's will.'

Allah's will. Was that why they had done it? Allah's will?

'And the will of the Sultan.'

Mahommed clung to Abdullah's words. He wasn't monstrous. It was the will of the Sultan. The will of Allah. He nodded, trying to make it true. 'He commanded me to fight.'

'And you have answered his call.' Abdullah picked up the rifle and gave it back to Mahommed. 'It is the will of Allah.'

When they reached White Rocks they lay on the ground behind an outcrop of quartz. It would provide some protection. They couldn't win this battle, but they could lose with honour. They reloaded their rifles, and waited.

Down below, beyond the Cable Hotel, they could see movement. Men were beginning to group. From that distance, they were no more than ants. There were a lot of them, maybe a hundred, two hundred. Maybe more.

Mahommed looked up at the sky, a washed out cloudless blue. 'Do you think it will rain?'

Abdullah followed his gaze. 'Not today.'

Mahommed looked away from the sky. 'I would like it to rain. I would like once more to feel the rain on my face. I would like to be cleansed.'

Abdullah said, 'It will happen. Allah willing.'

Hundreds of men crawled up the hill on their bellies towards them, all with guns. Mahommed lifted his rifle up over the rocks to look. Behind the men were horses, cars, trucks. A week ago these men would not have crossed the street for them. His eyes widened at the thought. 'So many, all coming to see us …'

Before Abdullah could reply, he was shot, a bullet catching the side of his jaw, shattering the jawbone, exposing ragged flesh. He was knocked back by the force of it.

Mahommed dragged him under cover. He put the rifle back in his hands. As he did so a bullet ploughed into Mahommed's ribs, through the bone and into his stomach. He heard the crack and felt the searing pain that followed.

Abdullah heard his gasp and turned, wanting to help.

Mahommed saw his friend's ruined face and shook his head. 'I am alright,' he said.

Abdullah saw a man running at a crouch towards cover. He found the strength to pull the trigger of his rifle. The bullet went off at an angle, wide. The kick pushed him back again and he fell to one side, dropping the rifle.

Mahommed barely noticed, seeing only the men coming towards them, floating in liquid heat.

He raised himself further. Abdullah reached out a hand to pull him back but had only the strength to brush it against his shirt before letting it drop again.

Mahommed swayed as he tried to stand. The pain had become part of him. His shirt also, mingling with the blood from his stomach.

The men were now in boats. Rowboats, skimming through a lake. They were surrounded by fine mist. Mahommed understood. It was all so clear.

'They have come from over the sea … of Loch Lomond …'

Alice was kneeling in one of the boats. She smiled at him and dipped a hand in the clear blue water.

'… to give us their war.'

Alice put both hands in the water, cupping them.

She brought them up again, letting the water fall slowly around her, splashing into the lake below.

Two more bullets hit him, one in the elbow. The other caught him in the chest as he was falling, puncturing a lung.

He lay where he fell, struggling to draw breath. He was aware of Abdullah, lying nearby, not moving. He tried to call his name but the only sound he could make was a whisper; Abdullah wouldn't hear it.

Putting his weight onto his good elbow, Mahommed began to inch his body over to him. They were only about two feet apart but movement of any kind unleashed arrows of pain. He needed to reach Abdullah while he could still talk. There was something he must tell him.

He pulled himself over the last bit of ground between them. He laid his head on him and curled into the warmth of his body.

He said, 'Abdullah … it is raining.'

Mahommed heard the gunfire, but dimly, from a distance, until finally it stopped altogether. He cupped his hands to catch the rain, but there was none. He didn't know where it had gone.

He moaned, his face contorting with pain. He felt blood fill his mouth, leaking from his whole body.

There were flies. Only a few of them stirred when someone kicked him. There were voices. He saw the policeman kneel to look at Abdullah.

He said, 'This one's gone.'

Mahommed became aware of the other man, one he used to know. Andy had been his friend, had called him Ghan. He was aiming his rifle at Mahommed's head.

'No.'

Andy kept the rifle aimed at him.

'No!' the policeman said again. He put his hand on the rifle to stop him and Mahommed saw Andy's disappointment.

They dragged him down the hill, the policeman taking one leg, Andy the other, letting him go only to argue with a farmer about taking him in. The farmer didn't want him on his dray; he had piglets in the back, which he was planning to deliver, and he didn't see why anyone should bother taking him to the hospital at all. Mahommed heard the argument go back and forth until it was resolved by the payment of a shilling.

He was picked up. There were more than two men now. He felt hands grabbing and shoving him, heaving him in among the mass of squealing piglets. He lay there, too weak to push them away. He heard more voices, but their words were only sounds strung together with anger.

He heard the crack of a whip; felt the wheels start to move under him. Every stone on the rutted track made them shudder. Mahommed, already cocooned by a blanket of pain, was barely aware of it.

With every movement he heard the piglets squeal.

He heard something else. A beckoning.

Come home …

The dray lurched again and Mahommed could feel the piglets' panic as they trampled over him, digging their hooves into his body. He retched, and found the taste of blood in his mouth, mingling with his disgust.

Come home …

Alice sat on the floor of the reservoir office, her back against the wall. She barely registered the sound of footsteps, the sound of the bolt being pushed open. When the door opened the room flooded with sunlight, blinding her, but she knew the man standing in the open doorway was Keith.

'I'm taking you home.'

His voice was distant. They were strangers. She didn't want to go with him. She didn't want to see the railway line again; didn't want to see or walk past the bloodstains on the ground around it.

She stood, doing as she was told. She didn't ask him anything; there was only one question on her mind and she didn't want to know the answer to it.

Instead she said, 'I couldn't get out. I tried to but I couldn't.'

He turned from her, already moving out. He said, 'Eileen needs you.'

36

Robert had gone back with the picnic train, skirting Doreen and Hector Cowie and climbing back on board at the last minute. He wanted to do so earlier but had been afraid someone might tell him to get off. When the train started back to town the motion made him want to be sick, but, not wanting to draw any more attention to himself, he forced himself to swallow the rising bile. He kept his eyes down. No-one sat near him. Only the flies, swarming on pieces of Irma's brain.

When the train reached the station he hurried off, avoiding the crowd waiting for news. He took the side streets. He did not want to see anyone he knew.

Adrian. He had to find Adrian. If he could just see him he could get through the rest of the day. He had a small amount of medicine left in his bottle at home, but nowhere near enough. He knew that once home, he wouldn't be capable of leaving.

Adrian would help him. If he'd been at the picnic like he should have been, he'd be helping him now. He might even have brought some medicine with him.

Oh, God, how he needed it.

Adrian's employees were at reception, arguing among themselves. Robert pushed past them, heading towards Adrian's rooms.

'You can't go in there.'

It was a woman, that fat cook of his. Her voice faded as her eyes travelled down the bloody muck on his coat. He instinctively wiped his hands over it before realising what he had done.

'I can go where I damn well like.' He was almost running now to get to the safety of Adrian's rooms. Adrian, he had to see Adrian.

It took him a moment to grasp how wrong everything was. The walls were bare of both paintings and testimonials. The shelves were bare of apothecary bottles. The desk was still there, but Adrian's chair was missing. A man was in the process of carrying out one of the patients' chairs.

'Put that down, it belongs to Mr Kadran.'

The man was unimpressed. 'And when he pays me the money he owes, he'll get it back.'

'Where is he?'

'You tell me and we'll both know,' the man said, carelessly scratching the chair on the door jamb as he went.

Robert tried to get his thoughts in order. This wasn't happening, it couldn't be happening. He went behind the desk and began pulling out the drawers. Medicine, there must be some here, there must be.

The fat cook came in and watched him. 'There's nothing in there.'

He ignored her insolent tone. 'Where's Mr Kadran? I need to speak with Mr Kadran.'

'He's gone.'

'Where is he!'

'I'll say it again. He's gone.'

He barely remembered how he got home. There were people on the streets; some of them looked at him strangely, he knew that much. Someone, a man, called out to him, but he didn't stop. All he wanted was the safety of his own four walls. He tore his coat off as soon as he was inside and rushed to the kitchen sink to vomit the contents of his stomach. He clung to the sink, unable to risk letting go.

His medicine. He needed his medicine. His bottle was in his desk drawer. There was nowhere near enough for the sickness that permeated every pore of his body but it would have to do. He let go of the sink and walked to his desk, moving slowly so as not to jolt his stomach. He kept his eyes averted from the coat lying by the door.

He opened the drawer. The medicine was there, lying on top of his sheaf of inspirational thoughts. He took it out and put it on top of the desk. He took out his writing. If there was consolation to be had, surely it could be found in this.

He found a page at random.

*The eagle soars above my head I know what it's
thinking thinking something flies and flies eagle flies
thinking something flies it flies up in the sky fly sky
fly sky …*

He didn't understand what it meant. He found another piece.

*Round and round the garden like a teddy bear
one step two step three step four step five step
six step …*

It went on for three pages, up to a hundred and thirty-four step. He was feeling even sicker than he had been. He riffled through the pages, desperate to find something that would help him. He stopped as he saw something familiar. *Fuck Irma fuckirma fuckirmafuckirm ...*

He pushed his words away, unscrewed the cap from his medicine, and drank what little was left. Then he put his head down on the desk and wept.

Edith kept Ibram and Partimah inside, close to her. From time to time she directed Zainie outside to see if she could find out what was happening. There were men coming and going, talking in huddles. She knew they would not give Zainie any specific information, but it might be possible to glean something in passing. She gave her strict instructions not to go too far away.

Edith looked around at the contents of the shack, making a note of the things that mattered to her. Some would have to be left. She would not tell the children they were leaving until she was ready. Telling them now would mean others would find out, and she had no interest in arguing her reasons. She bore them no ill will. Jemadar had been her protector. He had been kind; most of the others had been, too. But three parts of her were too many; it was time to leave one of them behind. And Zainie was getting older. Edith knew she couldn't keep her safe for much longer.

There was still some money. She didn't need it where she was going, but she would take it with her as insurance. If the part of her she thought was her biggest one proved to be empty, she might have to return. She didn't want that. She wanted her wanderings to take her home. But time erased things; memories became bleached. She hoped she hadn't left it too late.

Zainie came back and told her what she'd heard. Abdullah was dead. Many others had been killed.

Poor Abdullah. Poor silly old man. Edith wondered what mischievous spirit had shaken his mind, rattling it around until there was no sense left. Maybe that's what happened when you forgot which parts of you were the real ones.

Zainie also told her about Mahommed.

Edith thought about it. If there was a debt she owed to Jemadar, then it should be repaid. It would finish things properly before they left.

She found Jemadar's old white shirt and trousers. Zainie said that wasn't right, that it should be a *kafan*. Edith had said that was all very well, but neither she nor Zainie knew how to wrap it properly so how could they possibly explain it to Alice? And there was no point in asking one of the men to do it because the way things were, they'd probably be shot before they reached the hospital. The clothes were white and they were clean and that was going to have to be good enough.

37

Alice sat at the dining table. Eileen was curled up on Lewis's lounge chair; the rug she had knitted for Lewis around her shoulders. Between them was a silence neither could break.

Keith told her that Eileen had been waiting at home, afraid; that she had gone to the station and pushed her way through the crowd until she had found him; had said she didn't know where Alice was, that she thought she might be dead. That despite the heat, she had been wearing the rug, clutching it tight around her. Eileen stood and went into their room, the rug still around her shoulders. Alice knew she should go in to her, offer her some comfort, but she had none to give.

It was soft but insistent; the sound of something hitting the front door. The first time it happened she barely noticed. She heard the sound again. A pebble, or something like it. She stood, pushing her chair back, her body heavy. She could barely remember how to walk. She had to think about how it was done.

She opened the door to find Zainie, standing a little way off, pebbles in one hand, a bundle of white clothes at her feet. When she saw Alice, she let the pebbles fall.

Alice stared at her, waiting for her to say something. She could see the girl was nervous, but felt no curiosity; whatever Zainie was there for didn't matter to her.

Zainie said, 'We are told Gool Mahommed will die.'

Alice continued to stare at her. It occurred to her that she was supposed to say something, respond in some way. She put a hand on the door frame, needing to touch something solid. 'What do you want?' she finally said.

Zainie's voice was unsteady. 'He must be washed. He must be dressed.'

Alice shrugged. 'I'm not a Muslim.'

'If anyone from the camp goes, there will be trouble,' Zainie persisted.

'I don't care.'

Zainie sat on the ground and looked away. Alice saw that she was trembling.

'There is no-one else.'

'I don't care!'

Zainie didn't move. Alice leaned down and picked up a handful of gravel. She hurled it at her. *'I don't care!'*

Zainie looked straight at Alice. She was no longer trembling.

She wanted to make her go away, to shut the door in her face. She'd done it once before. If she did it again she would be beyond redemption.

Alice walked towards the hospital carrying the clothes, a basin, a towel and cloth, and a wrapped cake of soap. She had washed her hands, scrubbing at her ragged fingernails until they were clean. She had given the clothes a cursory glance, enough to establish that they were not Mahommed's; had run her hand over them, liking the soft feel of them even though they did not yet belong to him.

It was mid afternoon; the air dull and heavy with summer heat. Flushed and damp with sweat, it took her fifteen minutes to walk to the hospital. She didn't notice the heat, nor how it slowed her steps. She barely saw the people she passed on her way. No-one said 'Happy New Year' to her. They were clustered in groups; some angry, some downcast. She knew they had many things on their minds today. A single young woman carrying a basin would mean little to them. If it had meant something, it wouldn't have mattered to her. She was already scraped bare; there was nothing they could see that she cared about hiding. Her mind was empty of thought; she was working hard to keep it that way. Zainie had told her he would die; she knew if she allowed those words meaning, she would not be able to do this.

At the hospital, two policemen were stationed outside, barring entry. She didn't know them; they were reinforcements brought from elsewhere. She told them she was a nurse. They stood aside for her without question.

She paused, making a casual enquiry. 'Is the Turk still inside?'

One of the policemen nodded, happy to trade gossip. 'But don't worry, you won't be bothered by him. We've put him in a private room.'

'In case he tries to escape?'

'Not much chance of that.' He laughed, amused by the very idea. 'Not after what we did to him.'

Keith stood outside the closed door, guarding it. As she approached along the hall, her footsteps rang on the tiles, and he looked across at her. She saw how tired he seemed, part of this day for too long already. She understood why he might feel that way, and why he would not welcome her presence.

'You should be at home.'

She responded humbly, doing her best not to offend. She indicated the clothes. 'There's no-one else who can do this.'

'How can you even ask such a thing?' He shook his head, bewildered, as though her request was beyond all understanding.

'Because whatever he's done, he's entitled to go to his God in the way his religion requires.'

'But Alf? He wasn't entitled. Irma? She wasn't entitled either.'

She wanted to shout at him, tell him to stop, tell him that everything he said was true, that she would carry it for all time, but right now, right here, all she could do was this one small thing, and if she let herself listen to him she would not be able to do even that. She wanted to tell him he was right, but that one night in a darkened train carriage two shoulders touched, and what followed had nothing to do with reason.

She wanted him to let her through the closed door.

She ran fingers through her hair in an attempt to tidy it. She smiled at him. 'If you allow it, it would be a kindness I would remember with gratitude for a long time.'

He wasn't interested in her implicit offer. She could see he found her coquetry grotesque. He did want her once, she knew that, but he didn't now. All he wanted now was for her to go away.

'Please, Keith. Please let me do this one thing.' She reached out to touch his arm, not caring that he pulled away from her. She wanted him to see that she would not leave; that if he ordered her away she would fight him. 'Only this one thing. Please.'

He held her look for a long time before he turned away. He looked down the hallway at nothing in particular, making it clear that he would neither officially sanction nor deny her request.

'Anyway,' he said, 'he's probably dead by now.'

She didn't reply. She turned the door handle and entered the room.

He lay uncovered on the hospital bed, still wearing the clothes he was wearing when he was brought in. They were bloodstained and made ragged by bullets. Some blood still oozed from his wounds. Where it had dried, the cotton from his shirt had stuck to it. His eyes were shut; his breath shallow and raspy. She was not ready to see him like this. She had tried to prepare herself, but she was not ready.

There was a jug on the bedside table. She put the basin down next to it and took out the soap, the towel and the clothes. She filled the basin with water from the jug, and unwrapped the soap. Only after she had done these things did she turn to him again.

'Mahommed … it's Alice.' She barely recognised the voice as her own. 'Don't be frightened. I'll keep you safe.'

She reached out to brush her fingers against his cheek. She didn't know if he was aware of her presence, but if he was, she wanted him to know she would not hurt him.

She took the soap over to him so he could smell it. 'It's lavender. Eileen gave it to me for Christmas.'

She wet the cloth in water, lathering it with the soap before wringing it damply dry. She sponged it lightly over his face, patting away the red dust that mingled with his blood.

She rinsed the cloth and washed his hands. They had no injuries; she knew her touch would not cause him pain. She took her time with them, lacing his fingers with her own. They were dear to her; she wanted to feel them. She massaged his shirt free from the blood on his chest. She loosened it as best she could, leaving it partly on through fear of moving him more than necessary.

She washed his hair with the wet cloth, perfuming it with more soap. She took a comb from her pocket and combed his hair, cupping his head with her free hand.

'It's alright,' she said. Over and over, *it's alright, it will be alright, it will be alright*; a soothing murmur she voiced so that they could both believe it.

She pulled up a chair next to the bed and sat, taking his hand. She looked at his fingers. She looked at his face. These were things she needed to remember. She did not allow herself to think of what he had done.

She strained to hear his breathing, now barely audible.

She heard voices from outside, and turned to listen to them. She knew she would not be permitted to stay for much longer. She could not leave while he was still alive. She turned back to Mahommed, unsure if she was strong enough to do what she must.

But there was no need. He was gone.

She sat for a moment, looking at his lifeless body, dully trying to comprehend what had happened. She wondered when the pain would start, and, when it did, when it would end.

She stood and began to remove the rest of his clothing. She would finish washing him; she would dress him in clean white clothes. She had told Zainie she would do it. It was something to do.

★

She tried to say thank you to Keith but her voice failed her and she could do no more than mouth the words as she moved out past him.

She left the hospital with the sky already darkening. She crossed the road, following the protection of the evening shadows, and continued walking until her welling tears blinded her. She stopped, and put a steadying hand on the low metal fence beside her. She couldn't cry; not now, not here. Eileen was alone; she needed to go home to her, and mend what could be mended. If she let herself cry now, she might never stop.

She shut her mind to the day, willing it to a safer place. To a loch far away, where she dived in as deep as she could go; where the water kept her body close and whispered, *I will hold you*; where the sunlight fractured into rainbows that glanced through the water, bathing the darkness with colour no matter how deep she went. Where, when she thought her lungs would burst, the water gently lifted her back to the light above. Where she lay on her back and gave herself to the sun and the water, which drifted, carrying her to wherever it wanted her to be.

She stayed there for as long as she could. When it began to disappear, she took her hand from the fence and wiped her eyes.

She had shared this place once; had told him how to reach it. It was still there. It would be there after the scars on her hands had faded; after the memories of the day finally blurred; after sorrow at last released her. She would put on her magician's blue dress, and she would go there again, and he would be waiting.

ACKNOWLEDGEMENTS

Many thanks to Leon Saunders for reading every draft of the manuscript. I am deeply indebted to him for his patience, his generosity, and his incisive comments. Pam Baker read a draft at a time when I was floundering, and her care and encouragement helped me get back on track. Other friends, including John Alsop, Justine Gillmer and Sarah Duffy, read the manuscript at different stages and offered encouragement and helpful advice.

At HarperCollins, thanks to Stephanie Smith for seeing promise in a rough early draft and to Jo Butler for her enthusiasm and belief. Editors Nicola O'Shea and Katherine Hassett provided wonderful editorial guidance and I am extremely grateful to both of them.

The writing of this book was assisted by both a residential fellowship and a Varuna Award at Varuna Writers' Centre. They were much appreciated, as was the support offered by Varuna's Peter Bishop.

Last but not least, thanks to Georgie, Adrian, Rob and Mum for being my constant cheer squad.

Among other sources, two books were particularly useful in providing background for this book: *Tin Mosques and Ghantowns* by Christine Stevens (Paul Fitzsimmons, 2002), and *United We Stand* by Edward Stokes (The Five Mile Press, 1983).

Chris McCourt was born and educated in Sydney. After a brief career as an actress, she joined Crawford Productions in Melbourne as a trainee script editor, and has since written for many celebrated Australian television dramas including *GP*, *Fallen Angels*, *McLeod's Daughters*, and *All Saints*. Currently, Chris is a writer on the coming ABC drama series *The Doctor Blake Mysteries* and is a regular writer on the hit series *Packed to the Rafters*. *The Cleansing of Mahommed* is her first novel. She lives in Balmain.

www.ingramcontent.com/pod-product-compliance
Lightning Source LLC
Chambersburg PA
CBHW050112120726
47904CB00004B/1321